CORPSMAN UP

By

Paul Baviello

Corpsman Up

DEDICATION

To the Marines and Hospital Corpsmen of all wars, but especially to fellow Corpsmen Ivan Heller, Larry Padberg, Dave Porterfield, and Bob Aucoin, whose names are on the wall and in my heart for ever.

A special thanks to Dennis Seitz, who served with the Army's 25th Division, and Earl Fisher, a fellow Corpsman, who I served with in Nam, for their encouragement and being great friends. Julie, Gail, Janet, Lisa, Icylene for all your help. To all the outstanding Nurses at Jacksonville Naval Hospital in 1967-68, you trained us well. To the Marines I was unable to save and who are on "The Wall" I hope this book helps others realize the heroes you are. Lastly, to the Marines of Delta Company, 1st Battalion, 5th Marines, who kept me alive to write this book. I'm honored to have been there to witness your bravery. You will always be my brothers. Semper Fi.

Buzz Baviello

Introduction

What is it that makes men perform in battle? Is it gallantry, courage, or just plain guts that sends them storming up a bullet-riddled beach or leaping from foxholes into withering enemy fire? If these men are a special breed, then what label do we attach to the Navy's Hospital Corpsmen whose job it is to care for the wounded? Man's natural instinct is to protect himself and to survive, but Corpsmen, through all the wars, have consistently risked their own lives to rescue fallen comrades. Whenever Marines land, Corpsmen will be alongside to assume their responsibility of "keeping as many men at as many guns as many days as possible."

The Hospital Corps is the only group in the history of the Navy to receive a blanket commendation from the Secretary of the Navy for its heroic work. Since the founding in 1898 the Corps has distinguished itself. Robert Standley was the first Hospital Corpsman to receive the Congressional Medal of Honor in 1900. During World War I they became the most highly decorated Naval unit. In World War II Navy enlisted personnel were awarded fifteen MOH's; of which Hospital Corpsmen serving with the Marines earned seven. Five out of seven Medals of Honor to Navy people in Korea again went to Corpsmen serving with the Marines. In Vietnam, of the six medals awarded to the Navy, four were awarded to Navy Corpsmen. And lastly, the first Purple Heart awarded in the Persian Gulf War went to a Hospital Corpsman attached to the Marines.

As the bible says, "Greater love hath no man than to lay down his life for his fellow human." Hospital Corpsmen have shown that love to their fellow Marines for decades. On Iwo Jima, the percentage of Corpsmen killed was greater than that of the Marines. In Vietnam, over 700 Corpsmen died while coming to the aid of Marines. Was this sacrifice worth the price? The record speaks for itself. Over 95% of all wounded Marines recovered.

Although the Hospital Corps normally serves in hospitals and aboard ship during all conflicts and in peacetime, it is with the Marine Corps that they have made their greatest impact. They are extremely proud of their tradition with the Marines, and have become a respected member of the world's most elite fighting force. Ask any Marine who's been in combat, and he'll have lavish praise for "Doc". Corpsmen are accepted as Marines. They do everything Marines do and then some. They are given the highest privilege the Marines can bestow, the honor of wearing the Marine uniform with the Eagle, Globe, and Anchor. A Corpsmen attached to an individual Marine unit is given the responsibility of seeing to the welfare of his platoon. His opinion is highly regarded and officers have been known to take orders directly from an E-3 when it deals with the medical well being of the unit. Corpsmen have even taken on the role of Chaplain as they sought to help their Marines with personal problems.

Surprisingly, very little has been written about Hospital Corpsmen or Army Medics, especially since the world is always talking about ways to stop wars and killing. These men are the only people whose job in war is not to kill, but to preserve life. Hundreds of movies and books have been made depicting the heroic deeds of the soldiers in battle but Corpsmen have never received the credit they deserve, nor have they ever asked for it. Their rewards have always been the thanks of the men they've saved and their families. The Marines know their importance and so does the enemy. In the last few war, the Japanese, NVA and VC made Corpsmen the prime targets of their snipers. For this reason, they no longer wear the traditional Red Cross on their uniforms. A tremendous responsibility has been placed on their shoulders. Navy Corpsmen often do their jobs under intense enemy fire, alone and without any doctor's supervision and their decisions and actions can often mean life or death for fellow Marines.

Chapter 1

The reflections from the swimming pool lights bounced off the water, through a window, onto a darkened ceiling. Mike and Jody embraced on the couch in the living room; her head nestled tightly against his chest. She fingered the modest diamond engagement ring as Mike watched the dancing shadows flicker above him. The only sound in the hushed room was Walter Cronkite's familiar voice welcoming everyone to the late night news.

"Are you scared?"

Mike jerked his head toward her. "Huh, what'd you say?"

"Are you scared?" She pulled her head back so she could look into his eyes.

Mike continued to stare at the ceiling, and tugged nervously at the hair on the side of his head. He contemplated the question seriously. "Yeah, I am. But I don't think I'm scared of dying. I think maybe I'm more afraid that I won't do a good enough job and cost someone his life."

"Not you, I know you. You're too conscientious. You'll do everything you can to be the best."

"You know, I've never doubted my ability before, but this, this is war, and if I screw up, someone dies."

Silence came easy as they each retreated back into their inner thoughts for the next few moments.

"Mike, I love you. Please don't try to be a hero. Just come home. I don't know what I'd do without you." She dropped her head back onto his chest and squeezed. Tears began to well up in her turquoise blue eyes.

"Hey, hon, please don't do that," he said, stroking her long, blonde hair. "I'll be okay, really. The Marines take good care of their Corpsmen."

"Why do they have to send you to Vietnam?" she asked, a hint of anger now in her voice.

"They didn't send me, remember? I volunteered. Besides, I'm no better than any other guy that went over there."

"But why do you want to go? This war makes no sense."

"I don't know, I guess I feel I just have to do my part."

"I know. You're the kind of guy who always has to face things head on, no matter what the consequences."

"That's right, and I don't think I couldn't live with myself if I'd tried to get out of this." He wiped a tear from her cheek with his thumb. "Remember, someday I'll have to teach our kids about duty and responsibility. Do you think I could do it honestly if I avoided Nam?"

"God, I miss you already." She turned quickly and flung both arms around his neck. He could feel the wetness of her tears on his face as they kissed. Slowly he pulled away, her Ambush perfume lingering in his nostrils. Their eyes held each other captive.

"It's time for me to get dressed," Mike whispered softly.

"I know."

Sliding his arm from around her shoulders, he rose and walked slowly into the bedroom. The fresh smell of the recently dry-cleaned uniform filled the room. He meticulously put on each article. His chest swelled, as he looked in the mirror at his image in the green Marine uniform with the navy blue Third Class Petty Officer rank on the left sleeve.

At twenty-one, Mike Lombardo was the oldest of five children, four boys and a girl from a traditional Irish-Italian family. Growing up in Mamaroneck, a small town in Westchester County, New York, and attending Catholic school, instilled in him a strong sense of discipline and pride.

At five foot nine, his muscular body was proof of his athleticism, while his blond hair and hazel eyes always caused people to take a second questioning glance when they heard the family name. He proudly bore the names of the two men he respected most. Mike, his dad, a former Marine, and Patrick, his maternal grandfather, who had served with the 69th Regiment of the 165th Infantry, the infamous Rainbow Division, during the first World War.

Growing up, he'd often listened to the tales of the brave men in the "Fighting 69th", men like Father Duffy, Wild Bill Donovan, and Joyce Kilmer. He also loved hearing his dad talk about the Marines on Guadalcanal and Peleliu. Now he'd be joining them as the third generation in the family to serve the country in time of war.

He had been raised to believe strongly in God and Country, and nothing seemed more right.

Saluting his reflection, he smiled, tugged on the bottom of his coat, picked up his seabag and carried it out to Mr. Hollis' car. By the time he returned, Jody and her parents were waiting in the kitchen. Each held a glass of champagne. Mr. Hollis handed Mike the bubbly liquid and offered a toast to his safe return. There was really nothing more to say. Mrs. Hollis embraced Mike, and left the room, a stream of tears rolling down her face. Jody leaned against the counter, inspecting her empty glass. Mike moved alongside, wrapped his arm around her waist, and gave her a short tender kiss. Then together, they walked into the living room, where he picked up his cover and orders off the table. As he reached to turn off the television they heard Cronkite's voice echo:

"...Two hundred and forty-five servicemen were killed in fighting throughout Vietnam this week and that's the way it is..."

Grandpa,

In a couple of hours I'll be leaving for Vietnam. I'm going to miss all of you. The party you threw for me before I left New York was super. I'll always remember the flags, and the red, white, and blue decorations. But most of all, I'll remember the last talk you and I had in your den, and the tears in your eyes as you hugged me. How lucky I've been to have loving parents, wonderful grandparents, and to live in this great country. I guess going over to Nam is a small price to pay for all I've been given. I realize many people don't believe in this war and a lot of kids my age don't agree with me, but this is my choice. I don't know what will happen, but I think we need to help the Vietnamese people. I may not be right, but would I be right if I stood by and just watched the North take over? We didn't allow it in Korea or in the other wars, so why should we start now? Maybe it'll keep my kids from having to go off to war someplace else. Thanks for everything you've taught me. I know it's made me a better person. Take care of Grandma and give her my love. I'll try to write often. See ya in a year.

Love,

Mike

Chapter 2

"We will be landing at Da Nang in fifteen minutes. The local weather is heavy overcast with a chance of heavy rainfall, while the temperature is a humid eighty-five degrees." The pilot's voice woke many of the men from their fitful naps. Seats popped into the upright position as the stewardesses raced about the cabin, securing everything for landing.

Mike looked to his right when the starboard wing of TWA Flight 327 out of Kadena Air Force Base, Okinawa, dipped slowly. The men in the center and aisle seats contorted their belted-in bodies in order to peek out the tiny, rectangular windows. Unfortunately, the plane was captured completely within the grasp of the depressing, dull gray sky. While the engines hummed their rhythmic chant, the men strained to catch a view of the Nam from above.

The nose of the plane dipped shortly after Mike heard the "Ding" and glanced up at the red flashing rectangular "No Smoking" and "Seat Belt" signs above him. His thoughts suddenly turned to his two best friends Ivan and Larry. The inseparable trio had talked many times about going over to Nam together, but as fate would have it the other two got orders to Vietnam, while Mike was sent to Pendleton. Now all he had left was a picture; both had been killed during their first four months in country.

Closing his eyes, Mike looked toward the cabin roof. *Guys, I know you're listening. Help me get through this year. Help me to be a good corpsman, stay with me, don't let me be a coward, and get me home. I won't let you down.*

Suddenly, like Moses' parting of the Red Sea, the clouds disappeared. Lush green mountains, towering above the ocean to the west, gave a sense of calm and beauty to this war torn land. Now on final approach the aircraft passed over dozens of boats and sampans. Below, the water splashed a cold, unfriendly welcome on the white, sandy beaches. The lovely steel blue of the ocean suddenly changed into the muddy brown of the Da Nang harbor.

Like an eagle swooping in on its prey, the plane glided smoothly above the runway and sped past inverted horseshoe-shaped hangars, where camouflaged F4 Phantom jets slept, waiting to be awakened. The squeal of the tires touching the runway, followed by the roar of the engines reversing, sent a shimmy through the plane as it slowed.

Mike's stomach felt like one big knot and was aware of his racing heartbeat. Minutes later, while they taxied to the terminal he watched a green truck with stairs attached to its bed, roll up toward the front. The door swung open and a corporal dressed in cammies entered and picked up the cabin microphone.

"Welcome to Da Nang." His pause allowed the words to sink in. "All Marines and attached personnel depart and load onto the cattle cars outside. All others remain seated. Someone will be here shortly."

Slowly, and in an orderly fashion, the Marines and Corpsmen departed. Surprised by the lack of gunfire they filed past a covered area filled with men in various styles of dress. Most wore tropical khaki uniforms, some had on flowered print shirts, and only a few were scattered about in dirty utilities. A murmur of greetings buzzed around them.

"Welcome to the Nam."

"You'll be sorry."

"Anyone from Iowa?"

Feeling intimidated Mike and the other new arrivals smiled nervously and quickly made their way through the gauntlet of verbal abuse.

The rain fell hard as they climbed onto an open cattle car and left the compound. Mike's stateside utilities quickly turned a dark green, and he could feel their starch running down his arms. Despite his discomfort, he watched intently as the truck weaved its way through the maze of scooters, minibuses and military vehicles. They passed through an area known as "Dog Patch," where shacks made up of every conceivable material, from C-ration boxes to plastic ponchos, lined the roads.

Children, naked from the waist down and bare-footed, played in the mud puddles along the roadside.

An old woman in a conical straw hat balanced a bar on her shoulder with a rice-filled basket hanging from each end as she pranced in a quick walk-run alongside of the truck. Out in the field, another woman her black silk pants down around her knees, squatted to relieve herself.

The mixture of both human and animal feces, burned wood, mildew, animals, and cooking fires all combined to produce an extremely repugnant odor.

These people are so primitive. How can humans live like this? Mike felt so fortunate he lived in America. Now, more then ever, after seeing this country, he felt he was doing the right thing coming to help the people of Vietnam

Across an open field Mike saw the MAF transient facility, which someone said also housed the R & R processing center. The compound, enclosed by an eight-foot wire fence, contained two terminal buildings, a mess hall, and barracks for temporarily housing Marines waiting to go on R & R or back to the World.

The truck had barely come to a stop before the men dismounted and hustled inside the terminal on their left. Once everyone was inside, all the Corpsmen's orders and Service Record Books or SRBs as they were called were collected by a Marine and taken to the Division Surgeon's office for processing.

Expecting a long wait, Mike sat on one of the many well-worn wooden church-style benches. Still dripping wet and hoping to relax he pulled out Harold Robbin's novel "The Dream Merchants," that he'd started on the flight from Okinawa and opened to the dog-eared page. Four paragraphs later he realized he couldn't remember a thing he'd read. His mind raced as he looked around and took inventory of the busy structure.

Four large openings were cut into both the east and west walls. The structure reminded him of the barn on his grandpa's farm. From his seat he could observe the flight counter that ran the entire length of the north wall. The Army and Air Force personnel behind the counter worked at a leisurely, almost non-caring, pace. Dozens of grizzly combat veterans stood impatiently at the counter or lay sprawled on the benches. No one carried a weapon and new guys like himself were as conspicuous as a boy in an all girls' school.   Feeling very much alone, even in this crowd, Mike returned to the book where at least for a while he could escape his fears.

Around noon, a Hospitalman Chief appeared and called all the Corpsmen together.

"Lombardo, Michael P.; Gifford, William T." The Chief handed each man a sealed manila envelope.

Nervously, Mike stared down at the newly typed page attached to the outside.

                                                        132629
Nov. 1969
Memorandum Endorsement
From: Commanding General 1st Marine Division (Rein), FMF
To: Hm3 Michael Patrick Lombardo B124477 USN HM-8404
        Hm3 William Thomas Gifford B185667 USN HM-8404
Subj: Orders
        1. You reported at 0915 on 29 November 1969
        2. You will further report to Commanding Officer 1st Battalion, 5th Marine Regiment for duty.
        3. Your tour completion date is established as 28 November 1970.

                                                J. S. Romano

After introducing himself to Gifford, Mike turned back to the Chief who had finished passing out the assignments.

"Where do we go from here?"

"Outside is a Jeep," the Chief said, pointing with his thumb. "It'll take you to an LZ. From the Landing Zone you can catch a helicopter to An Hoa. Good Luck."

Mike looked through the doors out into the rain. *Damn, they are already sending us into a war zone and we don't even have any weapons.*

Throwing their seabags up onto their shoulders the two corpsmen headed toward the door. A lone Marine his face expressionless, wearing a poncho, stood in the rain alongside a roofless Jeep parked near the fence.

They had to splash through several large puddles to get to the Jeep. Gifford dropped his seabag to the wet ground and addressed the weary-eyed driver. "Are you supposed to take us to the LZ?"

"Yeah. Name's Williams." He extended his hand to each Corpsman. "So, you're going to An Hoa, huh?"

"That's what they tell us." Gifford wiped the rain from the bridge of his nose with his drenched sleeve.

"Where is this place?" Mike asked, his seabag still resting on his shoulder.

Williams grabbed Gifford's bag and threw it into the back of the Jeep before answering. "Well, it's about 26 miles southwest of here."

Mike dropped his alongside, stepped on the rear bumper and climbed into the back. He then made himself comfortable on the bags as Gifford settled into the soaked passenger seat.

"You'll be working in an area called the Arizona." Williams started the engine, turned on the wipers, and accelerated the Jeep forward.

"Why's it called that?" Gifford asked, as he held onto the side of the front window and turned sideways in the seat so that he faced Williams.

"Marines named it after the old Arizona territory. You know, that was the badlands at one time." Williams formed his fingers like a gun and pulled an imaginary trigger. "You catch my meaning?"

Already extremely anxious, Mike didn't like the sound of where they wee heading.

Neither of the newbees spoke as they rolled out the compound gate and turned right. They hadn't gone more than a hundred yards when Williams pointed to his left.

"That's 'Freedom Hill'. The long building in the middle is the PX, slop-chute, and merchandise store. You can buy anything from cars to suits there. The one to the left is the USO and the one to the right is the Red Cross and chapel. It also has an air-conditioned movie theater and fully equipped bowling alley. The amphitheater back there on the hill is where the Bob Hope show will be next month. Take a good look 'cause you guys won't get to see this place again for a long time."

"Why do you say that?" Mike asked, wide-eyed. "It looks like there's a lot of guys walking around over there."

"It caters largely to rear area troops. Besides bush Marines don't get into Da Nang very often." Williams focused his concentration on the road as the Jeep fishtailed around a big curve. "It's too bad," he continued, "but all the bennies seem to go to these rear echelon commandos and, Lord knows, they don't deserve them."

"Sounds like you don't care for the rear too much," Gifford noted softly.

"Hell, no. I was in An Hoa with Echo two-five. When I got my third 'heart' in the Phu Nhuans, they transferred me back here to Division. These dudes are real assholes. The grunts in the bush are good dudes. You take care of them; they'll take care of you. It's real family out there. Also there's too much dope back here. One piece of advice: Don't do grass or drugs in the bush. That's the fastest way I know to get someone killed."

And me too, Mike thought. "Is there much drug use going on over here? He asked.

"Like I said in the rear, yeah, mainly grass, but out in the field, no. If you catch a guy using, turn him in 'cause if the guys find out, he might get a quick medevac, if you know what I mean.

The two Corpsmen looked at each other and nodded thoughtfully.

Cruising down the road, Williams continued to play the part of tour guide, pointing out Division Headquarters up on the hillside and off to the right 1st Medical Battalion, a 300-bed hospital, staffed by Navy doctors, nurses, and corpsmen.

The pavement ended abruptly and the road became a sea of mud. After a short distance the Jeep came to a stop at an intersection. Five or six Vietnamese kids who had been playing along the roadside rushed the vehicle.

"Hey, Joe, you souvenir me one pack cigmo?" yelled one of the dark-skinned shoeless kids. Several others followed suit.

"Didi mau!" Williams took a swing at the closet boy with his open hand.

Jumping back, the kid flipped him the bird.

"You numba fucking ten. VC goin' to Bac, Bac you."

"Yeah Sure. Now, didi mau lin, you little bastard, before I squash you like a grape." Williams let out a huge laugh, as he turned left and accelerated.

Gifford looked over his shoulder and kept an eye on the kids. "What was that all about?"

"Oh, that?" Williams chuckled. "Nothing. You'll learn. Kids are always hanging around the troops. They try to hustle smokes, C's, or even their sisters. Sometimes they get to be a real pain in the ass, but most of time they're okay. Out in the bush they'll carry your gear or give you a back massage for some C's. I love to fuck with them once in a while and watch them get all bent out of shape."

"What was that you yelled at them?" Gifford asked.

"Didi mau?"

"Yeah."

"It means, get out of here or go away. There are only a few key phrases you'll need to learn. "Dung Lai" means stop, "Lai Dai" means come here, and "Nuck" is water. What more do you need to know, unless, of course, you want a piece of ass and that's "Boom Boom." Well, here you are."

As Mike was searching the surrounding countryside the Jeep skidded to a stop in front of a red and gold 1st Motor Transport sign.

"Here you go guys." Williams shift the gear into neutral and waited for Mike and Gifford jump out.

Mike immediately sank ankle-deep in the thick mud.

"The LZ is across the road' Williams pointed. "Can you see it over there?"

Both Corpsmen nodded. Mike was particularly nervous, and couldn't believe how open, primitive and exposed the position seemed. *The enemy could just walk right in before anyone could stop them I bet.*

"You guys take it easy and keep your ass down." William's gave them a wide grin and held his fingers up in a V. "Peace." He put the Jeep into a quick U-turn and sped off, sending a rooster tail of mud shooting from the back tires.

Sloshing their way across the road to the LZ Mike and Giff made themselves comfortable on a sandbag wall a few feet from the LZ matting. As he waited Mikes constantly searched the ridges and open fields around them. A feeling of nakedness and vulnerability only added to his already high state of anxiety.

An hour and eight cigarettes later, a CH-53 helicopter suddenly appeared over the ridgeline to the west. Swooping in, the seven large, rotating blades on the top created hurricane force winds as the back ramp lowered. Like Jonah from the whale, a crew chief emerged followed by four grungy Marines. The Chief's face, hidden behind a black visor, turned toward the drenched Corpsmen as they cautiously approached the helicopter.

Mike screamed to be heard above the noise, as the winds buffeted his face "This thing going to An Hoa?."

Pushing the visor up, the crew chief pulled the helmet away from one ear. "What?"

Mike yelled again, this time close to the crew chief's ear. "Going to An Hoa?"

"Bet your ass, Doc. Jump in."

Mike and Gifford strode up the ramp and anxiously made themselves as comfortable as possible. Seconds later, Mike felt the jet-powered helicopter blades increase their revolutions and felt the vibrations as the chopper effortlessly lifted straight up twenty feet. The pilot pulled up on the collective causing the nose to drop a few degrees, before moved forward, gaining speed and altitude with each yard. The crew chief immediately sat down on a red nylon seat and began reading an Archie comic book he had pulled from his large leg pocket.

The door gunner, with his visor down, scanned the vegetation below as he rested one arm on the 50-caliber machine gun that pointed out the side door. All the Plexiglas windows had been removed and the cold wind whipped through the inside of the bird. The air smelled clean but Mike's eyes, watery from the strength of the wind, were riveted on the crew chief, hoping to detect the first signs of danger.

Five minutes into the flight Mike relaxed a little and finally peered out the window. The beauty of the land below quickly mesmerized him. The dark greens of the mountain jungle provided a stark contrast to the emerald checkerboard paddies. He had never seen such vivid greens before. As he focused on people working in the fields he soon realized the helicopter was now in a controlled spiral toward the earth. As they banked to the left, he could see a sprawling base camp stretched out in the valley, entirely enclosed by multiple rows of concertina and razor wire. A thick, reddish dirt berm, with green sandbag bunkers at selected intervals, encircled the compound just inside the wire. Trestled observation towers stood at numerous points around the base. A mat runway ran almost the entire length of the northern side. The main section of the camp appeared to be a network of bunkers, tents, and artillery positions. Everything seemed to be painted with a brown coat of mud.

Damn, this place is so isolated. It immediately reminded Mike of a pioneer's wagon train circled against an Indian attack.

The wheels touched, and before the ramp was all the way down the two Corpsmen raced off, and seeking cover behind a sandbag wall, fully expecting to be shot at. They had arrived at the war - - or so they thought.

Grandpa,

Arrived safe. Sure is a lot different than I thought. Didn't have to fight my way off the plane. Sometimes, if you didn't know better, you'd never know there was a war going on, especially around Da Nang.

We spent Thanksgiving in Okinawa. Ate dinner in the mess hall and it actually was pretty good. We even had pumpkin pie. Hope all of you had a good Turkey Day. I sure missed playing pool with you and Uncle Jack like we do every year, but in 355 days we'll play for double the stakes. The big question, did Stepinac beat White Plains in the Turkey Bowl? We spent our days working in the Dispensary, giving shots to the guys "going south," but at night my friends and I would open and close the NCO club. It's funny, the guys going home were pretty quiet and serious; they just drank and talked among themselves, whereas the guys headed for Nam were the ones loud and causing all the trouble. You'd think it would be the other way around. One night three other Corpsmen and myself snuck off base and hit the hot spots in a town called Naha. We even got an official Japanese bath and massage. You know the kind where the girl walks on your back? You can't believe how relaxing it was. We all got pretty drunk, but before we did, we had a huge lobster dinner for only $5.00.

As soon as I get my new address I'll send it. Bye Grandpa.

Love,
Mike

Chapter 3

An Hoa, the base camp for 1st Battalion 5th Marines, was surrounded on three sides by mountains. Two major rivers dominated the area north of the camp. The closest, the Thu Bon wound its way northwest before turning east less than a klick from the base. The second river, the Vu Gia, was more north and flowed east through a valley dotted with villages and rice paddies before finally merging into the Thu Bon. The land between these rivers was hardcore enemy land known as the "Arizona Territory."

Six miles north of An Hoa sat the mountain range affectionately known as "Charlie Ridge." It is comprised of brush-covered foothills and triple canopy jungle that intelligence said is the home of the 984th Main Force NVA headquarters. Honeycombed with supply caches, bunkers, tunnels, rough terrain and thick vegetation the location made an ideal base camp for the enemy. From there the NVA and VC could easily infiltrate into the populated areas.

The only road into An Hoa from Da Nang, Liberty Road, had to cross the Thu Bon at Liberty Bridge. This 825-foot span located near Phu Loc 6 was continually attacked by enemy units, and on one occasion was actually blown up.

Mike and Giff spent two days processing into the battalion before being assigned to an individual line unit. Gifford was shipped by truck out to Hill 65 where he joined up with Charlie Company. Mike, whose unit was currently at An Hoa, only had a short walk in the rain to get to his company.

He approached the Delta Company office and saw that it was nothing more then a hardback hootch raised a few feet off the ground. The skeleton was made of plywood and screen material for the walls.

The roof was a garrison tent with its side rolled up above the screens. Around the base of the office were dozens of layers of sandbags in a perfect geometrical shape completely around the base of the structure.

Entering, Mike detected a dank and mildewed stench permeating from inside the crowded little room. The only sound was the tat-tat-tat of a pogue using the "hunt and peck" method on a typewriter. He placed a copy of his orders on the small field desk.

"Excuse me, I've been assigned to the company. Do I report to you?"

The clerk glanced up from his letter searching and then read the orders.

"Naw, go through there and see the 'Top', he's waiting for you." He handed the orders back without looking up again.

Mike moved in the direction the finger pointed, and now noticed office actually was made up of two separate rooms. As he passed through the blanket that was hung over the doorway to separate the two rooms he was surprised to recognize the face smiling at him from behind a desk.

"Hey, Top Kramer." Mike was relieved to finally see someone he knew.

At thirty-eight, Terry Kramer had been his First Sergeant for more than a year back at Pendleton. He was the stereotype Marine. A giant of a man, well over six feet, he had muscles that bulged despite being covered by his uniform. His square, firm jaw reminded Mike of "Sergeant Rock" in the comics. He had been a private at the Chosen Reservoir in Korea and already had served one tour in Nam. Wounded four times, in the service of his country, a nasty eight-inch scar, a souvenir of a Viet Cong bullet, provided the evidence of one wound. Back at Pendleton, the Top often gathered "his boys" around him and gave advice on how to survive the Nam. "Top' was constantly concerned about the troop's welfare and he treated the men like each was a son. At times, he could be extremely harsh but he was always fair. In fact, he reminded Mike a great deal of his grandfather, and whatever he did over here, it was important that both men would be proud of him.

Coming around the desk, the First Sergeant's huge hands grabbed Mike by the shoulders. "How ya doing, Doc? It's nice to see ya again." His fingers squeezed Mike's arm muscles as he shook him like a rag doll. "When the BAS told me the names of their replacement Corpsmen, I requested you."

"I appreciate that First Sergeant." Mike was feeling a little less a lone now that he finally found someone he trusted.

The two men spent the next several minutes recalling days gone by and what had happened with the company at Pendleton since Kramer had left.

As he poured himself another cup of coffee the Top called a clerk in from the outer office. "Take Doc over to supply and have them issue him his "deuce" gear and a weapon." Turning back to Mike, "When you finish, come back here. The Skipper should be here by then and I'll introduce you."

Excited to be finally getting a weapon to defend himself Mike nodded, and followed the clerk out into the mud and the rain.

Upon reaching the supply tent, he was given a complete issue of gear from boots to helmet. He stuffed it first into a willie peter (water proof) bag to keep it dry, then into a rucksack. The next stop was the armory, which was just twenty-five yards away in a large corrugated tin structure. The armor, a grizzly Gunnery Sergeant, painstakingly wiped the excess cosmoline off the weapon before handing it to Mike, then recorded the weapon's serial number as Mike read it off.

With the weapons log signed, Mike, and his guide returned to the company office. He dropped the heavy rucksack on the wooden floor and strolled into the office carrying his new weapon.

The Top, talking to a couple of officers, had his back to him and, as usual, a coffee cup in his hand.

"Excuse me, Top," Mike interrupted. "I've got my deuce gear. Now what?"

"Get over here, Squid." Top motioned with his cup. "Doc Lombardo, this is Captain Christopher, our CO."

Instinctively, Mike snapped to attention. "Pleased to meet you, sir."

"Good to have you on board, Doc. We sure need you. The company's been short Corpsmen since the 'Arizona' and, from what the Top tells me, you're a good man."

"Thank you, sir. I hope I can live up to the his expectations." He could feel his palms sweat and as usual, he was nervous in the company of brass.

"I've sent for Doc Mitchell. He's our Senior Corpsman and he'll assign you to a platoon." Looking down at the weapon in Mike's hand the Captain smiled. "I see you're carrying a "16." We must have a gungy squid on our hands, hey, Top?"

"Not really, sir." Mike raised the rifle and patted it with his free hand. "But I did get the idea from the Top." Sneaking a peek toward the First Sergeant, Mike thought he detected a hint of approval. "He told me when we were both back at Pendleton, that Corpsmen and officers were prime targets for snipers, and advised me to look as little like a Corpsman as possible. Besides, I guess if I'm not needed medically, an extra rifle might come in handy in a fire fight." Mike watched as the two officers nodded approvingly and heard the dull thud of boot heels on the wood coming from behind. Turning, he immediately spotted the caduceus emblem pinned on the man's shirt collar.

"Doc Mitchell, this is the new replacement, Mike Lombardo." The two corpsmen shook hands, while the captain continued to speak. "Get him squared away then get back here in an hour. We're having a CP meeting."

"Aye Aye, Sir."

"Doc, again, it's good to have you with us. My best advice to you is listen to the veterans, watch what they do, stay alert, and you'll get home in one piece. Good luck, son," Captain Christopher said before returning to his cluttered desk.

Mike said goodbye to the Top then turned and walked shoulder to shoulder with Mitchell out of the office.

"By the way, Mike, call me Mitch."

The Senior Corpsman was about the same height as Mike but much thinner. His dark hair was cut boot camp-style and he sported a neatly trimmed moustache. The accent was definitely Northeastern - - Maine or maybe - - Massachusetts. He had been the Senior Corpsman for little over two months and his main function was to serve as the liaison between the medical staff at the BAS and Delta Company. He was also responsible for ordering all the medical supplies needed by the seven Corpsmen assigned to the company.

"How long have you been in country, Mitch?" Mike asked.

Mitchell slipped in the mud. "Almost eight months. Damn, all this mud sucks." He wiped the mud from the hand that he had put down to keep himself from falling on his pant leg. "I'm gonna assign you to Second Platoon. The guy you're replacing was medevaced last week." Mike's eyes widened and Mitchell didn't wait for him to ask. "He took a bullet through the right shoulder, but he'll be okay. He's probably doing a lot better than we are right now. That's Second Platoon's area up ahead."

The side flaps of the old Korean War vintage garrison tent were rolled up. Several Marines sat on cots arranged in two neat rows along each side of the tent. Weapons, packs, flak jackets, helmets, web gear, and other assorted articles were strewn on the cots and wooden floor. Four of the men were engaged in a boisterous card game at the far end.

All eyes swung in their direction the instant they entered the tent, but returned immediately to what they were doing. Mitch directed Mike over toward a large, dark-haired man with a bushy Fu Manchu moustache lying on a cot, reading a paperback.

"Mike Lombardo, this big water buffalo is Doc Chris Graham."

Mike had to look up to see Graham's face as he stood. "Pleased to meet you, Mike." The handshake was vice-like and the voice seemed much too gentle and soft for the size of the man using it. His round face and burly features gave Mike the impression of a bear.

"So, where were you stationed last, Mike?" Graham asked as he sank back onto the cot.

"Camp Pendleton." Mike dropped the pack and rifle on the empty cot and sat.

"Were you at the hospital, or with a grunt unit?"

"Grunts."

Graham shook his head and winced "You poor guy. To go from that to this, someone must not like you."

"No, really, I enjoyed it. It was great duty, besides..."

"All right, all right, you two can get better acquainted later." Mitchell pulled a notebook and pencil from his shirt pocket. "What medical supplies do you want me to order for you?"

"Well, let's see." Mike thought for a minute. "I've got all the stuff in my Unit 1, but I'd like another three dozen battle dressings, a couple of small bottles of plasma, and a bottle of D5W, along with a few IV set ups." As Mitchell wrote Mike went over his own checklist in his mind. "Oh, yeah, what about pills?"

"I'll get you some aspirin, Benadryl, and a small bottle of Darvon. The BAS has made up a package of stuff for colds and other illnesses. I'll get that, too."

"Don't forget the most important of all," Graham interjected with a chuckle.

"What's that?" Mitchell's puzzled look showed he didn't understand.

"Lomotil."

"Ah, how could I have forgotten that?" His eyes rolled and grimaced as he remembered the pain. "I had the shits so bad for almost two weeks, I thought my asshole would fall off. Lomotil was the only thing that saved me."

"Mike, I'd also suggest you go back to supply and draw yourself another canteen cover. You can use it to carry the plasma in while on patrol."

"Thanks, Chris, I'll do that. Yeah, one more thing, what about morphine?"

"I'll have to draw it for you." Closing his notebook Mitchell stood.

"Chris, why don't you come with me and we'll get the supplies. Mike can stay here and get settled."

"Alright, sounds good." Graham put on his bush cover and extended his hand, which Mike shook again. "I'll catch you in a little bit."

"Good."

As soon as they were gone Mike changed out of the ripe stateside utilities he had worn everyday for the past week, into the pair of the clean jungle cammies he had just been issued. The card game at the other end was just breaking up.

"You guys are the biggest bunch of cheaters. I saw you trying to communicate with your eyes."

"Ah, take your losses like a man, and quit whining, will ya?"

"Naw, even with all your cheating you wouldn't have won if I had played the Jack."

Mike smiled at the good-natured bantering, but then fidgeted nervously as one of the winners, a shirt less, razor-thin black Marine, stared at him. Out of the corner of his eye Mike saw him reach into a box and start to shuffle in his direction. The man's muscles seemed to be chiseled into his skin, and immaculate white teeth gleamed across a wide smile.

"Happenin', Doc? Name's Ron Allen." He sat and handed Mike a warm RC Cola. "Where's you all from?" The words came out slow and heavy with drawl.

"New York. How about you?"

"South Carolina."

"The armpit of the United States," yelled one of the men from the other end of the tent.

Allen growled and flipped him off. Turning back to Mike, a grin spread across his face. "Is there anything you need?"

"Sure is. Do you know where I can get some bandoleers to hold my battle dressings and ammo magazines? Also, I'll need some M-16 rounds."

Without hesitating Allen pushed off the seat and walked slowly over to another cot. He pulled a green metal ammo can with yellow writing on the side out from underneath, and carried it back over to Mike's bunk.

A loud metallic pop rang out as he unlatched the flap. Lifting the lid, Allen took out five small tan cardboard boxes and tossed them onto the canvas next to Mike.

"One of those is tracers," Allen said, pointing. "Put one every fifth round. Here's a charger guide also, will help you load them faster. You can get as many empty bandoleers as you want in that wooden box down there."

"Thanks." Mike pulled the empty magazines from the rucksack and began to load the brass shells.

"How long have you been here?"

"Almost seven months, but it feels like seven years," Allen answered dryly.

The son of a cotton picker, Lance Corporal Ron Allen had been a platoon radioman for the last three months. Before that, he was one of the best in the company at walking point. He had been wounded once, but only slightly, when an RPG round exploded near him during a firefight. He was well liked in the platoon because of his infectious laugh and he always seemed to find the good in something or someone.

Mike retrieved a number of rounds that had fallen on the floor. "I keep hearing about a place called the Arizona."

"Oh, yeah, man," Allen said, bobbing his head up and down slowly.

"It's bucu bad. Back in May the whole regiment buckled with the NVA for a big man's ass."

"Buckled? What is that? Mike asked.

"Means we fought. You know buckled for your dust. We killed 300 to 400 of those little bastards on the first day alone. A couple of companies from 3/5 lost so many men on that op, they had to be relieved. You're lucky though. We just came out of there a few days ago so we won't be going back for a while."

"Where is it from here?"

"Just across the river." Allen said, pointing to the northwest.

Mike was working on his third magazine when another Marine, who looked like a schoolteacher behind his black-rimmed government-issue glasses, approached and tossed a mud-splattered paper at him. It floated almost to the floor before Mike was able to catch it. Quickly scanning the page Mike saw that it contained the "zulu" or service numbers for everyone in the platoon that he'd use for identification in case of medevac.

"I'll get with you later and go over radio procedures." The tone of the voice was definitely unfriendly.

"That'll be great," Mike said smiling. "It shouldn't take too long; I think I know most of them. You see, I was with the 28th Marines at Pendleton for the last year and a half, but I'm . . ."

"Okay, then fuck it, man. I got other things to do anyhow." His eyes glared as he spoke.

Mike was taken back by his attitude but, wanting to make friends with all the men, decided to try again. "Are we doing any good over here?"

"Fuck, no. All that shit about winning this war back in the world is bullshit. We fight and lose guys for the same area over and over again. We take it; leave it, and the gooks move back in and we have to go take it back again. This place is truly fucked. But you'll learn, boot." Without waiting for a response, he walked away.

Shocked, Mike looked at Allen and whispered nervously. "What did I say wrong?"

"Nothing, Doc. Don't pay much attention to Weller right now. His best friend got wasted a few days ago and he's been real bitter ever since."

"That's too bad." Mike paused. "What's the best way to treat a guy when something like that happens?"

"Just leave him be. He'll get over it. We all do. He really is a good dude. Just give him time, you'll like him." He stood and motioned with his hand. "Come on, Doc, I'll introduce you to the rest of the CP."

Mike was introduced to man one at a time and engaged in a brief conversation with each. Corporal "Rocky" Roads, the platoon guide, a stocky, cherub-faced young man with a heavy Boston accent, was the platoon comedian who never seemed to run out of funny stories or jokes. McGravey, the Platoon Sergeant on his second tour, had jet black hair combed straight back and sported a bushy moustache that extended down past the corners of his mouth. Neither his hair nor moustache would have met regulations stateside. Mike had already received a rude welcome from Bobby Weller, the head radioman. The third radioman, L/Cpl Gino Estes,the youngest of the bunch and the only one married. He was only eighteen and spent most of his free time reading "Superman" comic books, which his mom sent him from Brooklyn.

The last member of the group was one of the platoon Squad leaders named Sam Wilson from North Carolina. Standing 6 foot 1 he was the most educated of all the men in the tent. Having earned his Bachelors from North Carolina State University. He could easily have become an officer but chose to be enlisted like his two older brothers, father and grandfather before him.

Roads walked over and sat beside Mike. "Hey, Doc, did you hear the one about the Marine who wanted to learn more about Catholics, so he asks the chaplain if he could sit in on confessions?"

"No."

"The first Marine comes in and says 'Bless me, Father. . . I've been down in the ville and I've been to bed with a cyclo girl three times."

"The padre says, 'Say a rosary and put five dollars in the box when you leave.'"

"A second Marine comes in and says 'Bless me, Father. . . I've been down in the ville and I've been to bed with a cyclo girl three times."

"The padre says, 'Say a rosary and put five dollars in the box when you leave.'"

"The young Marine is all excited and says, 'I think I got it. Can I do the next one?'"

"The chaplain says, 'Okay.'"

"Pretty soon another Marine comes in. 'Bless me, Father. . . I've been down in the ville and been to bed with a cyclo girl once.'"

"The Marine, proud of himself, turns to the guy and says, 'You go back and do it two more times. We have a sale this week...three for five dollars.'"

Laughter filled the tent; even Weller cracked a smile.

"You know you got here at the wrong time, don't you?" asked Wilson, with a hint of a smile

"Why's that?"

"Haven't you heard about Jeanne Dixon's prediction?"

"No, I haven't."

"According to her, sometime in December the Battalion's supposed to be wiped out. Anyone with a four in their service number will be killed, and a seven will be wounded."

Mike wasn't sure what to make of the prediction. He never believed in that stuff, so he brushed it off lightly. "Shit, I guess I don't stand a chance. I wonder if I'll get killed first, then wounded, or wounded, then killed. My service number is B124477."

"You's in big trouble, man. Just stay away from me," Allen joked and held his hands out as if to ward him off.

"Well, one good thing, if it's true, I won't have to spend a whole year over here."

Estes put on his flak jacket and helmet before standing. "Doc, we're going to chow. You want to come?"

"Naw, I think I'll pass. Now that I have an address I want to write some letters so I can get some mail."

"Yeah, you can't believe how important a letter is over here," said Roads as he walked by.

"I thought we were in the rear? Why are you guys all wearing helmets and flak jackets?"

"Rockets. Never know when they'll hit. Colonel Webb says we all gotta wear them anytime we leave our tent area," answered Allen. "We'll catch you later, squid."

Pulling out some paper Mike laid on his cot. The area was quiet, except for the splatter of raindrops on the canvas tent as he wrote Jody about the events of the past week. Has it only been a week? It seems like months since I left.

As darkness covered the landscape eight candles, held in place by hardened wax, provided the only light in the tent. The earlier group of card players had begun another game. Finishing his last letter Mike decided to go over and watch. They were engaged in a game that was a combination of rummy, hearts, and bridge called Back Alley Bridge, which he had played often. Standing behind Allen he watched the radioman pull the nine of diamonds from his hand and snap it on the cot. Good play.

Suddenly, a monstrous explosion rocked the area, blowing out the candles and sending Mike scrambling to the floor. He lay trembling as the candles were relit. When he looked around he saw everyone still in the same place they were before the explosion, looking at him laughing. Somewhat embarrassed, he started to get up when another explosion rang out, sending him flying to the floor again.

"Stay down, Doc. You'll get tired getting up and down all night," joked Roads, still laughing.

Mike by now had made it to his feet and was brushing himself off, his face beet red.

"Listen, Doc. That's only H & I. You know, "harassing and interdicting" fire," Allen said kindly. "It's outgoing."

"Outgoing? Shit, how the hell do you tell the difference?" He jerked toward the ground again as another blast echoed, but caught himself.

"Incoming is usually rockets," Weller replied sarcastically, without shifting his attention from the game.

"It will sound like you're standing next to a train going by at high speed. Besides man, if you hear it hit, it's too late to do anything about it." Allen gave him a big grin and a wink. "Don't feel bad, Doc. We all went through the same thing, even Weller. You'll get used to it."

Time in An Hoa passed slowly, but by the end of the second week Mike received his first mail, which picked up his spirits. Each morning, right after breakfast, he and Graham would hold sick call. The most common ailment was what they called "gook sores." These nasty looking open lesions, usually started out as a small scratch and if left untreated spread into a very serious infection due to the unsanitary conditions in Vietnam. When it did the festering ulceration had to be scrubbed with a stiff brush and Phisohex until they bled. Antiseptic and a bandage were applied to keep it clean, and, when necessary, antibiotics were administered to fight the infection.

Sicknesses like colds and sore throats were treated routinely with pills. Anything they felt they couldn't handle was sent to the doctor at the BAS. The only other responsibility they had while in An Hoa was accompanying the platoon to guard the perimeter every other night. Most of the time, the Corpsmen had little if anything to do, except sit around, play cards, and bullshit. The Marines, on the other hand, spent much of their time trying to avoid the Gunny and his working parties.

Mike was becoming more and more comfortable with the guys in the platoon; even Weller had warmed up to him.

It was their turn for lines, so right on schedule at 1800 Allen, Graham, and Mike gathered up their poncho liners and buckling gear and headed out to the northern perimeter of the camp. When they arrived and entered the CP tent behind the berm, Weller and Roads were already there. Sergeant Mac was just finishing a meeting with the squad leaders.

"Okay, men, we'll have our normal four-man positions with one hundred percent alert until 2400, then twenty-five percent." Mac looked at each squad leader before continuing. "Make sure your 'girls' pick up their frags and pop-ups. Don't forget to remind them to hook up their claymores. Questions? Okay then, let's get it done. We'll call you on the land line when mid-rats get here." Before they had gotten too far away, he yelled an afterthought. "Don't let your people sleep."

Twenty minutes after meeting ended the tent flap flew open and a tall, well-built man entered carrying a case of Coke under one arm.

"Hey, Lieutenant, nice to have you back," yelled Allen.

"You've been skating for a big man's ass," Roads added.

Mike had just assumed Mac was in charge of the platoon and hadn't even thought about the lack of an officer.

The Lieutenant smiled. "Evening, men. Thought we could use some drinks tonight." He dropped the sodas on a cot and took off his rain suit.

"How was Da Nang, sir?" Graham asked.

"Great. I feel much better. Thanks for sending me."

Graham explained to Mike that the Lieutenant had been sent to 1st Med a few weeks prior because of a recurring high fever.

"Sir, this is our new Corpsman, Mike Lombardo," Graham said.

Mike stood as the Lieutenant extended his hand. "Nice to meet you, Doc. I'm Lieutenant Bach." He looked at Graham with a grin. "It's about time we got ourselves a 'squid' that knows what the hell's going on."

Lieutenant Kenny Bach stood a little over six four and had been an All-American defensive end at the University of Maryland before joining the Corps. As was typical of the service, they took a man with a degree in English Literature and made him the leader of grunts. Not that his men ever complained; they respected him and were thankful to have him. He didn't cut them much slack but as the men said, "He had his shit together." They knew he wasn't using the war to get medals or promotions. His only goal was to get as many of his Marines home as he could. The hardness around his eyes told Mike that he had seen a lot.

After talking to everyone for a few minutes he and the sergeant went to the far end of the tent and met among themselves. By the time they finished a loud and heated game of team Back Alley was in progress. The team of Mike and Allen had set Graham and Roads, and they were sticking the needle in and twisting it good, when a monstrous, earthshaking rumble shook the air. The camp's sirens started to blare. Cards flew in all directions. Mike watched those around him, making sure he wouldn't be the only one moving.

"INCOMING."

Grabbing his gear on the run, Mike followed the others as scrambling outside and into a nearby bunker. Four huge explosions shook the ground beneath them.

"Mothafucking rockets," Allen cursed, covering his head with his hands and scrunching into a ball.

Fear filled every cell in Mike's body as he tried to make himself disappear into the ground. Time seemed to stand still as he waited and waited for the next rumble of rockets. When the night remained silent he uncoiled and looked around to see how the others were reacting.

The Bach was the first to crawl out of the bunker. He quickly surveyed the area, and then yelled back inside. "Sarge, get all the men out of the bunkers into their fighting holes. Allen, get on the horn to 6 and see what's up."

Like a well-oiled machine the platoon swung into action.

With his body still trembling Mike exited the bunker, and immediately saw where the rockets had impacted. A huge fireball raged two to three hundred feet in the air at the opposite end of the base. A bright orange-yellow glow flickered on their faces as secondary explosions sent shockwaves echoing throughout the valley. Mike and Graham stood in awe for a few moments before heading into the tent to don their flak jackets and prepare their medical gear in case of attack.

Realizing that he might see his first combat at any minute, Mike's mine filed with hundreds of thoughts and emotions at once. Now he would find out once and for all, if he had guts or would he be a coward.

Allen was telling everyone what he had learned over the radio by the time Mike returned to where the Lieutenant had gathered the squad leaders.

"One rocket hit the fuel dump square on, which I'm sure you guessed. The other three landed in 2/5's area. They have 'bucu' casualties."

Well at least it is not any of our guys Mike thought.

"Alright, let's keep your people ready. The gooks may come, and they may not, but we don't want any surprises." Dismissing the squad leaders he, Allen, and Mac quickly made their way to their position on the berm. Mike and Graham decided to go along rather than stay at the CP tent.

Mike joined the Lieutenant in a bunker. He looked toward the fighting holes to his left and right and noticed that the Marines had their rifles resting on the front sandbags and pointed in the direction the gooks would come. He nervously squinted and scanned the blackness to the front of his position looking for any signs of movement. Then suddenly illumination was up all around the camp. It flickered an eerie glow, as it descended beneath its parachute. The dull light it cause played tricks with the shadows as all the bushes and trees seemed to move the longer Mike stared at them. The fear he experienced earlier had disappeared, as his focus was now on trying to spot enemy movement outside the wire.

Mike could hear the rhythmic thwomp, thwomp, thwomp of helicopters overhead. He turned and watched three choppers land in 2/5's area. They remained on the ground for four to five minutes before taking off again, silhouetted against the still-roaring flame. Thick, oily-smelling clouds, blown by the wind in their direction, made his eyes burn.

After more than an hour of waiting, the word was finally passed to stand down. As Mike left his fighting hole and walked back to the tent he noticed that the flames were almost out, but a nauseating smell hung over the area. Like tired, exhausted and walking like zombies, the men in the CP group went straight to their cots, rolled up in their poncho liners and went to sleep. Everyone except Mike... It was his turn for radio watch.

Grandpa,

Came under fire tonight for the first time. We were hit with 122mm rockets. Didn't last long but I couldn't imagine having to survive the shelling you had to withstand. How the hell did you ever cope with it?

I felt so helpless not knowing where those damn things would land. Actually, they landed a good distance from us but it sounded like they were coming right in on me. I'm okay so don't worry.

The sun came out today for the first time since I got here. Most of us spent the day laying around, soaking up the rays and trying to dry our musty smelling gear. With all the sun we did get a little bad news. We're going out to the bush tomorrow and, as with all good grunts, the bitching started right away and is still going on. Down deep, I think many of the guys were really getting tired of An Hoa and actually wanted to get out to the bush again. Now we can start kicking some ass.

Grandpa, 5th Marines has a great history. If I remember right, weren't they the same unit that you fought alongside at Belleau Woods and in the Argonne Forest? I remember you telling me how the Germans nicknamed them "Devil Dogs." I really find it kind of ironic, me going into battle with the very same Marine unit that was with you in the First World War. What are the odds on that? This country smells really bad and there is mud everywhere, just like at Verdun. I'm scared, but please don't let mom know. You know how she worries. Grandpa, I'm really proud to be serving my country and hope I can make you proud of me. From what I've seen I think my unit will measure up pretty good to the old "69th" and the "Devil Dogs" from the "big war". Well, at least when I come home we'll have a lot to talk about.

Mike

Chapter 4

Early the next morning, Second Platoon was flown out to Hill 52, five miles northwest of An Hoa. Two full canteens, first aid kit and K bar hung from a cartridge belt buckled around the waist. Along with that everyone wore a six-pound Flak jacket, four-pound helmet, and forty pounds of pack and ammo appropriate to each man's individual weapon. This was just the routine gear. Machine gunners and A-gunners had gun ammo crisscrossing their chest, Pancho Villa. Mortarmen carried the long, thin mortar tubes that weighed ten pounds on their shoulder, or a number of five-pound 60mm mortar rounds. Radiomen had the extra weight of the PRC-25 field radio with spare batteries. Added to this, everyone carried three C-ration meals, pop-up flares, claymores, and frags. The constant rain that saturated their equipment and uniforms as they waited for the word to move to another position four klicks east made everything even heavier.

"Okay men, lock and load." Lieutenant Bach shouted the order loud enough for all to hear.

Dozens of magazines were immediately freed from their pouches and jammed into rifles. The sound of bolts seeding rounds into the chamber was instantaneously followed by the "click" of safeties.

Mike could feel a chill run up his spine and his stomach start to churn. Nervously, his eyes tried to see everything at once and his heart pounded hard inside his chest.

"First squad lead out, staggered column, keep an interval." Bach's voice dominated the area despite the noise of the pouring rain.

Like a huge uncoiling snake they began to move slowly down the slippery hill.

From the Halls of Montezuma, to the shores of Tripoli. We will fight our Country's battles on the land, air, and, the sea. The tune and words echoed in Mike's head.

Reaching the bottom, the pointman turned left onto a muddy road where the platoon divided into two columns, one on each side. Every Marine in the platoon made a conscious effort to keep a good distance from the man on the opposite side.

Despite the thick pasty mud caked on their boots, the platoon moved along at a good pace. Thick, menacing, green hedgerows lining both sides of the narrow road drew everyone's attention.

They rounded a bend and a small ville came into view. White, wispy smoke ascended above the hootches before dissipating into the air. The clean fresh smell of the wet vegetation changed to the musty odor of damp straw, burned wood, and body excrement. The clucking of chickens and the squeal of pigs came from somewhere behind the row of hootches.

Mike watched and followed suit, as the pointman brought his rifle up to a ready position, and clicked the safety off. As he approached structures his eyes darted back and forth trying to follow every little movement. Walking cautiously, Mike wondered how many of these people were VC. Now the words of his Marines back at Pendleton came flooding back to him, that the people were farmers by day and VC at night.

Several villagers smiled waved, while others only stared or went about their business. Most of the women wore baggy black silk pants and white cotton button-down tops. Their hair, secured in a bun, was covered by a conical straw hat. Their teeth were stained black from their use of betalnut, which was chewed constantly to kill pain. The old men and young boys wore tan shorts and a variety of colored shirts. No one wore shoes.

A little boy of about ten, riding on top of a large gray water buffalo, suddenly, steered the animal onto the road in front of Mike. The horns were enormous and the power of the beast became obvious as it neared. The animal's head suddenly turned in Mike's direction and released a mean, throaty snort. Stepping backward slowly, Mike raised and pointed his rifle at the beast as it continued toward him.

Through the pouring rain, Mike nervously watched the boy give the animal a hard smack on the head and a hard jerk on the rope attached to the ring in the beast's nose. The buffalo responded without protest, and proceeded passively into the flooded field.

Mike's eyes stayed riveted on the animal until he was sure he was safe.

A hundred yards past the ville the platoon left the road and headed north. The entire area ahead stretched out in a checkerboard pattern of flooded paddies, separated by dikes. Rather then walk in the waist deep water the platoon moved single file on the top of the dikes. As they moved further into the field Mike could see the men ahead spread out in a zig-zag fashion following the earthen paths.

Goosh. Goosh. Mike could hear the sound echo with each step he took. The doughy consistency of the mixture of mud and animal dung forced Mike to exert extra effort with each step to free his boots from the gray quagmire. His legs not accustomed to humping this type of terrain had turned to Jell-O, and the weight of the pack cutting into his shoulders drained almost every ounce of strength he had left. To his dismay, the final leg of the journey had them climbing a steep hill in order to enter the perimeter of concertina wire and tanglefoot. At the top they were greeted with cheers by a platoon from Alpha Company, who had been occupying it for the last three weeks.

Relieved, Mike plopped down without removing his pack and leaned back against it. Despite the rain splattering on his helmet, Mike became cognizant of the fact that the hill was only about thirty yards in diameter and clear of all brush. The reddish earth, dotted with fighting holes connected by trenches, stuck out like a bald man in a barbershop. Flooded rice paddies stretched far into the horizon to the east, south, and west. Mike could hear the trickle of a river at the base of the northern end, while a klick farther north; "Charlie Ridge" towered above him.

Allen and Graham were already busy snapping their ponchos together in order to build a hootch to get out of the rain by the time Mike slipped his pack off. He helped them spread the ponchos over a topless sandbag square left by the previous tenants. Two steel bars stuck out of the ground on opposite ends and a third bar was lashed to the other two, so that it ran across the length of the sand bags. After draping the ponchos over the bar, they tied the four ends with cord to stakes in the ground, while Mike took his poncho and covered the remaining open space. With the inside now waterproof Allen crawled in through an opening in the sandbags and laid down a sheet of clear plastic so they could stow their gear.

The rain had finally stopped, and it was nearly time for lunch. Mike dug into his pack for one of the three rectangular cardboard boxes he'd humped all morning. He had long ago learned the art of fixing C-rations. As always he removed the dark brown foil package of essentials, and set it aside. It contained sugar, salt, powdered cream, matches, a box of four cigarettes, two Chiclets, a plastic spoon, and, most importantly, shit paper.

Pulling his dog tags out from under his skive shirt, he grabbed the P-38 can opener, affectionately called a "John Wayne," attached to the chain. He opened a small can containing four crackers and candy bar which he removed and set aside. Taking the empty can he punched holes with the John Wayne all the way around on top and bottom, then pinched the sides of the can inward converting it into a stove. With the hard part done, he opened a can of pork slices and lit the heat tab he had dropped in the tiny stove. A blue flame appeared, and a noxious odor burned at the inside of his nasal passages and eyes. In minutes the meat was hot and he used the crackers and cheese to make a sandwich. Dessert was a large can of thick, syrupy fruit cocktail, followed by a stale C-ration Kool cigarette.

Mike lit the cigarette just as the rain began to fall again. Within seconds the paper on the Kool was completely soaked. Mike flicked the soggy cigarette away, looked up at the cloud, and grinned, as the raindrops splattered on his face. *Only three hundred and fifty-five to go.*

The routine remained the same for the next few days. Day long squad-sized patrols went out in the morning, and at night LPs fanned out from the perimeter. Mike and Graham alternated going on the patrols. Corpsmen weren't required to go on LPs, so they spent their nights inside the perimeter on radio watch.

Despite not having had any contact with the enemy yet, the evenings were never dull. In one direction, Mike could watch illumination with its eerie glow float to the ground off in the distance. Turning around he'd see green and red tracers, spitting back and forth. He'd listen to the shells, from the big guns on Hill 65 or An Hoa, roar across the valley and land somewhere in the darkness. Every so often, he'd hear the swish of a pop-up flare soaring into space. Seconds later, the star cluster burst, each color meaning something different, and reminded him of Fourth of July fireworks.

Being the "boot" of the CP Mike always got the graveyard radio watch. The hardest part was staying awake, but tonight he would have no trouble. Earlier he had gotten two letters from Jody and the watch would provide him with the opportunity to read them again, alone. As soon as he called the first "sit rep," he pulled his poncho over his head and began reading by flashlight.

Grandpa,

Finally made it out to the bush. We're about 5 miles north of our base camp, on a tiny knoll called Hill 25. It rains all the time and we're constantly saturated. Just no getting around it. With all the walking we do in water, keeping my feet in good shape is a top priority. So I try to change my socks a lot. I've learned not to wear underwear since all they do is cause a rash. Usually when we do go out on the patrols all I have on is my rain suit pants and combat gear. I try to keep my clothes dry for when I get back. That way I can stay warm at night.

A few of the guys in my unit are some pretty hard dudes. They treat the Vietnamese we come into contact with real bad. You know, pushing, shoving, pointing weapons threateningly at them, and cursing them. They look like they're enjoying it, too. I'm not really sure how to react to it all, but it seems wrong to me. So far the people I've encountered with haven't warranted that kind of treatment. A couple of times I almost said something, but kept my mouth shut. I haven't been here long enough to know what these guys do.

I've been on a C-ration diet for a week now and have lost about ten pounds. I'm sick of C's already and we're supposed to be here two or three more weeks. Please have everyone send care packages with lots of good food. Oh, I forgot to tell Mom I need more socks and some Kool-Aid or instant ice tea. Any thing to kill the taste of the water. It tastes like shit!

Got a patrol, so I'll end now. Please do me a favor give Jody a call and reassure her. She sounds real worried. You're good at that kind of stuff. Thanks, take care and God bless.

All my love,
Me

Chapter 5

With the hidden dangers of Charlie Ridge looming up ahead, and the sun creeping slowly over the horizon to their right, second squad emerged from thick underbrush into a large monsoon-flooded paddy. As each man waded into the leech-infested water they discovered, to their surprise, that the water was over waist deep. The mud below their feet was soft and slippery, making movement slow and difficult. On several occasions someone would lose his balance and go completely underwater.

Mike's eyes continually searched the treelines around them. Pictures of Marines wading through the surf under heavy enemy fire at places like Tarawa during World War II flashed through his mind. He had no doubt that they'd experience the same fate if the gooks opened up on them while in such an exposed position. He prayed for everyone to walk a little faster.

Upon reaching dry ground Wilson, the squad leader, halted the patrol.

"Take five and check for leeches that might have hitchhiked their way across the paddy."

Quickly Mike removed his flak jacket and pulled down his pants. A half dozen of the black blood-sucking parasites had attached themselves to his legs and torsos. Applying the amber tip of his cigarette to the first leech, Mike grabbed the slimy creature with his first two fingers and thumb and threw it repulsively into the bushes. Having these things sucking on me is just another step farther from being a normal human being.

Despite blood dripping down his chest and legs from where the leeches had been, Mike casually put his gear back on and followed Allen as the patrol moved out.

By the time they approached checkpoint four, a ville two klicks east of the CP, it had started raining again. The downpour pounded onto the thatched roofs of the village. Freezing the squad in place with a raise of his hand the point approached the tiny hamlet cautiously. He looked and listened for several minutes before he was satisfied that the area was secure and signaled the squad forward.

"Okay guys, we'll take a 15-minute break here. Use the hootches for shelter and get in out of the rain," Wilson ordered before turning to Allen. "Call in checkpoint 4."

Entering the second hootch on the right, Mike shook the rain from his hands and wiped his face. The hootch was made up of one room about the size of a living room back in the world. The floor was dirt, packed hard like a well-used carpet. In the far corner a middle-aged woman was using an earthen fireplace, similar to the ones the early pioneers must have used in the old West. A large clay pot of rice sat alongside. The bed, chairs, and tables were all primitive, hand-made articles. The mamasan paid no attention, and went about her business as though he wasn't there.

Despite being an uninvited guest Mike grabbed a small stool, sat and made himself comfortable. Using his K-bar he began to clean the mud from his boots. As he scrapped at the foul smelling gray slime, he couldn't help but notice a baby girl clutching onto her mother's leg over near the fireplace. She had her black hair cut pageboy-style and couldn't have been more than a year-and-a-half. Like most babies in Vietnam, she was naked from the waist down exposing a number of ugly open sores on her pudgy brown legs.

"Hey, mamasan." Mike called to the women several times without a response. When she finally did turn he smiled and motioned with his hand. "You bring babysan here." The leather-skinned women leered at him suspiciously and pulled the child closer.

"Wilson," Mike had turned to his squad leader who stood in the doorway. "How do I let her know I only want to take care of her baby's sores?"

Sam Wilson slid alongside the woman, tapped her on the shoulder, and pointed to Mike. "Bac si. Bac si, make babysan numba one. Washy wash."

The woman nodded her head, relaxed, and walked the child over to where Mike was sitting. Lifting the little girl up onto his knee, he examined the red, festering lesions before he unzipped the Unit-1. Pulling out a green plastic bottle of Phisohex and a small bristle brush, Mike poured a generous amount of the white liquid soap over the wounds. Holding one of the baby's legs tightly in one hand, he picked up the brush with the other and began scrubbing. The little girl screamed in pain as he rubbed harder and harder. His stomach turned over inside as her wails got louder, but he knew the sores had to be thoroughly cleaned in order to heal. The crying turned to non-stop sobs when he finally finished and rinsed off the blood and crud. He allowed the hydrogen peroxide he poured over the raw wounds to foam for several seconds before applying bacitracin from a blue and white tube onto each using a cotton-tipped swab. Putting the wooden end of the swab between his teeth, like a cut man in a boxer's corner, Mike bandaged the wounds with Telpha pads and gauze. Once everything was done, he grabbed her under her armpits, lifted her up above his head, and wiggled her back and forth. Tiny teardrops ran down her innocent face as she continued sobbing.

"Hey, pretty girl. Sssh, don't cry, it's all over." The long stick in his mouth bounced up and down as he spoke. "Mamasan here." He handed the child back to her mother who held her tightly to her chest.

"Bac si numba 1," the woman said with a nod and smile. Mike returned the smile and patted the baby's bare bottom.

"Hey, Doc." Mike spun around to see Allen. He was grinning as he stood alongside a line of kids and their mothers. "Here's a few more for you. They must think you's a regular Marcus Willby."

"That's WELBY, smart ass. Where did they all come from?"

"I don't know. They started coming over a little bit after you began working on that kid."

Mike looked at Wilson. "Do I have time?"

"Go ahead, Doc, we'll make time. Allen, call the Lieutenant and let him know we're going to hold up here awhile and why."

For the better part of the next hour Mike treated an assortment of cuts, sores and rashes. A few had the reddish, circular pattern of ringworm, which two drops of Tinactin in the center of the ring would help clear it up in a few days. When the final patient was taken care of, Mike walked outside. The rain had stopped and he noticed the rest of guys in the squad playing and laughing with the village kids. Matt Roberts, a tall blond surfer from California who had drawn a picture of battle-dressed Marine riding a surfboard on the back of his flak jacket, was giving piggy-back rides to all comers.

Wilson looked at Mike and smiled.

"Looks like a damn nursery school, doesn't it?"

"Yeah, ain't it bitchin?" Mike nodded. "It is times like this that make being over here worth it don't you think."

"Yep, but I am sorry to say it ain't like this very often."

Both men broke into laughter when Allen fell over backwards, pretending to be knocked out when one of the little kids smacked him in the face.

"What's the chances of coming back here a couple of times a week, so either Graham or I can follow up on these treatments?"

"I'm not sure, but I don't see why not. I think this is a pretty secure area. I'll talk to the Lieutenant when we get back and see what he says."

"That'll be great."

"Now we'd better get moving. We've got a long way to go yet."

Despite the depressing gray sky, sunshine filled their hearts as they waved good-bye.

That evening word was passed that the Battalion Commander was extremely pleased when he heard about what they had done and wanted the visits to continue. Patrols returned to the ville four times over the next week and the men looked forward to going back each time.

It hadn't rained for several days so the trails were drier as 1st squad started out on another of the daily patrols. They'd be going back to the ville so Mike, who had gotten a care package from home, filled his pocket and bag with candy and food to share with the kids. Everyone was anxious to get to the ville, not only to play with the kids but also because, on the last visit, the villagers had cooked some real food for 2nd squad and they were hoping for some also. But before anyone could eat they had to sweep down by the river to check out reports of enemy infiltration.

Fours hours later, tired and with nothing to show for their efforts, they approached the ville, a mere hundred yards away. Suddenly an explosion thundered through the air. The shock wave hit them like the crash of giant surf. Having frozen for only a moment the squad took off running toward the billowy, black cloud of smoke that soared above the trees. Busting through a small treeline Mike saw what use to be a "six-bi" truck, now a mass of rubble. A large, gaping hole sizzled in the bed just behind the demolished cab, its jagged edges looked like fingers pointing upward. Bodies were everywhere, some as far as thirty feet from the truck. Despite a brief hesitation, to assess the situation, he sprinted toward the smoldering truck.

"Get me a medevac A-SAP."

Two charred bodies sat like statues in the cab. The stench of their burned flesh forced him to gag as he stepped up on the running board.

Realizing they were beyond his help he jumped down and rushed to the nearest living victim. The man's right leg had been blown off just above the knee and the remaining stump looked like a mass of raw hamburger. Got to work fast. He pulled the bottle of yellowish plasma from the canteen cover, and then tied a piece of rubber surgical tubing around the Marine's biceps. Uncapping the needle from the IV set-up, he pushed it into the skin where the vein had puffed up. The vein collapsed and he had to do it again. After failing a second time he quickly undid the tubing and repeated the procedure on the other arm. The needle entered the vein smoothly and the fluid dripped from the bottle into the wounded man's body. Following an injection of morphine, Mike stuck the needle through the man's collar and bent it as he'd been trained.

Two of the next three he looked at were dead; the live Marine had a huge, irregularly shaped chunk of metal protruding from the left thigh. The bone, broken by the blast, was exposed and pointed upward. Yanking off the Marine's belt Mike strapped the two legs together, immobilizing the broken one against the good one. He proceeded to tie a battle dressing around the wound before squeezing a syrette of morphine into the opposite thigh.

"Doc, over here quick."

Rushing to the spot behind a clump of bushes, he found five more critical cases lying in the tall grass. Moans and groans were all around him. *God, who do I treat first? Who has the best chance to survive? Have to decide fast.* The voice in his head was screaming at him as he stared at each of the wounded.

The entire left side of one face and head were missing. Two others had dark red blood seeping from a number of wounds over their bodies. Mike looked down in horror at a ghostly white figure that had a piece of shrapnel penetrating his skull and stumps where an arm and leg used to be. Mike moved first to a young Marine busy trying to stuff his sausage-like intestines back inside the gaping hole in his belly.

Soaking a large dressing with water from his canteen Mike tried to push the foul smelling, convoluted intestines in as best he could before placing the bandage over them. He wet the bandage again with water and shot the Marine with morphine. Racing from wound to wound he used the last of his morphine before returning to the double amputee. Knowing there wasn't much he could do for the young Marine medically, Mike sat and helplessly held his hand. He pulled the chain around the Marine's neck and read the dog tag, Roman Catholic. Bending over so his mouth was close to the young man's ear, he began, "Oh, my God, I am heartily sorry for having offended thee..."

The groans suddenly stopped and the boy's hand went limp. Dejected, Mike reached down and closed the Marine's eyes before covering him with a poncho liner.

The medevacs by now had started to circle overhead. Quickly, Mike made one last search of the area to make sure there were no more wounded. The red smoke that marked the LZ swirled around and up into the blades as the helicopter landed. Mike took charge directing which of the casualties should be evaced first, and assisted in rushing them on board. The medevac Corpsman took the plasma bottle from him and hung it on a hook dangling from the roof. Mike screamed at the top of his lungs, close to his colleague's ear.

"Tell them at 1st Med they've all had morphine. Didn't have time to write out tags."

The other Corpsman nodded and gave a thumbs up as Mike raced off. As soon as the chopper was filled, the bird took off and another landed. There was no rush loading this one; it would only carry the dead.

With the medevacs gone, the stillness was almost deafening, even the birds were silent out of respect. The area around the truck looked like one of the vacant lots in the Bronx Mike had seen many times. Spent medical supplies and military gear were scattered everywhere.

Lieutenant Bach and several others from the platoon, who had been back on the hill when the blast occurred, came charging through the brush and immediately made their way over to where Mike was standing.

"What's the bad news, Doc?" Bach asked softly.

Still jacked-up from the adrenaline high, Mike took a deep breath and ran his fingers back and forth across his forehead. "Nine KIA's and eight WIA's. Half of the wounded may not make it."

Bach scanned the area. Words were not necessary; he just walked away.

Feeling exhausted, Mike slowly trudged over to the side of the road away from the others. He dropped his helmet, sat on it, and lit a cigarette. His hands, covered with dried blood, trembled as he stared down at them. Like watching a slide show, he played back and tried to recall everything he had done for each casualty.

Allen came over and took a knee beside him. "Have a drink." He tapped Mike on the arm with the open canteen.

Mike continued staring at the ground and could only bring himself to shake his head no.

"You okay, man?"

"Yeah." He took a long drag on the cigarette, and let it out slowly. "What a fuckin' mess. God, I hope I made the right decisions." He flicked the cigarette away, closed his eyes and rubbed them with his fingertips. "You know, Ron, I've worked in emergency rooms back in the world and seen stuff just as bad as this, but there was always a doctor around to make the decisions for me. I just pray I did the right things for those guys"

"Doc, that was a tough one your first time out, but you did good. You stayed cool and calm. You didn't panic."

"You should have been inside here." He took his thumb and pointed at himself.

"You sure you're okay?" Allen put his hand on his shoulder.

"Yeah, I'll be fine. Thanks."

Getting up, Mike walked slowly to a puddle of muddy water and washed the sticky mess from his hands and arms. Several guys in the squad came by to see how he was doing and offer a word of comfort. He tried to smile and acknowledge them, but could only manage a small twitch from the corner of his lips.

With most of the blood finally gone he made his way over to where the Lieutenant had formed the men up for the move back to the hill and took his position in line.

"Spread it the fuck out, goddamn it," Bach yelled angrily. "Haven't we had enough casualties for one day?"

That evening just before sunset, Mike was called to the Lieutenant's hootch.

"Sir, you sent for me?"

Bach, who was doodling in the dirt with a stick, looked up and forced a smile. "Yeah, Doc, the guys tell me you did an outstanding job today. I just wanted to compliment you on that."

"Thank you, sir."

"By the way, do you remember treating an officer?"

"No, sir."

"Supposedly he was riding in the cab."

The image of the two blackened bodies flashed into his mind. "Well, there were two men in the cab. They never had a chance. Did you know either of them, sir?"

"Uh, huh. I think I knew the one riding shotgun. We were in Quantico together." Bach paused took a deep breath and drew a few more figures deeper in the dirt. His voice was angrier when he continued.

"Battalion's sending an S-2 team out tomorrow. They want us to escort them to the ville where we've been helping the people. Hopefully they'll be able to give us some information on how a mine could have been planted so close to their ville and no one warned us. Do you mind going along?"

"No, sir."

"Good. How are you holding up?" Bach seemed genuinely concerned.

"I'm fine now, sir." Mike paused a second. "Sir, I heard Sergeant Mac is taking a killer team out tonight? I'd like to go along."

"No, Doc, I'm sorry, you're not ready for that yet. Just go back to your hootch and relax. We'll handle it tonight. A few more months of this shit and you'll be ready."

Dear Grandpa,

This letter will be fairly short cause I'm going on another patrol in a few minutes. Had a bad situation yesterday. Truck hit a mine and most of the casualties were replacements for our company. They'd only been in country a few days and never got to fire their weapons. It was a real mess. 14 died. I did the best I could, but I wish I could have saved a few more. 3 of the guys died after arriving at 1st Med. The one that really hurt was the guy who died holding my hand. I didn't even get to finish saying the Act of Contrition for him.

Grandpa, I've got a question for you, and please be honest. Last night my unit sent out a four-man killer team. They dressed up like the VC and were supposed to move around all night hoping to surprise the enemy. I heard they went back to a little farm not far from here where they found VC equipment and ammo a few days ago and killed the people who lived there by fragging their bunker. Again, it's only rumors; I didn't see it. My question is, does stuff like that go on in war? Did you guys intentionally hurt people out of anger? It really didn't bother me when I first heard about it. It just seemed like their way of getting even. But, now, I'm not sure what to think. Don't tell anyone about it, okay, it's just between you and me. This war confuses me.

Mike

Chapter 6

The huey landed at the base of the hill. A tall, broad shouldered Major with a shaved head and clean, neatly pressed cammies was the first person to set foot on the ground. His boots that had been immaculately spit-shined were quickly covered with mud after his first few steps. He carried a black briefcase and wore a 45-caliber pistol in a shoulder holster. Close behind, a Marine holding a leash attached to a German Shepherd scout dog marched in step. The last of the trio was a much smaller Vietnamese man, dressed in extremely tight-fitting tiger-striped utilities. He had long, black hair with well-trimmed bangs partially hidden under a faded bush cover. Mike noticed several men in the platoon rushed to greet him right away.

"Who's that?" He asked Allen as they watched the men shake hands with the Vietnamese.

"That's Bai. He's one of our KCSs. He and another guy named Khanh usually worked with us in the Arizona."

"KCS, what's that?"

"Kit Carson Scouts. They're ex-VC who chieu hoi'd over to our side."

"Can we trust them?"

"Yeah, Khanh and Bai have saved us bucu times. They're good. From what I've been told, the VC killed his entire family when he wanted to quit fighting and return to his farming."

Mike frowned. "You've gotta be kidding. They killed their own man's family for that?"

Allen lifted the radio and slung it up onto his back. "That's the way I heard it and, from the way he treats the gooks, I can believe it. He's one mean bastard when he interrogates prisoners."

Bach's voice interrupted the conversation. "All right, let's move out."

The dog and his handler fell in behind the pointman, followed by Bai, then the rest of the squad. The Major positioned himself between Bach and Allen as they left the perimeter. It took nearly half an hour to reach the ville and the squad instinctively fanned out to set up security.

The "Mister Clean"-looking Major immediately took command and began issuing orders.

"Corporal Shraiberg, take Buster and have him search for tunnels."

"Aye, aye, sir. Buster, come." Shraiberg and the dog set off toward the closest hootch.

Mike watched the activity for a few minutes then decided it was a good time to check up on the kids. As he made his way to the hootch where he always worked he was surprised to see the people cowering in the doorways. Normally they'd rush out to greet him, but today they seem frightened.

Inside he sat in his usual chair, pulled a boy named Kiet up onto his lap and began unwrapping the bandages. He pointed to the healing sores. "Mamasan, babysan numba 1."

The sores were healing nicely and no longer needed to be scrubbed. He applied some ointment, re-bandaged Kiet, and patted him on the backside. Just as he turned to take care of another boy the dog started to bark loudly. He bolted from his makeshift dispensary, hustled outside and found Allen.

"What's up?"

"Dog found a tunnel. Lieutenant just sent for Sanchez."

Sanchez, the platoon's designated "tunnel rat," arrived moments later and immediately stripped to the waist. As he listened to the orders from the Major, the dog handler handed him a 45 and a flashlight. Holding the two weapons one in each hand he walked over to the tunnel entrance. He lowered half his body into the hole, paused, and flashed a smile before disappearing. All Mike could think of was he looked like Alice heading off to Wonderland.

Bai continued interrogating the people. He was livid as he screamed into the face of the village honcho. "You VC."

The old man, his eyes wide and his lips quivering, answered, "No VC. VC numba 10."

Bai moved closer and his voice was louder. He repeated the same question over and over.

Every time the old man answered the same, "No VC. VC numba 10."

Like a prairie dog on the Great Plains, Sanchez's head popped out of the hole and diverted everyone's attention away from the two Vietnamese. His face and chest were covered with mud as he pushed himself up to the ground level. "Shit, there's bucu stuff down there, sir. I saw weapons, ammo, frags, C-4, det cord. All kinds of junk."

"Okay, son." The Major's expression never changed. "I want you to go back down and start bringing it up." Executing a perfect parade deck about-face, he turned to Bach. "Lieutenant, let's get all these people rounded up and, Lieutenant, I want every hootch and bunker searched thoroughly."

"Aye, aye, sir. Okay, men, you heard the Major. Let's do it."

Like bees swarming the Marines scurried into each hootch, yelling and pushed the occupants outside. At times they prodded them like cattle with the muzzles of their rifles.

"Get your ass out of there. Move it."

"Hurry up, you 'Motha'."

"Shut your fucking mouth and move."

Several of the people had to be physically grabbed and pushed when they resisted. Men, women, and children were all brought to the center of the village while three Marines with bayonets on their rifles stood guard. The rest of the platoon went back to systematically searching each hootch. They checked everywhere: in clay pots, under thatched roofs, in fireplaces, and bunkers. Mike watched as Matt Roberts pulled the pin on a frag.

"Fire in the hole."

The big blonde surfer held the frag at arms length let the spoon fly and flipped it into the earthen structure before diving for cover.

Seconds later, the muffled explosion sent debris and black smoke flying out the entrance. Only then did Roberts enter and check it out.

Meanwhile, Sanchez was busy handing weapons out of the tunnel to Allen who stacked them off to the side.

The Major looked down at the pile of contraband then turned toward the gathered villagers. "Bai, someone in this ville knows who the fuck set that mine yesterday, and I want you to see if you can find out who it was."

Without a word Bai marched over to the crowd of people and began yelling at them. The women all started to wail and speak at the same time. It was a non-distinguishable jumble of words, spoken in a singsong manner. It got to be more and more irritating the louder it got. Finally, Bai gave up and returned.

"We get nothing from these people. They say VC come and force them to hide the weapons. They say they have no choice."

"Okay, we'll just evacuate this ville and take them all back for further investigation." The Major turned to Allen. "Son, get me Battalion."

Thirty minutes later two CH-53 helicopters landed nearby, and the squad urged the villagers toward the waiting birds. The woman whose daughter Mike had first treated passed by him. He rushed to catch up to her and walked alongside as she carried the baby in her arms.

"Hey, mamasan, how could you treat us this way after all we've done for your kids?"

"Khong biet." Scared and shaking, she never looked in his direction.

"What do you mean you didn't understand what I'm talking about? We've treated you people better than you've ever been treated by anyone, and you allowed them to blow up that truck. Why?"

"Khong biet."

"Fuck you, bitch. You know damn well what I'm talking about." Mike hadn't realized he was screaming only inches from the woman's face. He had to fight the urge to take the butt of his rifle and ram it upside her head.

"Chill out, Doc. It happens all the time. Don't sweat it." Bach had walked up from behind and grabbed him on the shoulder as the women moved away.

"Do they hate us that much, Lieutenant?"

"Wouldn't you if a bunch of foreigners came into your town, pushed you around, and tried to blow your old man away?"

"But we took care of their kids, sir. We didn't hurt them, we helped them."

"How many assholes do you think came in here before us and fucked with 'em, maybe even shot a few of their kids?" Bach looked compassionately at Mike. He realized that the real Vietnam was finally coming down around his Corpsman. "You know, Doc, maybe what you and Doc Graham did for these people kept our platoon from getting hit. That's something, isn't it?"

"I guess so, sir, but how can we ever win this war?"

The Lieutenant looked square into his eyes. "We don't."

Puzzled, Mike lowered his eyes and stared reflectively at the ground. He realized Bach was serious. "Then what's this all about?"

"To get back home. Alive"

With the last of the villagers loaded the choppers took off. The rotor wash whipped up dirt and grass into the Marines' faces. Mike held the top of his helmet with one hand and pulled his chin into his chest to protect himself.

When it was again quiet, Bach put an arm around his shoulder. "Doc, you've learned two important lessons in the last couple of days, and don't forget 'em. Men are going to die; some you'll save, others you won't and there's nothing you can do about it. Second, don't trust anyone over here but your buddies. We don't have control over the politics of the situation, so we just try to do our jobs as best as we can." He winked and gave Mike an encouraging rap on the back. "Come on, Squid, let's get back to the squad. We've got a war to win."

"Go ahead, sir, I'll be along in a minute."

 Pulling a Marlboro from the red and white box, Mike searched his pockets for his lighter. Spinning the roller ignited the spark for the flame that he put up to the tip of the cigarette. Clicking the lid of the lighter shut, he then looked down at the caduceus engraved on the side of the Zippo. The cigarette dangled from his lips as he contemplated what the Lieutenant had just said. Bach was right, I'm here to care for my Marines, nothing else, and regardless of the rights or wrongs of this war, I'm going to do that as good as I can.

He could see his reflection behind the two serpents wound around the winged staff on the shiny silver lighter, and noticed changes already. His eyes were sunken and lonely, his face had become gaunt and bearded, and there was a new maturity beyond his years. *So, this is your war. It doesn't make sense, but maybe that's what the grunts mean when they say, 'It don't mean nothin'.*

Taking a deep drag, Mike blew the smoke out forcefully and flicked the butt hard into the brush. "Fuck it."

By the time he returned to the ville, the men who had been ordered to burn the hootches and blow the bunkers were doing so. Explosions and the crackling sounds of straw on fire were everywhere. Plumes of white smoke climbed high into the air as the squad made their way back to the pos.

A week later Second Platoon was relieved by Bravo Company and made a four klick hump to Hill 65. Tired and weary they made their way up the switch back road and through the well-fortified front gate. They passed the mess hall off to their right before coming to a road that ran the entire length of the hill's crest. A sign with five white stars on a blue diamond enclosing the word "Guadalcanal," spelled out vertically on a large, red number one, sat in front of the battalion headquarters.

Turning right at the emblem of the 1st Marine Division they continued along the muddy road for a hundred yards until they arrived at a series of hardback hootches. There they noticed rest of the company who had been flown to the hill earlier. They had already settled in and scarfed up the best cots

"Lieutenant, billet your people in the last two hootches." The Gunny had come out to meet them before they even had a chance to stop. "Get them squared away, then get them to chow. The CO is holding an officer's meeting at 1400 hours, so make sure you're back by then."

"Okay, Gunny, anything you say," Lieutenant Bach was impatient. He never cared for the way the Gunny talked to officers, but was much too tired to start a hassle at this point. "Fall out, men. Drop your gear in those hootches, and then straggle to chow on your own. I've been told they're holding it open for us."

After lunch Mike and Graham held a sick call then accompanied several of the men who needed more medical care than they could provide to the B.A.S. It was late afternoon by the time they returned. The platoon right guide was passing out mail and Mike heard Roads call his name and tossed him envelope after envelope, so that by the time he was done Mike had a stack of eight letters to take back to his bunk. All thoughts of the last few weeks immediately disappeared as he lost himself in a world far away

"That from your girl?" Allen asked as he dropped down on the cot across from Mike.

"Yeah. God, I can't believe how much I miss her."
Allen laid his rifle across his lap, pushed out the locking pin and began breaking it down for cleaning. "Got any pictures, man?"

"Right here." Mike proudly handed him the picture. "She just sent me that. It's a new one."

"Yeowee! She's a real foxy mama." Allen continued to look at the picture as he handed it back. "How'd you ever get so lucky?"

"Actually, I owe it to some dumb 'jarhead'."

"How so?"

"Well, it was the fourth of July, 1968. A guy named Cloonan from my platoon at Pendleton and I went to the beach in San Clemente. This other guy Squires joined us about an hour later. He was already half tanked. All the time we sat on the beach he continued to drink wine from the two canteens he had with him. About noon two good-looking women walked by and set their blanket down about ten feet from us. Squires and Cloonan had the situation well in hand before I could move. Anyway, being the odd man out, I just put my head down and tried to catch some Z's. The next thing I hear is, 'Get away from me you jerk.'
When I look over the taller of the two girls is stomping down to the water. Cloonan and the other girl quickly follow, Squires is just sitting there staggering in the sand. I decided to find out what happened. Cloonan and the two girls are standing in waist deep water and the tall blonde is washing her hair. To make a long story short,

Jody wouldn't talk to or acknowledge Squires, so he finally just poured some of the wine on her head. Well, me being the nice guy I am, I apologized and the next thing I knew, we had spent the rest of the day together. Six months later we were engaged."

"Man, that's cool."

"How about you? You got a girl back home?"

"Naw could never seem to find the right one for the kid." Allen never looked up as he continued scrubbing the bolt with a toothbrush.

Mike put the letters down, then grabbed the barrel of Allen's weapon and a bore brush. Pushing the rod into the barrel he rammed the brush up and down several times. "What do you think we're going to be doing here?"

"Probably like always. Provide security for the road sweep east to An Thanh, or run patrols. At night we'll stand lines, or guard the bridge outside Tam Hoa."

"Is that the one we crossed today?"

"Right on." He took the barrel from Mike, inspected the bore, nodded approvingly and began the reassembling process. "Thanks, Doc." As soon as the sling was re-attaching, he leaned the weapon against the wall and stood up. "Hey, I'm going over to play cards with a couple of 'Brothers' in 3rd platoon, you wanna come?"

"No, thanks." Mike picked up the pile of letters, touched them under his nose, inhaled and smiled. "I'm going to fantasize some more. Thanks anyway."

"Okay, catch you later." Allen stopping at the door and quickly turned back to Mike. "You wanna go to Midnight Mass tonight? I heard the Chaplain's going to hold it in the mess hall."

"Yeah, I think I might. Come and get me before you go."

"Will do. See ya."

Christmas Day wasn't much different than all the others since he had arrived in Nam. The rain pelted the tin roofs and the wind howled through the screens making it unusually cold. The one difference was that Mike received two large packages from home. One contained a giant six-foot Christmas stocking that Jody made along with cans of beef stew, ravioli, chocolate pudding, and peanuts. She'd also packed his favorite chocolate chip cookies and two pans of banana nut bread, which was devoured by the guys in the platoon almost as fast as he opened it.

The other package was from his dad. It had two large sticks of pepperoni, Ritz crackers, cookies, a dozen packages of Kool-Aid and hot chocolate. His mom put in a tiny plastic Christmas tree with a note. "Our family has always had a tree at Christmas, and it's not going to change just because you're over there." She also included the half dozen pair of socks he had asked for. But the nicest surprise was the two fifths of Seagrams his Grandpa had hidden inside.

Lounging around the hootch that afternoon the platoon shared the bottles of Seagrams and listened to the Bob Hope Show from Da Nang on the radio. The show was fantastic. Everyone laughed at the jokes and enjoyed the music, but the best part came when Connie Stevens sang "Silent Night". At first they only listened, but soon some of the men started singing along, a few more joined in until finally everyone was singing. Mike looked around at his new family as he sang. Their teary eyes seemed to be transfixed on something far away, as though they were looking through a window into the past, or possibly the future. The song seemed to bring a sense of tranquility to each of them.

What kind of men are these? They can be hard and mean, never blinking an eye at mutilation or death. Most of the time the only things they think about is killing gooks or getting laid. But now, singing this simple song as reverently as any choir, they seemed so gentle and caring. It's a shame we really are only little boys who've had to grow up too soon and face the horrors of this world long before we're ready.

".... sleep in heavenly peace."

Hi,

Thanks for the booze, Grandpa. All the guys thank you, too. Christmas went good. Ron Allen and I went to Midnight Mass. I'll tell you, it was as good as any Father McManus served. I assisted as altar boy, and even surprised myself by remembering all the Latin. Our Chaplain is a super guy; you'd get along with him good. His name is O'Rilley, and his family also came from county Cork. Maybe you knew them?

Christmas Day we had a big dinner at the mess hall, turkey with all the trimmings, and the Battalion XO played Santa Claus. He passed out presents and letters sent to us by school kids back in the world. I got a tiny plaid blow-up pillow that'll come in handy.

I don't know if this sounds corny or not, but I really care about the guys in my platoon. I'd do anything for them and they for me. I'm so proud to be here with them, but I guess you know all about combat camaraderie. I don't know if I'll make it or not, but I want you to know I think we should be here fighting this war, and so do most of the guys. When you see the little kids it makes you want to fight harder. We're here so they can grow up like us, free. Why is that so hard for people to see?

In her last letter Mom told me what you said to that antiwar protester in White Plains who was carrying the NVA Flag. The guys really got a kick out of it. She also said you were so angry, she had to pull you away before you got into a fight -- GET SOME, GRANDPA. Maybe when I get home, you and I can go out on a KT and go after a few of them together?

Next week we're going on a sweep in the mountains to hunt for a suspected NVA headquarters so I probably won't be writing for a few days. Take care.

God Bless
Mike

Chapter 7

The monsoon rains came down heavy in the chill before sunrise as Delta Company waited at the LZ. The men had been told that for the next three days they'd be searching "Charlie Ridge" for an NVA headquarters. It was never easy in the mountains but this time of the year it was going to be especially hard. Realizing that, many of the men, in an effort to avoid going, reported to sick call right after chow. They each believed they could convince Mike and Chris that they were sick enough to be sent to the BAS and that would keep them in the rear. But because of the large number of Marines that showed up and with almost everyone in the platoon having some form of illness, the two Corpsmen decide to be extremely tough and sent only the very worst cases to see the doctor. Of course, it didn't win them many friends.

Sitting hunched in the rain, cupping an already soggy cigarette, Mike watched the sky lighten and noticed a half dozen CH-46 helicopters and Cobra gunships begin circling overhead. He watched as they landed one by one in the foggy, dark gray dawn, pick up a full load of men, and disappear into the cloud-covered mountains to the northwest. When it was his turn to board he walked up the ramp into the belly of the bird and made himself comfortable on the red canvas seats for his ride into the mountains.

Upon landing, Mike learned that the mountains were much colder than the lowlands, and it became colder still when a strong wind began to blow. He rolled down his shirtsleeves and turned up his collar, before walking across the LZ to wait the arrival of the rest of the company. He found an old fighting hole dug months or years before by some other unit and made himself as comfortable as possible by removing his pack and sitting on the edge of the hole. He couldn't do much about the rain except let the downpour play a steady beat on his steel helmet. His finger pressed lightly against the trigger of the rifle that lay across his lap; his eyes darted back and forth scanning the jungle just beyond the perimeter. The foliage was so thick that a person only fifteen feet away would be nearly impossible to see. His heart pounded rhythmically as he stared into the jungle of tall, defoliated trees whose tops disappeared into the low clouds and fog. The last time he remembered feeling this edgy was when he was a young boy and had stayed up late by himself to watch "The Werewolf."

"What's happenin', Doc?" Allen slapped him on the back.

A surge of adrenaline rushed through Mike's body as he jumped and swung the rifle around. "Damn, you scared the shit out of me. Don't be doing that."

Allen laughed hard. "Sorry about that, my man. What's ya doing?"

"Nothing, really. Just looking and wondering where the gooks are."

"They're out there, probably watching us right now."
Mike moved his head quickly from side to side as his eyes widened. "You think so?"

"You best believe it." Sitting down alongside his pal, Allen removed his helmet and rubbed the top of his head. "Doc, why in hell did you ever become a Corpsman? Don't you know it's a dangerous job? A man could get killed doing your job" Ron's warm grin spread across his face

Mike chuckled bravely, "Oh, it's a long story."

"We ain't going no-where." Casually, Allen pulled a can of peaches from his leg pocket and opened it with his P-38.

"Well, you see, I tried to enlist in the 'Crotch,' but my knee was still too weak from an injury in spring football practice. They told me to work on it and come back in three months to have it tested again. In the meantime, I got my draft notice, so I rushed over to the Navy recruiter and he took me right away."

"Why didn't you just let them draft you?" Allen said before he spooned a yellow peach slice into his mouth.

"No way. If I had to come over here, I wanted to be with a GOOD outfit. Too little discipline in the Army, that's why they get their ass kicked all the time."

Mike pulled a pack of cigarettes from his pocket, and shook it so a few of the filter tips extended beyond the top of the red and white pack. "Want one?"

"Yeah, thanks." Tossing the now empty can into the brush, Allen grabbed a cigarette, and leaned toward Mike who held the lighter for him.

"Anyway, I get to boot camp and, after three weeks, I really hate it."

"Boot camp or the Navy?"

"Both. But there's nothing I think I can do about it, so I just went with the program. They even made me a squad leader."

"Get some, Doc. A born leader."

"Well, we finished our eighth week and we go on a twelve-hour liberty."

"WHAT?" Allen stiffened. "Y'all got liberty in boot camp?"

"Yeah, didn't you?" Mike teased.

"Fuck no. We were lucky to get enough time to piss. Well, I'll be, you 'squids' got it dicked, man."

"Yeah, sure." Mike looked around. "I've really got it made, don't I?" Flicking the smoke away he slid into the hole and, while standing ankle deep in mud and water, he leaned against the side and faced Allen.

"So, where'd you go on liberty, to the slop-chute?"

"No, we went to a place called Kenosha, in Wisconsin."

"You mean you even got to go off base?"

"Yup, I had a really good friend named Connie that went to school up there, so two of my buddies and I went to visit. When we get there we go into the dorm. A girl at the desk picks up the phone and tells Connie we are there. She tells us to have a seat; it will be a few minutes. So, there we are sitting there in our dumb looking ill-fitting navy blue sailor outfits and our heads shaved looking like total jerks.

We start to notice this steady stream of girls coming down the stairs. They pretend to do something in the lobby, and then run back up stairs. My buddies and I, we're loving it."

"After eight weeks and all those women, I can imagine, man. I'd a been going ape shit."

"Yeah, I know, you Marines get horny looking at water buffaloes."

"Hey, 'squid', don't you be capping on my Corps." Allen pretended his pride was hurt. "Continue, man, continue."

"Finally, Connie comes down along with a friend. She had borrowed a friend's car and we all go over to this pizza joint near the college. We spend the next few hours drinking beer, eating, and have a really great time, but unfortunately they have to leave for some big sorority bash.

After we walk them out to the car we still have five more hours to kill so we decide to go back inside and continue drinking."

"Man, now I know you're dinky dau, Doc. I can't believe it. Liberty, women, and drinking during boot camp, and you don't like the Navy."

Mike smiled. "A few more pitchers and we're all pretty toasted. I start complaining and bitching about how much I wish I coulda gotten into the Marine Corps. My buddy Ivan jumps in and suggests that I still could. He had heard that because of all the casualties over here they were accepting volunteers for the Hospital Corps and FMF duty. I suddenly get excited about the possibility, and before I know it, Ivan and I make a deal to go in the next day and sign up."

"Did your partner live up to his end of the deal and volunteer, too?"

Mike hesitated. "Uh huh. He was killed over here in 68. He was with Echo 2/5, but I'll tell ya I've never regretted that decision. So now tell me why did you join the Corps?"

"Ah, anything's better than sharecropping." Seemingly agitated Allen climbed out of the hole. "Hey, man, I gotta go... check the batteries in the radios. I'll catch you later."

The next morning, after being ordered not to erect shelters, everyone was completely soaked. The rain and biting cold continued while they waited for word to move out. Mike's teeth chattered, and the longer they waited, the colder he got. Standing around in small groups, hands in pockets and shoulders scrunched into necks, most of the men shivered uncontrollably. When the word to move out finally came it was no surprise that they all cheered.

The incessant rain and foot traffic had turned the trail into a quagmire. Cold and wet Marines, covered with mud, slipped and fell down the hill as they descended into the valley. Most of them were extremely angry and irritable until they stumbled upon a base camp some time around noon. They soon forgot the conditions as they located and began searching bunkers, huts, and tunnels.

From the weapons and documents they found Delta Company learned that the camp belonged to the Headquarters of the Q72 Battalion. They also discovered a file that listed all VC members in the Duc Duc area. The camp was so large that it took the Company most of the day to destroy all the bunkers, tunnels, and weapons.

It was late afternoon before the sun peeked through a break in the clouds and Delta Company moved out. Third Platoon was on the point and hadn't gone more than three hundred yards when the CO's voice came over Allen's radio.

"Delta 2, Delta 2, this is 6, over."

"6, this is 2 actual, go," Lieutenant Bach answered into the handset of the PRC-25 on Allen's back.

"Ah, 2, be advised we have NVA regulars moving in our direction. I want you to take your platoon to coordinates 673-851, and set up a blocking force. First Platoon will move farther ahead and sweep toward you, while I keep the rest of the company up here on the ridge and block any escape this way, over."

"Ah, roger 6, out." The Lieutenant passed the handset, wrapped in a clear plastic battery bag, back to Allen and yelled back toward his men. "Pass the word, squad leaders up."

He pulled a laminated map from his flak jacket pocket and marked the position with a grease pencil before carefully studying the terrain on the map.

As soon as all the squad leaders had arrived he explained the plan and got the platoon moving down the hill.

Reaching their objective squad leaders expertly deployed their men in a treeline located on the edge of a clearing. Chris Graham raced toward one end of the line, as Mike found cover behind an old fallen tree at the other. Laying chest down in thick, brown mud he was only able to see the clearing through a small space under the tree. His stomach started to churn, and his heart pounded so hard against his sternum he thought it would burst. He had forgotten about the cold as the adrenaline warmed him. Rifle bursts from First Platoon jerked his head in their direction and he squinted to see any movement in the mist-shrouded brush on the other side. The sounds of a horrific firefight raged still some distance away, but it was definitely moving toward him.

Damn, I wonder if any men have die. I am so scared. How am I going to react? I don't want to die. Please God watch over me.

He pointed the black front site toward the far treeline, but had trouble keeping it steady as the volume of firing increased and got louder. Despite the rain, he felt his hands sweat on the rifle and he had to swallow hard several times to get enough saliva to flow.

Cautiously, he raised his head and looked up and down the line of Marines, hoping to be reassured they were as frightened as he was. His finger tightened on the trigger. The sounds of the battle were now only yards away and bullets began to whistle through the dense vegetation across from him.

Suddenly, dozens of pith-helmeted NVA soldiers popped out of the treeline like a row of jack-in-the-boxes.

"OPEN FIRE"

The world all around Mike erupted with a litany of automatic weapons and M-79 rounds. Red and green tracers whizzed in every direction. The distinct "cracks" of the NVA's AK-47s could be heard above the steady staccato of the Marine M-16s. The explosive bark of Mike's rifle sent a stabbing pain into his ears as he poured rounds in the direction of the enemy. The smell of gunpowder filled the air, and the smoke cut down on visibility. Mike rammed a second magazine into his rifle and lowered the sight on a green-uniformed blur running across his front. He squeezed and a second later he saw the blur fall almost as if someone had yanked its legs out from under it.

"Corpsman. Get a Corpsman over here."

The cry came from somewhere off to his right.

Oh, shit, no. Despite a split second hesitation Mike took off in a crouched run, clutching his rifle in one hand and Unit 1 medical bag in the other. A hail of bullets kicked up clods of mud all around his feet forcing him to take cover. He felt his sphincter muscles tighten as he peeked to see where the casualty was.

"Over here, Doc."

Pushing off the ground once again he ran toward the voice. Several AK-47 rounds snapped a branch off a tree above his head. Mike's dive to the ground caused his helmet to pop off and roll a short distance away.

Instinctively, he reached out and put it back on before crawling over to the wounded man. He had been hit in the upper arm, just below a "Death Before Dishonor" tattoo in blue letters. Dark red fluid pulsated from a gaping hole, shooting a stream of blood through the air with each beat of the heart. The sticky liquid warmed Mike's fingers as he probed the wound searching for the bleeding artery. Trying to grab it and hold on to it proved to be as difficult as attempting to catch a greased pig.

When he finally snared it, he squeezed tightly which stopped the bleeding. Unsnapping his surgical kit with his free hand Mike pulled out a silver surgical clamp and locked it on the severed blood vessel

"Take it easy, man. You're going to be fine now."

"Oh, fuck, Doc, it hurts. It hurts bad."

"Yeah, I'll bet it does, but you're going be okay, really." Even though he himself was terrified Mike wanted to keep the wounded Marine calm and out of shock. Despite bullets still exploding into the trees and bushes around them Mike decided it was best to make light of the situation. "You know Veljacic, you're lucky. I usually don't make house calls."

The Marine chuckled through his pain. "And to what do I owe this occasion?"

Mike rolled onto his back, yanked out a battle dressing and ripped the clear wrapper open with his teeth. Turning back he struggled to stretch out the long cloth ties before placing the tan dressing over the wound, so that the words "Other Side To The Wound" faced him. "Well, first off you've got a great looking sister and I was hoping that if I take care of you you might fix me up. On top of that I got nothin' better to do today and so seeing as I was in the area...."

The scream of a bullet speeding by caused him to stop and pull his head into his shoulders like a turtle. Reaching into his large leg pocket Mike pulled out a blue plastic cigarette case and slid the top off. He took out a small squeeze tube attached to a capped hypodermic needle, and yanked the cap off with his teeth. A quick jab and the needle penetrated the skin, sliding easily into the deltoid muscle.

"Thanks Doc, you sure I will be ok?"

"I'll stake my reputation on it and if you don't...."

"Corpsman."

Again he had to break cover and dodge bullets. When he did reach the casualty, he tasted the spaghetti he had eaten for breakfast coming into his mouth. Streams of blood trickled from a clean, round hole in the man's forehead into wide, lifeless eyes. His open mouth freeze-framed his last utterance. The entire back of the skull was gone, gray matter and pieces of brain floated in a pool of frothy blood. Mike tried to compose himself as he pulled out a poncho, and covered the body. Feeling helpless and alone he turned and began firing at the enemy as fast as he could pull the trigger. There was no longer fear, only anger.

Suddenly it was silent. It had stopped as quickly as it had begun.

"Allen, call First Platoon and notify them we're sending a squad into the treeline to search the bodies. " The Lieutenant then ordered third squad forward and he watched long enough to see them disappear into the thick brush.

It wasn't long before Roberts reappeared at the edge of the trees and yelled across the clearing. "Hey, Lieutenant, all's clear. We got 4 or 5 dead gooks in here. There's also a few wounded gooners. You want us to blow them away?"

"Naw, you'd better not." He turned to where his Corpsmen were getting their casualties ready for medevac. "Doc, they've got wounded, one of you come with me and see what you can do for them."

Graham grabbed his bag. "Mike you finish up here, I'll go."

Thirty minutes later, the entire squad emerged carrying several wounded NVA on ponchos. Wilson walked over to where Mike sat and held up a green web belt with a red star on the buckle.

"Hey, Doc, shoulda come in there, man, we got bucu souvenirs. Look at this, I got me a gen-u-ine NVA officer's belt." He looked proudly at his treasure.
"Almost everyone got something, flags, wallets, weapons, packs, canteens, pith helmets. You name it, we got it."

"Sounds more like you found a damn surplus store," Mike quipped as he got up and began walking a wounded Marine up the hill for medevac.

Halfway up he paused to rest and glanced down onto the valley floor one last time. The NVA bodies scattered about in the mud, were left there for nature to care for. *I wonder if their families will ever know they're dead?*

Disturbed by the thought he dismissed it quickly, grabbed hold of the wounded Marine's arm and continued to the top.

The medevac was waiting when they arrived, and the NVA wounded were the last to be loaded. How ironic. Former enemies who had just tried to kill each other, now flying together to a place where all that mattered was keeping a person alive.

Once everything was secure and the choppers had gone the CO determined it was too dark to continue so he ordered the company to set up a perimeter for the night. Everyone began erecting low hootches among the rocks to give them some protection from the rain and bitter cold.

Mike and Graham still had one more job to do before they could get out of the weather and eat chow. Separating, they set out to check on the general condition, but more importantly on the feet, of each man in the platoon.

"How you guys doing? Mike squatted to see the men under the poncho shelter.

"Fine, Doc." Lopez and Stone were both from second squad.

"Good. Now get those boots off and let me see your feet."

"Come on, Doc, it's too cold," Stone objected.

"I don't care if it's snowing," Mike said impatiently. "Get 'em off ASAP."

Unlacing the wet boots was extremely difficult, but pulling them off was even more of a struggle. With the boots off the two men peeled the drenched socks down over their wrinkled feet.

Moving close Mike inspected Lopez's feet first. "Oh Damn, I don't know, it looks pretty bad. We may have to amputate at the ankle."

Lopez jerked his foot away and sat upright. "Come on, Doc, you're kidding, aren't you?"

Mike allowed himself an appreciative smile. "Yeah, but if you don't keep changing those socks, I won't be. Now let the air get to them for awhile before you put on dry socks," slapping Lopez's leg lightly he started to get up.

"Hey, Doc." Mike bent down again. "Yeah what?"

"Ah," Stone hesitated, "I don't have any."

"You what?"

"I don't have any dry socks."

"Why not?"

"I didn't feel like humping them. You know, we were only going to be out three days."

"Sometimes you frickin' guys piss me off. You never learn. I ought to let you suffer." Sliding his pack from his shoulders Mike opened it and took out a pair of his own that he had wrapped in a plastic baggie.

"Here, I want them back when you're done. Washed."

"Thanks, Doc, I owe you one. It won't happen again, I promise."

"Yeah, I'll bet. Catch you guys later."

Mike made his way to several more hootches, and it wasn't until he and Graham were sure everyone had been seen that they headed back to the CP area. Allen had built a hootch for he and Mike to share, while Graham partnered up with Roads. Totally exhausted, Mike crawled under the low hung poncho, and removed his boots and socks before pulling a can of food from the pack and cooking dinner. The icy breeze followed the contour of his bare feet as he lazily stirred the can of franks and beans.

"You've been awful quiet since the firefight."

"I know, Ron. It's taking me some time to get over it, but that's my job, isn't it? You know, when Hymes was killed today, I prayed that I'd get one of those little fuckers in my sights. I actually wanted to see the bullet tear into one of those gooks' chest, then stand over him and watch him die."

"I know where you're coming from. We've all been there a few times. It's not hard to kill over here, is it?"

"No, it sure isn't." He hesitated as he spooned a frank into his mouth and thought. "I don't know, I feel different, like something's been taken away from me. Something I can never get back, no matter how hard I try. All of a sudden war seems so ridiculous. We're out here trying to blow them away, and them us. For what?"

"I'll be damned if I know, but if you keep thinking about it, you'll go dinky-dau real fast. I think I'm long past the feelin' stage."

"Ron, you think it is true someday that after we die our spirits will be united with our bodies?"

"Don't know Doc, that is what they say will happen."

Mike thought on for a moment then added, "Well, which body will be united?"

"Huh?"

"Well, if you are old will it be a young body? Or will the guys that lost an arm or leg or were just blown away over here, will they be united with their whole body?"

"Geez Doc. That is some heavy shit. I never thought about it. I don't know."

"Before I came over here I never really thought much about dying. That was for old people but the more death I see the more I want to live, go home and go out on a date again, eat pizza and tell my parents how much I love them."

"I agree." Allen looked at his hands as he rubbed them together. " I have so much I want to do when I get back to the 'World'."

"Yeah me too. I can only hope we get to choose the body we are reunited in and we can see our friends whole again."

As Mike spooned the last of his meal into his mouth his mind flashed to the dead NVA lying in the rain.

"Ron, promise me, if I ever get wasted you won't leave my body in the jungle. Somehow find a way to get to me and bring me back, so my mom and dad will have me to bury and not just an empty box."

Allen eyed him curiously. "Ah, don't be talkin' like that. You know Marines don't leave their dead."

"Promise me, it's important."

"Okay, I promise. Now, we'd better get some sack time. You've got the 'four to six' watch. Hey Doc, don't worry Bro we ain't going to let anything happen to you. Night."

Mike smiled weakly and pulled the poncho liner over his face. Between his thoughts and the continuing cold, getting to sleep was extremely difficult, but he finally got a few hours.

Dawn brought with it more torrential rains. Heavy white clouds covered the surrounding hills and visibility into the valley was limited to no more than fifty meters. Sitting in the hootch Mike was heating water for hot chocolate when the radio along side of Allen crackled with a transmission.

"Break, break, all platoons send your Pappa Lima's up to the CP, ASAP."

Allen yelled toward the next hootch. "Hey, Lieutenant, Captain wants you up at the CP most ricky-tick."

"Okay," Bach answered like he had just awakened from a good drunk.

"What the fuck does he want now?"

Mike and Allen could hear him grumble to himself as he laced his boots and crawled out of the hootch into the rain.

"Guess the Lieutenant don't like being out here anymore than we do," Allen said, grinning. "Will you hurry up with the cocoa?"

Mike took a sip from the can before he handed it to Allen. "What do you think's up?"

"Don't know. Maybe the war's over." Allen gulped the sweet light brown liquid. "Umm, that tastes good. Nice and hot."

They passed the can back and forth, until all that remained was the unstirred cocoa that had settled at the bottom of the can.

"Squad leaders up." There was a tone of urgency in the Lieutenant's voice.

The Lieutenant was on one knee, a map resting on the thigh of the other leg, when Wilson, Jones, and Hughes arrived and squatted. "Okay, plan's changed. Battalion's got information that the gooks are going to hit Hill 65 in force tonight. They want us to hump out of here and be in position to be a reactionary force if they do."

"Why don't they just come in and fly us out?" Wilson asked, mildly irritated.

"Can't get in, too much fog and clouds. So we're stuck." He looked at his watch, one of the green plastic ones that were issued to all officers, and wiped the rain off the crystal. "Skipper wants to move out in one-five minutes. Get your people shaking; we've got a lot of ground to cover. Questions? Okay, let's do it." As soon as the squad leaders left, he turned to Graham. "What's the men's' condition, Doc?"

"Last time we checked they were pretty bad, especially their feet. Most are in the first stages of immersion foot and the cold is really getting to them."

"What are you able to do for them?"

"About all we can do is make sure they change their socks as often as they can, but I don't think anyone has dry socks left. We've tried putting moleskin and tincture of Benzoin on the blisters, but there's not much else we can do except get them dry for a few days, and that ain't about to happen, is it?"

"Nope. Well, Doc, I'm sure you're doing everything that you can. Keep me informed." Bach buckled up the last strap on his pack and with a grunt, hoisted it onto his shoulders. "All right, Second Platoon form-up on the trail."

For twelve grueling hours the company made their way down the mountain. The terrain was extremely harsh, and many times they were forced to cut and hack their way through it. The daylight faded into night, and the men began to trip, stumble, or fall in the darkness. The CO finally halted the column when the pointman fell over an eight-foot cliff. It had become impossible to see. Hoping to light the trail, the Captain called for arty illum. Within minutes the shells roared over head and the illum popped out. The parachute allowed the light to float down to the earth slowly, but the clouds and fog were much too thick, and it didn't help.

Hungry, tired, cold, and wet the grunts sat tightly bunched on the trail, one behind the other, cursing everything under the sun. Seconds turned into minutes, and the minutes became an hour. Angered by the foul up several of the men pulled out their poncho, covered themselves, and just went to sleep.

A mosquito buzzed into Mike's ear and startled him awake. Throwing off the poncho, he was surprised to see daylight. He stretched to work out the kinks, and then remembered where he was. He looked around in a mild panic and noticed that the entire company was sleeping. No security, no LPs, no one on guard, only the CO and his radioman awake. Three or four RPGs and we'd all have had it. Mike sat up and lit a cigarette. It tasted good in the early morning chill and it helped warm his cold, numb hands.

The rain had stopped and the clouds appeared to be higher in the sky. When it was finally light enough to see, the company moved out again, and within a few minutes walking time they were able to see Hill 65 and the paddies down below. The pointman soon found a well-used speed trail that followed the course of a rapidly flowing stream, and once on the trail they moved much faster. The sounds of the raging water a few feet away thundered through the jungle.

Mike had to laugh as he watched the back of Allen's head bobbing back and forth, as he carried on a private conversation with himself.

"Fuckin' intelligence, never gets nothin' fuckin' right. Makes us hump out of the fuckin' mountains all fuckin' night, and nothin' fuckin'happened."

"Hey, Ron, what do you think of your beloved Corps now?" Mike teased.

"Fuck you and the horse you rode in on, 'squid'. You can be . . ."

Before he could finish his diatribe, sounds of automatic weapons fire radiated back from the head of the column. Instinctively, they dove to the ground and faced outboard. The shooting up front was quickly joined by two M-79 grenade explosions. It wasn't long before the word filtered back that the point had ambushed a squad of rice humpers and killed them all.

"I'll bet they was carrying rice from the villages down below up to their compatriots in the mountains," Allen said turning to Mike. "They was probably just ditti-boppin' along and the last thing they expected was to run into a Marine unit, particularly at this time of the morning."

"Yeah, I guess we really ruined their day."

Both men released a nervous laugh as the word to move out was passed. Mike adjusted his pack straps on his shoulders as he passed the ambush site. The flies had already begun to swarm around the four dead bodies that lay scattered just off the trail. The rice had been dumped over the bodies, and it mixed with the already coagulating blood.

An ace of spades, with the inscription "D 1/5" written in big black letters, stuck out of one of the dead men's' mouth. Mike had heard about units marking the dead, but it was the first time he'd actually seen it. That's stupid. If the gooks ever marked one of our guys like that, we'd really be pissed and want to go after them, not fear them. He turned for one last look at the bodies, and saw Sergeant Mac jerk the card from the dead man's mouth, and put it into his pocket.

They reached Hill 65 shortly after noon, and for most of the men the first order of business was to change out of the muddy, smelly utilities into something dry. The removal of their boots and socks was like a special reward to sore feet for carrying them the last few days.

Again Mike, Graham, and the rest of the company Corpsmen had to treat their individual platoon's medical needs before they could relax or change. They discovered many feet swollen, and on several the furrows of skin had cut so deep into the soles that made walking painful. For the better part of an hour the Corpsmen cleaned, soothed, and bandaged cuts, and scraps on knees, elbows, and hands. They treated dozens of blisters, and wrapped several sprains. Three of their men had to be referred to the BAS with more serious problems. One, Graham felt, had developed phlebitis. His leg had swollen, the skin was red and hot, and the foot had puffed up to twice its normal size. The other two were sent for possible broken bones. While they worked, sandwiches and hot coffee were brought over from the mess hall and were gobbled up quickly but not before the Marines made sure their Corpsmen got the first choice.

It took almost two whole days before most of the men were fully recovered. Mike and Graham had just finished sick call and were sitting around when their senior Corpsman, Doc Mitchell, entered the hootch. The grin on his face advertised that he had good news.

"Hey, Chris, pack your gear, buddy. Your replacement is in."

Graham shot upright on the cot. "Don't be jiving me, man."

"No, I'm serious. They're trucking him out here right now. Get your stuff together and . . ."

Graham didn't wait to hear the rest of the sentence. He was jumping up and down, shaking hands with everyone around. "Yeah. I'm finally outta the bush."

Corpsmen normally only spent six months in the bush with a line company, then six months in the rear with a BAS or at 1st Med. Graham had been with Delta Company six and a half months.

"When do I leave?" In his excitement the words seemed to run together into one long word.

"Right away. Get down to the LZ; you catch the next bird to An Hoa. You're being transferred to the BAS"

Graham had said his good-byes and was heading out the door before Mike had time to lace his boots. The two men walked quietly to the LZ. As soon as Graham saw the helicopter flying toward the landing pad he extended his hand.

"Mike, ol' buddy, take care of second herd, they're a good bunch. We made a good team, you and I, a real 'dynamic duo'. Take care of yourself, too."

"Thanks, Chris, I will. It's been a real pleasure for me working with you. Thanks for all your help."

The helicopter touched down and Graham took a few steps toward it before he stopped, and turned back to Mike and gave him a big hug. He had to yell to be heard. "Hey, next time you're in An Hoa, I buy the beer."

"You're on. Now get out of here before someone changes their mind."

Mike watched as his partner disappeared into the waiting bird before strolling slowly and dejectedly back to the hootch. As he entered the screen door he saw his new partner unpacking his gear. Rich Barker was a short, blond-haired, fair complexioned man of about twenty-one. He had come directly to Nam from a stateside hospital, and carried about twenty pounds of extra weight around his middle that caused him to look even shorter than he was. Dressed in clean jungle utilities, fresh from the package, and boots black, not white and well worn like everyone else's, he looked totally out of place.

Barker had never been with the Marines before, other than Field Medical School, so he'd have a lot to learn, and now, after only two months in the Nam himself, Mike had that responsibility. Baker didn't bother to smile as Mike went over and introduced himself. The first thing he noticed was how Barker's handshake was limp and weak, and the hand itself was small and baby soft. As Mike struggled through the normal get acquainted process, Barker never changed his sour expression and his answers were always short and curt. Mike looked at the sideburns halfway down the new guy's face, and the hair growing over his ear.

"You know, Gunny's going to get all over your ass about your hair; I think you should try to get it cut before he sees you."

"No way. I'm following Navy Regs. There's nothing he can do about it."

"Yeah, there is. You're not with the Navy now, and the Marines won't let you have it like that." He was getting irritated at trying to make Barker feel welcome and wasn't in any mood to argue about it, so he decided to change the subject. "Well, what do you think of the Nam so far?"

"It sucks."

Reclined on the cot, Mike clasped his hands behind his head. "You're right about that, but you're lucky, at least you're with a good outfit."

"Fuck these Marines, I think they're all assholes."

Mike bolted upright and looked around as if to see who might have heard Barker. "Hey, man, you'd better watch what you say. They don't take too kindly to being called assholes. What's more, I don't like it."

"I don't care what they think. They're nothing but a bunch of uneducated hired killers who take orders like robots. First chance I get, I am getting out of here. Besides, I don't believe in this immoral and illegal war."

"Oh, and how are you goin' to do that?"

"I was promised in my contract that I would be an Operating Room Technician and I have already made an appeal to see that it is honored. My mother has a Congressman friend of ours working on it right now."

Mike walked over and put his face only inches from Barker's. "Listen, pal, what you think and do is your business, but as long as you're in this platoon, you'd better do the job, or I'll cut you a new asshole. Do you understand me?" His jaws tightened and his eyes bore into Barker. "You're gonna be a lonely son of a bitch."

"No sweat, I won't be here that long." There was a touch of arrogance in Barker's voice.

"Have it your way."

Mike was furious and he left before he took a swing at the jackass. He found Allen in the next hootch and they challenged Roads and Weller to a game of Back Alley.

Hi Grandpa

Sorry I couldn't be there for your retirement banquet. Mom and Dad said it was really neat, and tons of people showed up. Geez, 40 years in law enforcement. I can't imagine doing anything that long. I'll never forget the day you made Chief. I was so proud of you. That was also the day you locked me in a cell for an hour just so I'd get the feel of what it would be like if I got sent there. Remember that? I'll tell ya, you sure made an impression on me. Anyway, congratulations. Now you can just sit around and get old.

Chris Graham's been transferred to the rear and I have a new partner who I don't like much. Truthfully, he's a jerk.

You wouldn't believe how beautiful this country is. If there wasn't a war it would be a great vacation spot. Maybe after this is all over you and I can open a travel agency and book trips here. I know all the local "hot' spots. I can see the advertisement now: "Spend an explosive week on Goi Noi Island, before crossing Liberty Bridge for a few days' fishing in Alligator Lake. Disneyland, Dodge City and the Arizona Territory are all within easy walking distances."

Well, I guess I'm getting kind of stupid so I'll close for now. Take care.

Mike

Chapter 8

After the abortion on Charlie Ridge, the next few weeks saw the company go through a normal transition. Captain Christopher was relieved as CO and assigned to Battalion S4. The executive officer, Lieutenant Bittner, was promoted to Captain and made the company commander, while Lieutenant Bach took over as the XO. Top Kramer was transferred to Division, and Sergeant Mac boarded a Freedom Bird for home. Second Platoon received a new platoon sergeant named Greene and were expecting a new Second Lieutenant any day.

Replacements began to trickle in slowly. Delta Company always had a special ceremony welcoming new men into the unit, and by the end of the week there were enough new faces to hold the ceremony.

The company was given permission to use the Enlisted Men's Club at 6:30, a half hour earlier then it normally opened. Upon entering, the tent everyone was reminded to grab two cans of beer and circle up. Everyone, that is, except the new guys. Once the CO arrived, the Gunny stepped forward.

"OK, listen up." His voice boomed as only a good Marine DI's could. "All you new guys lie down on your backs."

Scared and bewildered the ten new Marines slowly, and nervously followed orders.

The Gunny Continued, "We have a tradition in this company that you are about to experience. You are about to join a fraternity like no other in this world. From this day forward you will be a member of the best company in the First Marine Division. No matter where you go, or how old you are, you will always be family to every man who served as a member of 'Deadly Delta'." Gunny paused to let the words sink in before continuing. "As one of our new brothers we would like to sing you a little song of welcome."

Gunny looked around at the assembled veterans, smiled, and then winked. "Ok on the count of three. One. Two. Three."

The voices echoed loudly and strong to the tune of 'Campdown Races".

> Oh you're going home in a body bag
> Doo Dah, Doo Dah
> Oh you're going home in a body bag
> Ov'r the Doo Dah day
> Shot between the eyes,
> Shot between the thighs.
> Oh you're going home in a body bag
> Ov'r the Doo Dah day

At the end of the song, everyone standing emptied the contents of his cans of beer on the unsuspecting men lying on the floor. After the laughter and much good-natured banter ceased, the men were helped up and everyone proceeded to get drunk.

February brought with it the end of the monsoon season. No longer would the Marines have to contend with the constant rain and mud. Instead, the heat offered a new challenge to their endurance and sanity. The oozing muck of December and January was being replaced by powdery, red clay that seemed to attach and cling to everything, equipment, clothes, but mostly onto perspiring skin. The mercury soared to new heights at times and stayed consistently above the one hundred degree mark. The heat's intensity felt like it sucked the oxygen from everyone's lungs. Even in the shade they couldn't escape the grueling temperature, as it found a way to even invade the last sanctuary of relief. It was a monster that grew as the day went on.

Where-as the rains would often wash away many of the horrid smells and bring a freshness to the land, the heat grabbed the odors and held them captive - a stagnant reminder of the hell hole they were in. Nightfall brought no relief either, as streams of sweat continued to pour over their bodies making sleep difficult.

Delta Company had been lucky. So far they hadn't been called on to do any major humping in the heat but their good fortune was about to run out. In three days the battalion would be deploying into the infamous, and deadly Arizona Territory across the river, to relieve a badly battered Second Battalion.

The night before they were to leave, Mike sat alone in the tent writing letters, while the rest of the guys enjoyed a night at the club drinking beer and watching a movie. With the last envelope sealed, he dropped the letters in the bag, blew out the candle, and went to bed. No sooner had he closed his eyes than one of the PFCs in the platoon rushed into the tent.

"Doc, Doc, come quick. Doc Barker slipped and fell on the way back from the club. He's bleeding pretty bad."

Grabbing his Unit-1 from under the cot, Mike followed him until they came upon the group gathered around Barker. Kneeling, Mike shined his tiny flashlight on the injured area and discovered an eight-inch gash in Barker's calf, exposing muscle and bone.

"How'd this Mike dabbed at the wound with four-by-four gauze pads before applying a pressure dressing.

"Don't know. Guess I tripped over something and fell onto that stake."

Mike eyed him suspiciously, leaned closer so the others couldn't hear. "If I ever find out you did this intentionally, I'll see that you get court martialed."

"Hey, man, what do you have against me?" He paused for an answer but none came. "Just because I don't want to die in this fucked up war. Is that it? Or is it because I don't want to be with the Marines? If that bothers you, I'm sorry." He winced as the pain shot up his leg.

Mike continued working on the wound without saying a word.

Barker's tone softened. It was almost apologetic. "Mike, believe me, it really was an accident. Besides, I wouldn't have the guts to injure myself."

"Yeah, sure." Deep inside Mike wanted to believe that Barker was a good guy, but he just couldn't. "Okay, a couple of you guys carry him down to the BAS."

"You think he did it on purpose, Doc?" asked Allen, as he walked behind with Mike.

"I don't know, and we'll probably never know, but I'm sorta glad he won't be with us in the Arizona. He'd be more trouble than he's worth."

Ron Allen nodded in agreement as they reached the door to the BAS. None of the men from the platoon who helped carry Barker said anything as they put him on the treatment table and left.

Mike saw the hurt and pain on Barker's face and realized it wasn't just from the wound. Despite his dislike for him, Mike couldn't leave without saying something.

"Hey, Rich, you take care and don't make it with too many nurses." There was a long awkward pause. "I know we don't think alike, but I really can't blame you for not wanting to die over here. I hope you get your transfer. This place isn't for you." *Hell, it isn't for anyone.*

Baker forced a smile. "I'm sure that was hard for you to say. I appreciate it. It means a lot to me. You know, in the short time I've been with the company I can see why you like being with the Marines. They have changed my opinion somewhat and kind of grow on you." Baker gave a hint of a smile before a bolt of pain shot up his leg. I know they don't think much of me, but please let all the guys know I will really miss them." Fighting his own emotions, Barker took a deep breath and looked directly at Mike. "I want you to know, I would have done my job when the time came."

Mike patted Barker on the shoulder, raised his fingers to form a V.

"Peace!"

Back in the tent, Mike sat off by himself and stared at the flickering candle on the empty ammo crate. *Now I'm now the only Corpsman in the platoon and tomorrow we head into the Arizona. That means I'll have to go out on every patrol and night ambush. I wonder how long I'll be able to keep that up? Just my luck, but it don't mean nothin.* Blowing out the candle, he crawled under his poncho liner and closed his eyes, but it was well after midnight before exhaustion took over and Mike was finally able to drift off to sleep.

The sun was barely above the horizon as Mike watched the Phantoms scream out of the sky toward the Arizona. The distinct rumble of the diving jets was followed seconds later by eruptions of black and gray clouds, and the echo of explosions across the valley. Each plane made numerous passes and, on their final run, they covered the area with napalm, sending a wall of orange flames across a wide front. With each explosion the men of Delta Company cheered their approval.

"Get some."

"All right, crispy critters."

With the jets finished, a dozen helicopters appeared, and circled like vultures looking for dinner. They landed in groups of three and filled their bellies with combat-ready Marines.

Anxiously, Mike watched out the window as they flew over the Son Vu Gia River toward the Arizona. Touching down in the dry rice paddy, the Marines raced out the back of the choppers toward pre-assigned positions and secured the LZ for the rest of the battalion.

There was no incoming fire, so Allen and Mike found a small tree and lay in its shade. Mike unscrewed his canteen lid and took a drink of the already hot water.

"Okay Ron what happens now?"

Allen's eyes remained riveted on the surrounding treelines for any sign of enemy movement. "We'll leave here as soon as the whole battalion gets in and make a move to the Hot Dog."

"The Hot Dog? What's that?"

"Oh, it's a long elevated strip of ground surrounded by paddies over to the west. We call it that 'cause on the map it looks like a hot dog."

"Will all the companies stay together the entire time we're out here?"

"Nah. From what I understand, Charlie's going down to the An Bangs and Alpha's going over near Football Island."

"Jeez, you guys got names for everything." Mike smiled and put the canteen back in its pouch.

"Yeah, well, it makes it a lot easier to identify places that way."

An hour later the battalion headed toward their first day's objective. The fields, which had not been worked in some time, were overgrown with weeds and grass. Bomb and artillery craters pockmarked most of this once-fertile land, and Mike was impressed with the sight of almost five hundred Marines spread out on line moving across the paddies. He felt good and ready for action. Anyone who tried to mess with this much firepower would surely get waxed.

It took most of the day to reach the objective, and several more hours to dig fighting holes and erect shelters. Shirts stained with perspiration clung tightly to weary bodies as men too exhausted to heat their food chose to eat it cold. The sun's intensity slowly dwindled in the west. Several grunts left the lines to hook up claymores and set out trip flares. Long shadows engulfed the perimeter, providing them with some relief from the searing heat.

As darkness settled in, the Marines took up positions on the perimeter. They were ready for their first night in the Arizona.

The next morning, with the sun casting a dim light on the paddies to the east, Allen and Mike sat in the early morning dew eating their pre-patrol meal. Randy Sullivan, the new platoon leader who had joined them only a few days before, came over and sat down.

"Coffee, sir?" Mike handed the Lieutenant the canteen cup filled with the coffee he had just prepared.

"Thanks, Doc."

The men in the platoon already felt comfortable with Sullivan. He had shown he was willing to listen to the suggestions of more experienced men before deciding on a course of action, but at the same time he proved he was sharp enough to make split second decisions when they had to be made.

"Where'd you go to school, sir?" Mike asked, before shoveling a bite of boned chicken into his mouth with the plastic spoon.

"I went to the University of Colorado. How 'bout you guys? Did either of you go to college?"

"I did," Mike mumbled, his mouth still filled with food. "Went to the University of Dayton for a year. Didn't learn much, though, I wasted my time, too much partying."

Sullivan shifted his gaze toward Allen. "How about you, Ron?"

"No, sir, I had to work to help the family, so I never got the chance, but I'm sure going to go when I get out."

"Did you play any sports in college, Lieutenant?" Mike asked.

"Sure did. I was shortstop on the baseball team."

At five feet ten, Randy Sullivan looked more like a third baseman than a shortstop. He had thick muscular legs and a barrel chest. His closely cropped brown hair was already starting to recede further than most men his age. He had always wanted to be a Marine and joined the Platoon Leaders Program as soon as he could after reaching the Boulder campus.

"How come you didn't turn pro, Lieutenant?" Allen asked as he laced his boots.

"Oh, no, not me. I really wasn't that good. As a matter of fact, I was just barely good enough to get a scholarship. But at least it got me a free education."

"Yeah, and now your favorite Uncle Sam is giving you an all expenses paid vacation in this tropical paradise," Mike grinned. "What do you think of the platoon so far, sir?"

"Really seems like a great bunch of guys. I think we can work well together. I know I have a lot to learn but I'm fortunate that Lieutenant Bach had you men well trained. It makes my transition much easier and hopefully allow me to avoid serious mistakes as I learn."

Allen gestured to catch Mike's eye. "Hey, Doc, we'd better start making our way down to Wilson's squad for the patrol. He said he wanted to leave before the sun got too hot."

Mike wiped the perspiration from his forehead, looked toward the sun, and chuckled. "You gotta be kidding. What do you call this? It's already hotter than hell."

"Yeah, well, it'll get hotter, so let's didi."

After putting on his gear, Mike helped Allen with the radio, and as the two men started to leave, Sullivan walked over and put a hand on each of their shoulders.

"You guys be careful out there, ya hear?"

"Yes, sir." Both men answered in unison.

Second squad was waiting at the edge of the perimeter by the time they got there, and as soon as Wilson saw them he called to his squad.

"Lock and load."

While he waited for the four men ahead of him spread out, Allen glanced back over his shoulder at his Corpsman who was next in line. "You know, Doc, I think the Lieutenant's going to die a little each time one of his guys gets hit."

"Yeah, I think you're right, but he'll probably change. We all do. Remember how I was my first few weeks, always second-guessing everything I did."

A big toothy grin crossed Allen's face. "Oh, yeah, and now you're just a salty, cold dude. I saw you smiling when you gave Green and Morgan their penicillin shots for the clap."

"That's right, fucker, just wait till you get a dose. I'm gonna use a square needle."

Allen flipped him off, spun on his heels and left the perimeter. Mike followed about ten yards behind, his eyes riveted on where Allen stepped.

You really are getting salty, Mike thought.

Walking down the trail, Mike noted that he now carried the rifle like the veterans. He held it in one hand by the mid point where the flash guard intersects the receiving chamber, his thumb passing through the rear sight handle. Bandoleers of battle dressings and magazines crossed his upper torso and his flak jacket hung open in front, exposing a shirtless, hairy chest. Sweat streamed down his face and arms and glistened on his bronze, well-tanned skin. His faded camouflage pants were unbloused, but rolled up to the top of the well-worn boots. His helmet cover, like most veterans, was frayed, tattered, and covered with slogans. On one side he had written:

"Yea, though I walk through the valley of the shadow of death, I shall fear no evil, 'cause I'm the meanest mother in the valley."

While on the other side he had graffitied,

"Footprint of an American Chicken"

His muscular body had become solid and firm, having lost all stateside fat. He walked with the confidence and assurance of someone who knew what he was doing. The immobilizing fear from the first few weeks was now well hidden. Although he was still scared, he now knew what he should fear. Most sounds and explosions did not register a flinch; he had learned which ones meant danger. He was finally accepted into the inner circle of veterans who could act cocky and make fun of the new guys. He'd been bloodied, and he knew for the rest of his life a part of him would always be in Nam.

The squad moved steadily along a speed trail paralleling the "Hot Dog" for about half a klick before heading south across a large paddy. They entered the treeline on the far side and soon came upon a stream. Slowly, one by one, they crossed the thirty yards of waist deep water. As Mike waded across, he removed his helmet, scooped up the cool water, and poured it over his head. Acting as an air conditioner a slight breeze helped cool his overheated body.

Two hours passed before they reached the halfway point of the patrol. The terrain hadn't been extremely hard, but the heat had sapped their strength and slowed their pace considerably.

Moving east toward the next checkpoint, the pointman discovered a well-used speed trail and followed it for about two hundred meters before coming to a clearing.

Halting, he signaled Wilson forward, when he spotted a number of unexploded artillery shells lying in the open. Together the two men quickly assessed the situation.

"We'll have to blow them. If we leave 'em, 'Charlie' will use them for booby traps. Wait here."

Wilson moved into the open field, while the rest of the squad watched from a distance. He cautiously checked each shell for trip wires. Not only did he have to worry about one of the rounds being booby-trapped but also for ones that might planted in the clearing. After a few anxious moments and satisfied it was safe, he called for the rest of the squad to join him.

"Okay, guys, let's gather the rounds and stack them up in the center of the clearing. Pop, I want you to take some C-4, pack it around this stuff and blow it."

"Roger that." Wilson pointed to the right. "The rest of you get down in that trench and take cover."

Reaching the ditch, Mike noticed a company of Marines a half a klick to the west. "Hey, Wilson, who's that over on that hill?"

The squad leader looked, and then checked his map. "That's Charlie Company. They must have finally reached their new pos."

"Shouldn't we let them know we're down here and we're going to blow this stuff?"

"Not a bad idea, Doc. Hey, Allen, call the Skipper and tell him to notify Charlie Company of our position and what we plan to do."

"Good as done."

Wilson and Mike jumped in the ditch joining the rest of the squad, followed minutes later by Allen who slid in along side them.

"Skipper says don't worry about Charlie Company. They know we're down here."

"Good. The rest of you, hug your asses to the ground." Wilson double-checked to make sure everyone was under cover. "Okay, Pop, go ahead and light that motherfucker."

"Fire in the hole." Pop ran as fast as he could and leaped into the trench feet first.

The explosion sent debris flying in all directions. Fragments of rock, dirt, and stone rained down on them, and the smell of cordite filled their nostrils. They were just climbing from the ditch when....

THUNK, THUNK, THUNK.

Instantly, heads spun in the direction of the familiar sound of mortar tubes popping. Wide eyed, Mike tried to locate the whistling projectiles as they passed overhead. The first round impacted seventy-five yards away. Quickly, the squad scrambled back into the ditch. Allen rotated the radio on his back toward Mike.

"Doc, change the freq on the radio, quick. Switch it to 42.40. Hurry, damn it."

Turning the knobs, Mike watched as the numbers on the dial click into position; finally the precise digits appeared in the tiny window. "Got it. Go."

"Charlie 6! Charlie 6!" Allen screamed into the mouthpiece. "Check fire! Check fire!"

The rounds were being walked in, now only 50 meters away.

"God damn it, somebody answer." The panic in Allen's voice intensified.

The projectiles continued uninterrupted toward the ditch.

40 meters---- Allen urgently repeated the call

30 meters.---- "Keep trying," pleaded Wilson

20 meters.--- Mike curled up into a ball, held his hands on his head, and closed his eyes. *Please, God, don't let me die like this.* The ground shuddered, and a blast of dirt fell on top of him. Mike knew the next one would be in the ditch. *Should I try to run or stay?* Time seemed to stand still as he waited for the pain he knew was coming.

The radio crackled, "Delta 2 Alpha, this is Charlie 6, over."
"2 Alpha, go."
The mortars had stopped.
"Ah, 2 Alpha, we're sorry about the mistake. We had no word you were in our AO. Be advised we have a squad headed toward you, do not fire on them. I say again, do not fire on them. They should be reaching you in about zero one mike."
"Ah, roger that, 6."
"Did you sustain any casualties, over?"
"That's a negative, over."
"Thank God. Okay, 2 Alpha, this is Charlie 6, out."
Allen was on the radio, explaining to the CO what had happened as the squad from Charlie Company appeared at the far end of the clearing.
Still shaking, Mike rose and lit a cigarette. He watched as a very angry Wilson rushed over and talked briefly to the Charlie company squad leader before the strangers headed back to their company. By the time he returned to the rest of the squad they had gathered around Allen. He was just starting to explain what he had been told by the Skipper.
"Seems the CO took it for granted that Charlie 6 knew we'd be here because he was at the Battalion briefing when the Colonel outlined our patrol."
"Is that why he didn't call them?" Wilson asked.

Allen nodded "That's affirm."

Pop shook his head. "Stupid motherfucker".

"Son of a bitch almost got our asses blown away. I'll put a frag up his if he ever does that again."   The voice echoed from the back of the group.

"Okay, enough of that," Wilson ordered. "Let's saddle up and move out. We've got a long way to go, and besides it don't mean nothin."

The first week in the Arizona was both physically and mentally demanding. The lack of face-to-face confrontation compounded by the large number of booby traps casualties put everyone on edge. Tempers were short and fear overcame all emotions. In the last four days alone, Mike had to medevac eight men from booby traps, two of which were traumatic amputations of both legs. He was already exhausted. Each day he'd return early in the morning from the night ambush, have just enough time to eat and hold sick call, then head back out on a six-hour patrol. On more then one occasion he nearly became the victim of friendly fire. Twice, rounds from either Battalion's 81 mortars or Four Deuces in An Hoa landed almost on top of their ambush. The constant stress was taking its toll on him and he knew it. His eyes developed a faraway, sunken look, and he snapped at everyone who came to him with minor ailments. When he got the chance to sleep, he couldn't. He no longer joined in the usual B.S. sessions with the guys. He realized he didn't have any other options. Patrols and ambushes couldn't go out without a Corpsman, and he was the only one they had. He had no choice.

Putting on his flack jacket and helmet to go out on yet another patrol, Mike tried to dismiss his fears by looking up at the beautiful royal blue sky, sprinkled with a few puffy, white clouds. It thought it was a perfect day for a stroll along the beach, Jody under his arm and a can of beer in his hand. That is, if he was back in the world. In Vietnam he had to settle for walking Indian-file behind Wilson as they started down the trail.

"Where we going today, Wilson?" Mike asked.

"Wherever the darts fall."

"Darts?" Mike laughed. "What the fuck are you talking about? Don't be trying to get sent in as a heat casualty 'cause it ain't going to work."

"Naw, that's how they decide where to send us on these patrols. Didn't you know that, Doc?" He paused and chuckled. "Yeah, some asshole pogue sits in front of his PX fan, with an ice cold Coke he pulled from his PX refrigerator, and throws darts at the map on the wall. Wherever the darts land, that's where they send us. His aim is our destiny."

Mike smiled to himself. "I can almost believe it."

The patrol passed through the deserted ville of Phu Loi 1 and called in the first checkpoint. They were halfway across a large paddy, heading east toward Phu Loi 2, when the swish of a moving RPG round preceded the explosion. Bursts from automatic weapons cracked high over their heads.

Reacting immediately, the members of the squad returned fire. A paddy dike provided the only cover as the volume of enemy fire increased. Bullets kicked up dirt all around.

Wilson lay on his stomach behind the dike and scanned his map, as casually as if he were reading a comic book. "Weller, get the Lieutenant on the horn."

Weller, who alternated patrols with Allen as radioman, contacted Sullivan, and then passed the handset to Wilson, as the rounds whistled through the air.

"Delta 2-6, be advised we're taking heavy small arms and RPG fire from Phu Loi 2. Request two rounds of H.E. at coordinates 822-509, will adjust, over."

"Roger, 2 Alpha."

Refolding the map, Wilson tucked it back neatly into his flak jacket. "Listen up." His voice was unusually calm for the situation. "As soon as the mortars stop, we're going to assault the treeline in fire team rushes. Romano, your team gets the green weenie; you'll go first."

"Gee, thanks. I love you, too buddy."

The Lieutenant's voice echoed from the radio. "Shot out."

The shells screamed over their heads and impacted to the left of where the enemy firing was coming from.

"Come right five zero and fire for effect," Wilson ordered confidently. The next series of mortar rounds whistled then landed directly in the treeline, only forty yards from the pinned down squad. The blast sent stumps, branches, and earth high into the air.

"GO, GO, GO," Wilson barked as the last shell hit.

Romano's fire team jumped up and raced toward the enemy position, rifles blazing. Cruz on the "sixty" and the rest of the squad laid down a solid wall of covering fire. The second fire team was already up and moving by the time Romano's team had reached the cover of the next dike. Temporarily stunned, the gooks finally returned fire and caught the team in the open. Two of the men went down instantly. "Cowboy" was able to crawl on his own to the safety of the dike, while Lopez lay, not moving, where he had been hit.

"Corpsman."

Terrified Mike had his face pressed as low to the ground as possible, leaped from behind the dike at the same time as Wilson. Both men sprinted across the open field. Bullets cracked and whizzed all around as they snatched Lopez under the arms and dragged him to cover.

Lying as flat as possible, Mike ripped the plastic wrapper off a battle dressing with his teeth. The hole made by the bullet in Lopez's chest gurgled as air escaped. To seal in the leaking air, Mike placed the plastic wrapper over the hole, and then tightly tied the dressing over it. He made sure there were no other wounds before administering an injection of morphine.

The third fire team had made its way up to them. Weller was already busy calling in the medevac, as Cronin pumped about ten blooper rounds into the treeline.

Wilson popped a full magazine into his rifle. "All right, you heroes, on the count of three we're gonna rush the fuckers. Let's cut these motha's a new asshole. One, two, three."

Sprinting across the last twenty yards, they let loose with their best bloodcurdling war cries and disappeared into the brush.

Once the firing had stopped, Mike, who had stayed with Lopez and Cowboy, got up, sat on the dike, and lit two cigarettes. He gave one to Cowboy, who had been hit in the arm, and smoked the other himself. The rest of the squad rejoined him moments later.

"Hey, Doc, what happened to your back?" Weller's breathing showed he was still pumped with adrenaline.

Touching the back of his shoulder, Mike was surprised to find his hand wet with blood.

"Damn, you've been hit." Weller inspected the wound more closely, than gave him a tap on the head. "Looks like you got a neat little flesh wound, not bad at all. Bullet must a just barely grazed you."

Mike still couldn't believe he'd been hit. "Mind cleaning it for me?"

"Okay. Do I get to give you a tetanus shot, too? I've always wanted to repay you squids."

"Just shut up and get busy." He handed Weller some antiseptic and a large three-inch Band-Aid. As Weller cleaned the wound, Mike thought how different it was from the first day he and Weller met, when he treated Mike with distain and lack of respect.

Wilson walked over and grinned. "Shit, Doc, you ain't gonna to claim a heart for that tee-tee thing, are you?"

"I don't know. I'm not even sure it was from a bullet. I never felt a thing. What should I do?"

"If you don't put yourself in for one, I'll do it for you. You owe it to yourself. Two more like that and you're out of here." He turned his head toward the sound of helicopters, still not visible in the distance, then back to his Corpsman. "You know, Doc, that was a damn stupid thing you did, running out there to get Lopez like that."

"What do you mean? You were right there with me. What was I supposed to do, leave him out there?"

"First thing you should have done was see if he could crawl back to you. If not, then you get one of the other guys to go out and get him."

Mike shook his head. "No way. I'm not going to ask someone else to do my job. Besides, the guys were plenty busy with other things."

Wilson smiled and placed a hand on Mike's good shoulder. "You're okay, squid, a little gungy, but okay. Next time, though, let one of the snuffies do it. If you get hit, who'll take care of me?"

"Well, we'll see."

With his body Mike shielded Lopez from the rocks and sand kicked up by the medevac, then with help from Wilson, lifted him by the arms and legs and carried him on board. Meanwhile, Cowboy was able to walk on by himself. After laying Lopez on a litter, Mike shook his hand and wished him well and raced off the back end. As soon as Mike was clear the pilot took the bird up. Before the medevac could get out of site, the CO radioed and ordered the rest of the patrol canceled, much to the relief of the men.

Later in the day, as Mike lay in his hootch, his wound began to throb and his hands shook. Only now was he realizing how close he had come to getting hit bad. He was fighting tears and really feeling sorry for himself when the Lieutenant knelt and poked his head in the hootch.

"Hey, Doc, how you doing?"

"I don't know, sir. I guess I'll be okay."

"Just wanted to let you know you'd better get your gear packed now, cause as soon as you get in from the ambush in the morning we're moving up to the Northern Arizona. We're goin' over to search for a suspected NVA hospital in a place called 'Dodge City'."

"Oh, fuck," Allen cursed.

Just by the way Allen said it, Mike knew it was bad. "Sir, can I talk to you alone?"

"Sure, Doc, let's go down there."

Mike crawled out, and they trudged over to a fighting hole. The two men sat on the edge, lit a smoke, than fumbled for the right words.

"Sir, do you happen to know when we're going to be getting another Corpsman in to take Barker's place?"

"No, Doc, no one has said anything to me about it. Why?"

"Well, sir, I'm not a fucking machine." He hesitated, looked down and watched his boots as they dangled back and forth in the hole.

"Sir, the rest of the guys get to stay in the perimeter and rest every other day and don't ever have to go out on a patrol the day after a night ambush."

The Lieutenant listened sympathetically.

"I'm not sure I can take much more of this. Patrols every day, booby traps, snipers, and ambushes. In all, I may get to rest maybe two hours each day. I just feel sooner or later the odds are going to catch up to me. They almost did today, and now we're going to Dodge City. I need someone to cut me a huss. Just a day or two of not having to watch every little step I take. I'm drained, Sir. Emotionally and physically drained."

"Doc, I understand what you're saying and I'll see what I can do, but you know we can't send out patrols without a Corpsman."

"Yes, sir, I know." He kept his eyes down so he wouldn't have to look at the Lieutenant. "I'm not trying to get out of anything, it's just if maybe they could hurry a replacement for Barker."

"I know you aren't...."

"Ah, shit, sir, I realize I have a job to do but I've been getting these bad feelings lately."

"I think I know what the pressure must be like for you. I'll talk to the CO and check on getting some help out here for you."

"Thank you, sir, I really appreciate it. Hope you don't think I'm trying to skate."

"Naw, don't worry about it. Maybe the Skipper will allow me to send out an LP tonight, rather than an ambush. That way, you can get some rest. How's that sound?"

"Fine, sir. Thanks." The Lieutenant left Mike sitting by himself, staring into the paddies to contemplate his thoughts

Reality in Vietnam is nothing more than a booby trap, cold C-rations, and the next treeline. What all this all boils down to is just a personal little war of squad-size patrols and ambushes. Even with all the high tech stuff, it's still us ground-pounders who have to search out and close with the enemy. We're forced to survive the rice paddies and mountains in one hundred and twenty degree heat or monsoon rains, while others who don't care sit in air-conditioned offices back in the rear. Along with that we have to battle gook sores, diarrhea, jungle rot, rats, mosquitoes, lack of mail from home, and endless periods of boredom and depression. For what? For a grunt there is no past or future, just the present, and the only truth is our friends and the day we go home.

Dear Grandpa,

Things have gotten pretty intense lately. We've lost quite a few guys, mostly from booby traps, an, I've joined your very exclusive club. Yep, that's right. I got a Purple Heart. Don't worry, though, it's only a scratch, but don't tell Mom. She'll get all scared. You know how she is.

Grandpa, I am so scared I just want to get home and go back to school. The longer I'm here the more I realize how I've changed. We are like animals, with no compassion for anyone or anything. Just the other day I had to take care of a wounded NVA prisoner, and I treated him as rough as I could. I wanted him to hurt and hurt bad; to get even somehow. Almost every day one of our units "buckles" (fights) with the gooks. But even seeing the enemy, I still don't understand why we are here. It's like we're fighting this war alone. We never see the ARVNs. As a matter of fact, last week they flew my platoon down to an area called the An Bangs to provide security for a downed chopper. To our amazement, as we came running off the helicopter, a squad of ARVNs went running on. Can you believe that? We stayed and they got flown back to the rear. To make it worse, it wasn't even a Marine chopper. It was theirs.

Well I am finally twenty-two. The guys celebrated my birthday by giving me a C-ration pound cake with a match stuck in it. It was really great of them to do that 'cause over here guys kill for pound cake. Think I'll catch a nap. Bye for now. Give everyone my love.

Mike

Chapter 9

Like an egg sizzling in a frying pan the sun hung above the horizon in the eastern sky and bombarded the earth with intensity. Mike was already drenched with perspiration, as he watched the re-supply chopper arrive, drop the cargo net, then land in the center of the perimeter.

With the sun directly in his eyes and the dirt and sand being kicked up by the rotor wash, Mike was unable to make out the face of a lone figure dragging his gear down the back ramp until he was only yards away.

"Chris, what the fuck are you doing here?"

"They sent me out to give you lightweights a hand. Seems these 'juggies' can't get along in the Arizona without ol' Doc Graham."

Mike placed a hand on Chris' shoulder. "Hey, Chris, man, I didn't mean for them to send you out here. I was hoping to speed up a replacement for Barker, or Barker himself."

"Forget, Barker, he's long gone, back in the world, so I hear, and there ain't no replacements coming in cause of Nixon's troop reductions. So, seeing as how I was the boot in the rear, I was elected."

"Hey, man, I'm really sorry. I never thought my bitching would bring you back out. You know I wouldn't have done that."

"Fuck it, Mike, it don't mean nothing. It's not your fault. Besides, one Corpsman can't make it out here the entire time."

"Really, I'm sorry."

"Shit, forget it." The two friends walked along toward the CP. "Tell me, what's the new Lieutenant like?"

"Good dude. Really got his shit together."

"He must really like you."

Mike frowned. "Why do you say that?"

"I heard he raised a stink about you being out here by yourself. That's why I got out here so fast."

"Really?"

"Yeah. Hey, I Heard you got a Heart."

"Naw. What I got, didn't rate a Purple Heart. Not compared to some of the wounds these Marines get. I am still not sure I will wear it."

"I think you should, but I understand. Now what's been going on?"

"Well, we're getting ready to move up to the northern AO in a couple of hours, so don't get too comfortable."

"Oh, great, I get here and we move. What's the casualties been like?"

"Mostly booby traps. Remember Pop?"

"Uh huh."

"Well, he was walking point the other day and he tripped an 81 mortar booby trap. He lost his foot and hand."

"That's too bad. He was a super guy."

"You're right, they all are. Come on, I'll introduce you to the Lieutenant and the rest of the guys. Platoon's almost all new since you left."

"Sounds good, let's do it. How's that girl of yours doing?"

With Second Platoon on point, the company had moved a little more than a klick across an open paddy before the lead element disappeared into an extremely dense treeline. Thorns and branches scratched and sliced into bare arms and shoulders. Equipment became entangled in vines and was forcefully yanked free. The gurgling of a flowing stream could be heard somewhere on the other side of the thick underbrush. The temperature continued to rise with each step they took into the brush.

Mike's head felt as though it was expanding and contracting on every heartbeat. The thick humid air was void of even the wisp of a breeze.

By the time the pointman Mann found a speed trail, his hands were covered with blisters from having hacked his way through thirty yards of bamboo and vines, and he was in the first stages of heat exhaustion.

Once on the trail his movement was much easier and the cooling breeze gave him some welcomed relief.

Mike had just turned onto the trail when he heard the explosion. "Corpsman up."

The weight of the rucksack slowed him as he ran, so he worked one arm free and let the pack fall to the ground with a thud. Breathing heavily, he halted for a moment at the edge of a clearing, and saw Cronin and Perez kneeling over a body on the opposite side. Instinctively he looked left, and then right, as if he were crossing a street back in the world, before he dashed into the open. He had only taken five steps when a rifle's bark sent him leaping into a nearby bomb crater. Landing on his side, he did a perfect roll to the bottom while bullets splattered the ground above him. Seconds later, his helmet tumbled down, and settled beside his foot.

"Doc, Doc," the Lieutenant yelled. "You okay?"

"Yeah, I'm fine."

"Good. Stay right where you are until we can find the sniper."

"Can't do that, sir. Mann might be hurt bad." Using his elbows he crawled to the top of the crater and peeked over the rim in the direction of the three men. "Listen, sir, there's another hole closer to Mann. Give me some cover to keep that fucker's head down and in two dashes I can make it."

Sullivan pondered his options for a moment then yelled back, "Okay, Doc, go ahead. Second Platoon, get up here on line. Move, move, move"

Their equipment banged hard against their bodies as the remainder of the men in the platoon raced swiftly up the trail holding their rifles in one hand and helmets on with the other. Within minutes they were lying side by side with rifles pointing in the general direction of the sniper.

"Open fire," screamed Sullivan.

The noise was deafening as the hail of bullets sliced tree limbs in two and shredded foliage. They maintained their rate of fire until Mike had reached the other side safely. As soon as he was sure his corpsman was working on Mann Sullivan maneuvered the platoon in fire team rushes toward the suspected location of the sniper.

The shrapnel from the booby trap had ripped several jagged chunks of flesh and muscle from Mann's lower legs. Luckily, the heat from the explosion had cauterized most of the wounds, reducing the amount of blood loss. The trauma did not appear to be life threatening, but part of the tibia on Mann's right leg was exposed, and Mike could see he was becoming ashen and going into shock.

"Allen, get me a medevac ASAP." Mike yelled as he covered Mann with a poncho liner and elevated his legs.

Meanwhile the firing had stopped, and after a thorough search of the area, Sullivan was satisfied that the sniper was long gone. By the time he returned with the platoon, the rest of the company had set up a hasty perimeter for an LZ.

Mike sat on the scorched trail where the booby trap had blown a small hole and filled out the medical treatment tag. Then secured the tag onto Mann's collar and enlisted four volunteers to help carry him, just before he heard the medevac arrive. Kneeling, they each grabbed a corner of the poncho and the moment the ramp dropped they rushed Mann on board, and gently set him down on the cold steel floor.

The CO had the company moving again even before the helicopter had disappeared over the horizon, and they reached the objective around noon. The sun was torrid forcing most of the men to build temporary sun hootches to shield themselves from its intensity. For the rest of the day the men in the company just sat doing nothing. No Patrols, no OP's, no digging fighting holes. This made many curious and wonder what was going on. Their answer finally came at sundown when the word was passed to saddle up.

Using the cover of darkness the entire company moved silently down the hill, and headed back across the large rice paddy they had stared at most of the day, to a treeline a half klick away. Then for the next hour they settled into their nighttime position, digging holes, setting trip flares and claymores, and sending LPs in four directions.

Mike had been given the ten to twelve radio watch so he laid down next to the PRC-25 and struggled to find a comfortable position, yet one not so relaxing that he'd fall asleep. Looking up at the sky he listened as the crickets carried on their nightly musical and laughed as he heard several of the men snoring.

The night would be perfect if it wasn't for these incessant mosquitoes, he thought, and applied more repellent. He couldn't help but recall the jokes he'd heard back in the world about how the mosquitoes over here were so big they could land at Da Nang airbase, refuel, be loaded with bombs, and take off before anyone realized the mistake. Now he knew what they meant.

The illuminated dial on his watch told him it was time to get another Sit-Rep from the LP, so he picked up the telephone-like handset and squeezed the black rubber button on the side.

"Ah, Delta 2 Alpha, Delta 2 Alpha, sit rep, sit rep. If all conditions normal, key your handset twice. If not, key it once, over."

Silence. Mike bolted upright.

"I say again. Delta 2 Alpha, Delta 2 Alpha, sit rep, sit rep. If all conditions normal, key your handset twice. If not, key it once, over." There was urgency in his voice this time.

Finally he heard the two "shushes" echo from the earpiece, which allowed him to lie back down.

The minutes dragged on, as he waged a constant and losing battle with sleep. His eyelids continually got heavy, and his head nodded forward until it involuntarily jerked, pulling him out of the light slumber.

Several times he was forced to sit up and slap himself in the face to order make sure he'd stayed awake. He tried eating, chewing gum, and even thinking about Jody, but the entire watch was a real struggle.

When his watch was over, Mike inched over, woke Sullivan, and was asleep before the Lieutenant had time to take a leak.

It seemed like he hadn't been asleep very long when he felt someone shake him by the boot.

"Doc, Doc, wake up, man."

"What? What's up, Ron?"

"LP's got movement. Get your gear and get down to the lines."

Mike watched Sullivan take down the info from the LP as he hooked his cartridge belt around his waist, and slipped into his flak jacket. The squad leaders were already there and waited for the Lieutenant to finish.

"Here's the dope. LP's spotted a platoon-sized unit moving this way."

Mike could hear the anticipation and excitement in Sullivan's voice.

"Wilson, I want you to put a 'sixty' on that finger over near your squad. Jonesy, put the other one in the last hole in your squad. Tell

your people I want them to hold their fire until the 'sixty' opens up.
Questions? Okay, get back to your squads and keep them quiet. Men,
this is our chance for a little payback. Let's do it."

Mike positioned himself near the center of the platoon and
shared a hole with Hayes and O'Brien from third squad. He quickly
freed four magazines from his bandoleers, and placed them on the
freshly dug pile of earth in front. Casually, he slid the hellbox for the
claymore closer to Hayes and waited. The full moon illuminated the
open field well and it wasn't long before everyone could see the enemy
figures moving toward them.

O'Brien nudged Mike with his elbow and whispered as he
looked down the sights of his rifle. "This is going to be a turkey shoot,
Doc."

"Why do you say that?"

"Look how tightly they're bunched. They're just ditty-boppin.
They have no clue we are here. Skipper sure made a smart move
switching positions after dark. They must think we are still set up on
the hill"

"Come on, baby, walk a little faster."

Mike heard the voice pleading from the next hole. He felt his
hands begin to sweat as he released the safety on the rifle, and pressed
his cheek on the cool plastic stock.

The dark clad figures continued to advance, each step taking
them unknowingly closer to death. Their faces appeared calm, the
night was calm, and then all hell broke loose. A short burst from the
"sixty" started the killing. At a distance of only twenty meters, the
enemy pointman never knew what hit him. The blasts from several
claymores cut down a few more before the gooks realized they were in
a world of shit. Green enemy tracers mixed with red Marine tracers as
they whizzed back and forth. Frags and mortars exploded with their
menacing "Crump" in the paddies. The "swoosh" of an NVA, RPG
sailed over the lines and crashed somewhere in the middle of the
perimeter. Illumination popped high in the sky, lighting up the night
even more, and exposing frantic NVA soldiers scurrying to save
themselves. They were defenseless and they knew it. Several tried to
make a run for the safety of a treeline, but never knew they didn't make
it, as the withering rifle fire relieved them of all their fears. Artillery
illume soon replaced the mortars, allowing more H.E. to be directed

onto the slaughter. From the other side of the perimeter men from first and third platoons raced over to join the carnage. Up and down the line the ecstatic Marines were standing up out of their holes, screaming, tossing grenades, and firing down on the trapped enemy soldiers. Delta Company had sounded the "Deguello." No prisoners would be taken.

"Cease fire." The order was passed repeatedly along the lines.

When the sky lightened, Second Platoon left the perimeter, and moved slowly, and cautiously, into the paddies to check the bodies. Mike joined Sullivan and Allen out in the open. He watched as Wilson, standing on a dike, reaches down to take an AK-47 away from an NVA body. The rifle suddenly raised and released an entire magazine of rounds into the air.

Mike jumped to the ground as he caught a glimpse of Wilson falling backwards. As a last ditch hope, the enemy soldier took off for the treeline to the right. A trio of Marines directly behind the fleeing gook calmly flipped their selector switches to full and emptied their rifles in his direction. The rounds struck their target in mid-stride. As each bullet hit, the body jerked spasmodically. The force propelled the man forward twenty feet before he finally crashed to the ground.

Charging over to Wilson, Mike expected the worst. He stepped up on the dike and looked down at the body of the squad leader laying spread eagle, face up in six inches of paddy water.

"Ahhh, what's up, Doc?" Wilson smiled.

"You hit?"

"Naw, but I think I shit my pants."

The others who had gathered around roared with laughter before helping him up.

The rest of the bodies were searched thoroughly and dozens of souvenirs taken. Determined not to be denied this time Mike hurriedly rushed over to one of the mangled bodies. Kneeling, he unfastened the NVA soldier's red-starred buckle and yanked it through the loops. The lifeless body twisted and turned as the green web belt slid from around the waist. Holding it up he admired his prize before heading back to the CP.

The sun had risen to eye level by the time everyone returned to the perimeter. The men were jubilant and alive with energy despite the lack of sleep and continually recounted the ambush for the next few hours. They had been lucky; the entire company had suffered only one casualty, and that was a flesh wound.

Graham peeked over the top of the magazine he was reading when Sullivan returned from a platoon leaders meeting around noon. "What did the Skipper say at the briefing, Lieutenant?"

"Well, it seems as though we got ourselves twenty-six confirmed kills."

"Get some, Delta Company," yelled Allen who was preparing a gourmet lunch of pork slices mixed with spaghetti and flavored with Tabasco sauce.

The Lieutenant smiled proudly. "We also captured twenty AKs, two mortars, and a B-40 launcher with rounds. The Captain figures they were replacements because of all the new gear and letters we found. They probably came from the mountains and were trying to link up with a unit somewhere in the area."

Allen chuckled as he looked out of the corner of his eye at Sullivan. "Must have had a boot lieuie leading them, hey, Lieutenant?"

"Don't think so." Sullivan started to walk away but stopped and looked directly at Allen. "I think he must have been a ridge runner from South Carolina. Everyone knows they are not too smart."

Everyone laughed except Allen, who smiled weakly and tried to think of something clever to say, but nothing came out.

"Well, I'll be. The Lieutenant actually shut him up," Graham said, shaking his head. "Hey, Ron, better watch out. This officer's smart, he's going to keep you on your toes, Blood."

"Fuck you, squid. Go check someone's pecker. This is between MEN." Smiling, Allen pushed himself off the ground. "If you gentlemen will excuse me I'm going to the potty."

The next morning was Sunday and, as they did every Sunday, Mike and Graham got an early start handing out the large pink malaria pills. It took a while because they had to stand and watch each man to make sure he swallowed it. If they didn't, most would throw them away The common notion was that all the pill really did was give them the shits, and many figured a bout of malaria would get them out of the bush, which they reasoned wasn't a bad trade off.

Once he had finished, Mike leaned back against his pack and puffed on a C-ration Winston. "You want to go out with the patrol today or ambush tonight?"

Mulling over the choices, Graham pulled the cigarette from Mike's hand and took a drag. "I'll take the patrol."

"You're sure now - - I don't really care."

He patted his belly and handed back the smoke. "Yeah, I need the exercise."

Three patrols, one per platoon, left the perimeter at the same time, but in separate directions. Only a few hundred yards outside the perimeter, the patrol from First Platoon suddenly radioed for a medevac. They had taken three WIAs from a single booby trap. As the medevac chopper landed, the patrol from Third Platoon, which had headed east, became engaged in a firefight with an unknown size force and was taking heavy small arms fire. Mike sat alongside Allen in the shade of their hootch and listened to the company net as the squad leader reported they had two KIAs and one WIA. The battle raged for several more minutes before Mike saw medevac choppers arrive. Minutes later, second platoon's patrol with Graham along called in their first checkpoint. Allen slept while Mike manned the radio, and for the next three hours all remained quiet except for the reporting of successive checkpoints.

"Delta 2, this is 2 Alpha. Be advised we have reached Charlie Papa 6 and are on our way in "

Mike acknowledged the transmission. "Roger 2 Alpha, got the beer waiting."

No sooner had he put down the handset when a huge explosion sent a rocket of black smoke soaring above the brush and trees. Weller's frantic voice echoed from the radio.

"Delta 2, Delta 2, we have casualties, request emergency medevac. I say again. We need a medevac ASAP, over."

"Roger, 2 Alpha," Mike answered. "Can you advise us of your situation, over?"

"Wait one." There was a short delay. "Be advised we have three Whiskey India Alpha and one Kilo India Alpha."

Having been awakened by the blast, Allen took over and called for the medevac. A crowd had begun to gather at the CP. Concern etched on each face as they waited for further word on their friends.

Minutes that seemed like hours passed as the radio stayed quiet, adding to the tension. By the time the medevac choppers finally contacted the patrol, Weller's voice seemed calmer. A pair of Cobra gunships circled above and provided cover. Higher up, a second CH 46 orbited. Within minutes the wounded were on board and on their way to Da Nang.

"Delta 2, this is 2 Alpha. Be advised all wounded have been evaced and we are moving out, over."

"Ah, roger that." Allen unkeyed the handset.

CRRR-RUMP!!

Mike's head spun in the direction of the new explosion. Bile filled the pit of his stomach as he watched the dark puff of smoke begin to rise above the trees. Oh, God, no.

"Delta 2, be advised we have multiple casualties, and need another medevac quick. Doc Graham's been hit, over."

Mike snatched his gear and started running in the direction of the patrol.

"Where do you think you're going, Doc?" Sullivan yelled.

Mike froze. "Chris is hurt. They don't have a Corpsman. I'm going out to help them." He was irritated that the Lieutenant was wasting time.

"Get your ass back here. You don't go anywhere unless I tell you. We don't need any more casualties. Reluctantly, Mike followed orders as Sullivan paced nervously. "Ron, see if they need any help."

"2 Alpha, do you need our squid, over?"

"That's a negative. Be advised we have six more wounded, over."

Heads slumped. No one could believe that out of the thirteen men who left on the patrol, ten were now casualties.

As was the routine maneuver, the Cobras circled, while the second medevac landed. It was on the ground no longer than it had to be. As it lifted off, it was raked by heavy small arms fire from the surrounding trees.

Once the medevacs were safely away, attention focused on the three men still one hundred yards out. The danger of more booby traps was the biggest concern, but there was now the possibility of ambush from the snipers who'd fired at the chopper. Anxiously, the company waited and watched the trail. Minutes later, a figure appeared out of the dense underbrush, followed at some distance by two others. As each man entered the perimeter, he was handed a cup of cool water taken from the nearby well, and escorted to a shady area. Looking emotionally exhausted, the CO joined them and sat down beside Wilson.

"Thank God, you're all back. Okay, son, now tell me what happened."

Sitting on his helmet, Wilson removed his flak jacket. "Well, sir, we hit our last checkpoint and were heading in. Holden was on point. He was about to enter some scrub brush, and the next thing I remember is getting up off the ground."

"Were your men spread out?"

"Yes, sir. Douglas was in front of me. He took a piece of shrapnel in his thigh. It was real tee-tee. Waterbull was wounded in the neck and arms, but he wasn't too bad either. But Chief, who was right behind Holden, was killed outright. He had . . ."Wilson's lip quivered uncontrollably as he tried to get the words out. "Damn, I can't believe it. Half his motherfuckin' chest was gone. It looked like, like someone had taken a big bite out of him. His face was gray and his eyes stared at me, like he was asking me what happened."

"Here, man, have a smoke," Mike said, lighting a Marlboro and handing it to him.

"By the time I got up to Holden, Doc Graham was already working on him. Both his legs were blown off at the hip. Doc stayed with him and started an IV, while the rest of us went back and took care of the others. We loaded our guys onto the medevac and waited until it was clear before I gave the word to move out. I watched Doc walk over to pick up Holden's gear just before the booby trap sent him flying in the air. Sheehan, Ackerman, Ski, Salazar, Majors, and Ramos were all clustered together and took much of the blast. Weller, Shepherd and I were behind a mound which protected us, I guess."

"How bad was Chris?" Mike interrupted.

"I don't know. He had big chunks of flesh missing from both his legs and he lost a lot of blood. Some of the other guys were pretty bad, too, but not nearly as bad as Doc. Still, he wouldn't let us work on him until he was sure each of the guys was taken care of. I know he was hurting, but he never once cried out. He kept telling us how to treat the other guys. He's one tough dude." Wilson pulled a plastic case from his pocket and handed it to Mike. "Doc said to give this to you."

"Thanks, Wilson." Mike grabbed the case containing what was left of Graham's morphine.

"He also told me to tell you that the drinks are on you when you get back to the World."

Mike smiled weakly. "How are you holding up?"

"I'm a little shaky but I'll make it."

"Good job, son." The CO patted Wilson on the shoulder. "You take care and get some rest. If you need anything let me know."

Wilson walked by Mike and in a low voice said, "Yeah, get me out of this fucked up place."

Back with the platoon CP, Allen was sharpening his K-bar on a Whetstone. Weller and Greene sat off by themselves, talking quietly. Sullivan had his map out, but his eyes were unfocused and his mind seemed to be elsewhere. Mike went over and sat in the grass next to Allen. He lowered his head and wrapped his arms around his drawn up knees, still holding Graham's morphine case.

"I should have been on that patrol, not Chris." Mike raised his head and looked at Allen. "Ya know if I hadn't opened my big mouth to the Lieutenant, he would never have been out here."

The statement caught Sullivan's attention immediately. "Listen, Doc, it's not your fault. If Graham didn't get it this way, he'd a gotten it some other way. It was meant to be. His number came up, that's all."

Mike shook his head. "I can't buy that, Sir. He was safe in the rear. He was working in the BAS with only four months to go."

"No one's ever safe over here. You've been in An Hoa when rockets come in. He could have gotten it from one of those."

"But you don't understand I'm the one who bitched about needing a partner, and that's what got him sent back out."

"Yeah, and I'm the one who told the Skipper I wanted another Corpsman and he complained to battalion, so we're all at fault. If that is how you want to look at it."

"I still should have taken that patrol," Mike said, slamming the morphine case to the ground. "He wasn't used to being back in the bush yet. Especially here in the Arizona."

"That's bullshit and you know it." Allen was emphatic. "Doc Graham's been in the bush long enough to know how to act out there. He was no FNG"

Sullivan agreed. "He taught you, didn't he?"

"Maybe you're right. But I still think he wouldn't have gotten hit if I hadn't complained."

"He also wouldn't have been out here if Doc Barker hadn't gotten hurt. It's fate, man," Allen reasoned.

Mike nervously clicked the lid of his Zippo open and closed while he puffed on the cigarette hanging between his lips. "Sir, what the fuck are we doing here, anyway? Yesterday we blow away twenty-five of them and today we lose a bunch of our guys. What's been accomplished?"

Sullivan hesitated a moment. "I don't know, but I think you have to look at the big picture to understand that question. We've been sent here to stop communist aggression - - no more, no less. Everything else is hogwash. Look at it this way. Ever since World War II, the communists have been, like the bully on the block, trying to take and take. President Truman decided back in the late 40's we'd stand up to them, and every President since has followed the same course." He eyed both men to see if they were comprehending. "We've stood up to them in Berlin, Korea, the Cuban Missile Crisis, and now Vietnam."

"I can understand that and go along with it, Sir, Allen said. "But what I don't understand is why don't they let us fight this war to win? I mean if we're going to be here, let's do it right."

"I agree with you totally, but I can't answer that."

"Yeah and what about all the long-haired freaks and demonstrators back in the world?" Mike said. "Why do they hate us so much? They preach peace, love, and all that bullshit, but I never see them protesting the fact that our guys are being torn apart by booby traps or pungi sticks, or that the gooks murder teachers, village chiefs, and ordinary civilians. All they do is strut around campus carrying the NVA flag, shouting the praises of Ho Chi Minh, while at the same time burning our flag." His eyes narrowed. "They must think we are some kind of assholes. I wish they'd come over here, then maybe they'd have more respect for us."

"No. No, you don't. Have either of you read Shakespeare's 'Henry V'?" Sullivan asked.

Both Mike and Allen shook their heads in the negative.

"Well, there's a scene in it just before the Battle of Agincourt. They are totally outnumbered, so one of the characters wishes they had more of their countrymen who are back in England to help them fight the battle. The King hears him and says something like, 'No, our loss is enough for our country to suffer.' Besides, he explains to them with fewer men, there would be greater glory. He then tells his men that those that survive the battle will every year on the anniversary be able to stand tall and show their scars as one who fought there."

"It sounds to me like this Henry guy had his own Vietnam," Allen joked.

"My favorite lines are very appropriate for us, I think. They never really meant much to me before, but now I realize they are so true. Henry says, 'We few, we happy few, we band of brothers. For he today that sheds his blood with me shall be my brother'."

"Wow, get some. That's really true, isn't it, Lieutenant? That is awesome. We are and always will be brothers as far as I am concerned, sir." Mike said as he looked proudly at his friends sitting near him.

"I can't remember the rest of the words, but basically he tells them that those that are not there will curse themselves and hold their manhood cheap next to the men who fought on Saint Crispin's Day."

"Do you really think it could be like that for us some day when we get back to the world?" Allen asked.

"I don't know Ron, but I sure hope so. You guys deserve it."

A Marine walked up from behind. "Excuse me. Lieutenant Sullivan?

"Yes."

"Capt'n wants to see all platoon leaders up at the CP right away."

"Okay, I'll be right there." He grabbed his rifle and helmet. "Doc, if you want to continue talking about this some more, we can after I get back."

Allen looked at his friend. "You okay now, Doc?"

"Yeah, I feel better after talking to you and the Lieutenant. Thanks."

You wanna play some two man Back Alley?"

"You're on. You deal."

The game was half over by the time the Lieutenant returned. "Skipper got word from Battalion. They want us to pull back. They feel this area is too heavily booby-trapped, so they're going to bomb the shit out of it. We're heading over near Football Island to Hill 11 to relieve Delta Company. We'll be leaving in the morning so the Skipper only wants LPs out tonight. Sergeant Greene."

"Yes, sir."

"Tell Wilson to send me two men."

"Aye, aye, sir."

"One last thing, Holden died before they could get him to the hospital and Tommy Sheehan was killed; he caught a round through the head when the snipers fired at the medevac."

Grandpa,

We've been real busy lately but I wanted to get a quick letter off. Don't know how to put into words what I'm feeling right now. Chris Graham was medevaced yesterday along with a bunch of other guys. He got it pretty bad but he'll survive from what I hear. Grandpa, if I don't make it back I want you to know I did the best I could, and I am so proud to be associated with these men over here. They are the greatest bunch of guys I have ever met. I love you all so very much and I am so lucky for the family I have.

The rains have stopped and it's bucu hot. Usually the temperature gets well above 100 degrees, and at night the mosquitoes drive us nuts. The repellent helps somewhat, but it stinks. The ground here has gotten real hard and is a virtual wasteland. I don't think anything will ever grow here again.

I heard that Woody Hayes and some football players were in An Hoa the other day visiting but we didn't get to see them. That's typical though; it's always the pogues that get all the benefits. You wouldn't believe how many people over here never leave a base camp or see combat. The guys were telling me that the last time they were in the Arizona, Martha Raye came out and visited them. They said she is an honorary

Colonel in the Green Berets. Supposedly earned a
Purple Heart, too. There is another lady named Chris
Noel, who is always out in the field visiting the grunts.
As far as I'm concerned they're the real heroes. I hope I
get to meet them, just once, to say thanks.

Mike

Chapter 10

Hill 11, although only eleven meters high, was an island in a sea of dried up paddies, the only high ground for over a klick in any direction. Two hundred yards to the south, a trail ran the entire length of the Son Thu Bon River from the mountains to the eastern end of the Arizona. Beyond that was Football Island with its thick vegetation, and a favorite hiding place of the NVA. Several major speed trails intersected near the hill, making it a crossroads for most of the foot traffic through the valley. The only ville of any size in the vicinity was along the river, only a mortar shot away. Strategically, Hill 11 was an extremely crucial position.

During the first week on the hill Second Platoon lost an average of one man per day from booby traps. Morale was down and everyone was increasingly frustrated at the lack of contact with the gooks.

Mike thought Sullivan's decision to change the time the patrol scheduled for the next day to before dawn was a great idea. First off by doing so they would back by noon, allowing the men to avoid the heat of the day. Secondly, by sending them out that early, Mike figured they might catch the gooks by surprise and the men could get some kills as payback.

The moon glistened off the dew providing good visibility as Cronin led the patrol across a large paddy toward the speed trail along the river.

The slight morning chill was a welcome relief from the inferno of midday.

As Mike and the rest of the squad entered the treeline, a low clinging fog settled along the ground, but Cronin, who was on point, was still able to find the trail that ran along side the river. Turning west, he led the squad cautiously toward the ville. A few hundred yards down the trail he heard voices coming from somewhere ahead in the darkness. Freezing in his tracks, he halts the patrol with a hand signal, than motioned Wilson forward.

Kneeling on one leg Wilson removed his helmet, turned an ear toward the sounds, and listened. Certain there were people close by he pointed at three of the men, and motioned for them to follow him quietly.

"Dung lai." Wilson's voice echoed through the morning haze. There was a short pause. "You guys, get up here on the double."

Racing forward, the rest of the squad found Wilson and the others standing over three silent figures, clad in black, sprawled face down in the mud of the riverbank. The muzzle of a rifle was pressed firmly to the back of each of the VC's heads.

Wilson waved his free hand at his men. "Okay, a couple of you guys, let's get 'em up on the trail."

Cronin casually walked over and planted the toe of his boot hard into the ribs of one of the prisoners, and pointed up the embankment.

"Didi mau len."

Even in the dark Mike could see that the VC were terrified and obeyed immediately, but were still pushed and shoved roughly from behind as they tried to scramble up the slippery bank. To his surprise the prisoners were all women in their early twenties or late teens.

"Allen, call the Lieutenant and see what he wants us to do with them." Ordered Wilson. "Roberts, you and Kev tie them up and search 'em good."

Roberts handed Mike his weapon, pulled out a strand of comm wire and cut it into three pieces. Then, forcefully yanking their hands behind their backs, he bound them tightly before doing a quick search of their bodies. Finding nothing, Kev turned his inspection to their packs. Inside the first he discovered paraphernalia to construct simple booby traps. Opening the other he pulled out a package wrapped in brown paper. Quickly tearing off the paper, he opened the box and found a note written on yellow legal paper.

"Hey, listen to this bullshit. It says, 'Compliments of the students of Berkeley, California. Success to your cause."

Mike snatched the box. "Let me see that." The box was filled with an assortment of medical supplies and medicines. His jaw tightened as he felt a deep hurt inside at the thought that his own countrymen were against them and helping the other side

Allen had been standing ankle deep in the mud, talking on the radio to Sullivan the entire time. "Wilson, Lieutenant says to bring the gooks back right now, and don't forget to blindfold them."

"Okay."

"Hey, Doc, give me hand." He reached up for Mike's hand and pulled himself up the embankment. "Thanks. What's all the commotion about?"

"Take a look in that box and peep out what our fellow Americans are sending to the HEROIC PEOPLE OF NORTH VIETNAM."

Allen's eyes narrowed as he shook his head. "Those motherfuckers. Maybe we should be back in the states blowin' them away. Might get this fucked-up war over faster that way."

"Yeah, well, we can't worry about that now, let's get movin'." Wilson ordered Cronin to take the point while he, Mike, and Allen each grabbed an arm of a prisoner and led them down the trail.

The hike back was extremely slow because the blindfolded women constantly stumbled or fell. The day was unbearably hot by the time they turned them over to the captain so Mike returned to his hootch to put on shorts and shower shoes before checking on Seitz and Ryan who had come down with a bad case of the flu.

At Dusk ambush Mike and Wilson's squad headed back to the same area they had been at that morning. In order to keep from being spotted the trek took forty-five minutes, so it was well after dark by the time they arrived. Most of the men quickly rolled up in their poncho liners and went to sleep. Mike had the first radio watch and he felt unusually relaxed as he looked up at the clusters of stars. *What a beautiful night.*

A quiet breeze coming in from the sea reminded him of the times he played hide-and-seek as a kid. As he was enjoying the sights and sounds of the night, the company's position back on Hill 11 came under mortar fire. Mike heard at least eight rounds impact in the initial salvo, followed shortly by eight more.

For the next several minutes the night was quiet and Mike began to wonder if anyone had been wounded. Then the net came alive with radio traffic back and forth between the Skipper and the platoons.

From the conversations Mike determined no one had been hurt, but all the shells had landed inside the perimeter.

Illumination filled the sky as the CO prepared for the ground attack that usually followed. When nothing happened, the night was again allowed to turn black, and Mike was able to return to his daydreaming.

An hour later he heard "killer team" from first platoon report that they had ambushed and killed several NVA. Just before he was relieved, the sky clouded over and the rain began to pour from the sky. The last thing he heard before falling off to sleep was the LP from Third Platoon reporting movement.

It was still raining at 0400 when Allen woke Mike. He quickly gulped down some water from his canteen before the squad broke the ambush, and headed for the ville along the Son Thu Bon. Arriving at the outskirts, Wilson maneuvered the squad on line and waited. When it was light enough to see, he signaled for them to move out. He, Allen, Mike, and Bai, the Kit Carson scout, positioned themselves near the middle. With muzzles pointing forward, and bayonets fixed the Marines moved as quiet as possible through the brush.

Mike's heart pounded hard in his chest. He could hear the swiftly flowing river gurgling only a few yards to his left, as he spotted row of eight or nine hootches, mingled amongst the vegetation. A dog started barking causing fingers to tightened even more on the triggers. Cronin was the first to reach the outskirts and was attacked immediately by a brave canine. The assault was thwarted by a strong kick to the face, sending the mongrel yelping in full retreat.

Halfway through the ville the men were startled when an old man with a white wispy goatee appeared from a doorway.

The Marines dropped quickly to their knees and every rifle in the squad leveled on the Vietnamese man. Several more villagers came out of their houses as Bai approached the man cautiously.

Allen made his way to a young mamasan. "Mamasan can couc."

"No can couc, An Hoa boom."

The "can couc" was the Vietnamese ID card that civilians were supposed to have but usually lost.

Allen poked a strong finger in the woman's chest. "Mamasan, you VC?"

Mike could hear the fear in her voice and she kept her eyes riveted on the ground.

"No. No VC. VC numba ten."

"Where VC?"

"No khong biet."

"Yeah, sure. Didi mau."

Frustrated Allen turned to Mike. "That's the standard response we get from the people out here in the Arizona. They try to tell us that their card had been blown up by artillery from An Hoa.

Mike laughed nervously. "That's as good an excuse as any I guess. I bet the only people who have a ID card are the VC."

"Yeah with the black market the way it is I am sure you are right."

Wilson listened as Bai interrogated the old man. Realizing he was getting nowhere, Wilson dismissed the old man and sent him back to his hootch before continuing the sweep.

They were nearing the last hootch when four figures emerged and took off running into the brush. "Davis, get your fire team after them," screamed Wilson. "The rest of you, follow me."

With Davis' fire team thrashing their way through the jungle of vines and bushes, the others raced down the speed trail. The trail ended at a clearing and they arrived in time to see the VC disappear into a treeline on the farside. Instinctively, everyone dropped to the ground and opened fire. The "sixty" chopped down vegetation like a chainsaw.

Seconds later, Davis scrambled out of the brush and linked up with the rest of the squad. "You want us to go after them?" he asked, still breathing hard from the chase.

"Naw, they're long gone by now. Let's didi back to the ville and have a talk with that old geezer."

Arriving back in the village they forcibly rounded up all the people and brought them to the center of the ville. The papasan was escorted over to Bai. Mike couldn't understand what questions Bai was asking but to every one the old man answered, "Khong biet " or "No VC."

Bai's face grew redder and angrier with each question. Suddenly, before anyone could stop him, the butt of Bai's rifle came up and smashed into the old man's chin with a dull thud. The papasan dropped to the ground in a heap, as Bai hovered above him like Cassius Clay taunting his fallen victim.

"Do Mau Mi."

More than one Marine smiled as blood dripped from the gash under the old man's chin, streaking his beard red.

"Doc, you better patch up the little bastard," Wilson said matter-of-factly.

"Yeah, okay," Mike answered. "Ain't this the shits? Every one of these people are probably VC, and we'll get our asses busted for popping the old fart."

"Remember, Doc, we're here to win their hearts and minds. Now you make sure you give that boy your best bedside manner, ya hear?" Allen said sarcastically.

"That a crocka shit." Filled with anger and outright hatred fro the lying old man Mike put a bandage over the wound without cleaning it. He hoped it hurt a lot though.

Wilson was still on the radio when Mike finished. "Roger that, 2 alpha out." Handing the headset back to Allen, a disgusted look crossed his face. "CO says he wants us to bring everyone we suspect back there, so let's get them moving."

Like drovers on a cattle drive they herded the people who didn't have ID cards across the open paddies. Helicopters, blades spinning, sat waiting as they arrived at the perimeter.

Quickly the first of the villagers were pushed into the bellies of the choppers. Walking down the ramp Mike saw the captain talking, through his interpreter, to a few of the civilians off to one side before they too were loaded. Mike returned his hootch.

He had just removed his boots when Wilson came by.

"Hey, Doc, Gunny wants all of us at the CP."

Irritated, Mike didn't say a word.

"Doc, you hear me?"

"Yeah, yeah, I'm coming." Angrily slipping his feet into the boots, he walked lethargically to the company CP without bothering to lace them.

Captain Perry was finishing a conversation with the Gunny, and he didn't appear too happy. "Okay, men, sit down. People, I want to know what the fuck happened out in the ville." He looked hard into each man's eyes. "Every one of those people complained about someone hitting some old man with a rifle. Is that true?"

There was a long silence. Mike couldn't believe what he was hearing. Here they were risking their lives in this goddamn war, and the CO was looking to bust someone for butt stoking a lying VC.

The words jumped defiantly out of Mike's mouth before he knew he was saying them. "No, sir. They're fuckin wrong, I patched the son of a bitch up myself and saw the whole thing. When we came back into the ville the old fucker saw us and tried to sky out. He knew he had lied to us about the VC in the ville. I saw him look back, and as he did he tripped and fell, smashing his chin on a rock."

"Are you sure that's the way it happened, Doc? The people tell a different story."

"Yes, sir. Sir, them people are all VC, what else do you think they're going to say? When we questioned them before they told us there were no VC around. Then two minutes later four run out of a hootch."

The Captain's tone softened. "If I ever find out something else happened, there'll be hell to pay. Do I make myself clear?"

"Yes, sir." The answer was in unison.

"Okay, dismiss."

While at the CP Mike decided to find the Senior Corpsman and put in an order for medical supplies. As he knelt to tie his boots, he heard the CO and Gunny speaking on the other side of a hedgerow

"You know, Gunny, I'd like to personally decorate the son of a bitch who popped that gook."

"Me, too, sir. How about Doc Lombardo? He didn't blink an eye when he told that story about the old guy falling."

"We've got some great boys in this company, Gunny. I'm very proud of them."

"Yes, sir, they're good Marines."

"Gunny, when we get back to An Hoa, I want to have a big party for these guys. Set it up with the Top to use company funds, okay?"

"Aye, aye, Skipper."

"Good, after all this they deserve it."

For the next week it seemed as though the enemy had packed up and left the Arizona. There was no contact and no one had to be medevaced. Things were going so smoothly that the Skipper permitted the men to have a swim call. The swimming hole was nothing more than a large bomb crater only a few yards outside the perimeter. Security around the thirty-foot luxurious Ho Chi Minh-style pool was rotated by platoons every half hour, and many of the men used their rubber ladies to float around in the warm sun. Even though the water was a little muddy and they had to share with a few leeches, everyone loved it.

Second Platoon was the last to swim so it was late in the afternoon by the time they finished. Mike, wearing his green 1st Marine Division shorts, carried his helmet under one arm and the air mattress under the other as he followed the winding path up to his hootch. He saw Allen sitting up, sweating, under the hot poncho and called out.

"Hey, pal, you should've come for a swim."

"No way, man. Us bloods and swimming don't get along."

"Well, here, at least you can take a bath. You smell like shit." Mike flung the water he had brought back from the pool in his helmet at Allen, hitting him square in the face. Seconds later he was forced to use all his agility to dodge the boot, canteen and C-ration can of peaches that came flying at him from inside the hootch. "Okay, okay, truce." Mike laughed as he flashed a peace sign.

"All right, truce, but you was lucky. Next one would've been right on target."

"I guess I know now why they made you a radioman. You can't hit shit." Allen started to throw his helmet, but Mike put his hands up and fell on his knees laughing. "No, no, no, please don't, I'm too young to die."

"Okay, I'll spare you this time."

Crawling in the hootch, Mike stretched out on the still damp air mattress, and closed his eyes. "Boy, this is the life."

Hi Grandpa,

This is one screwed up place. You can't tell friend from foe. The people are real nice to you one minute, but then as soon as you leave the ville they're shooting at you. I really have grown to dislike the people out here. They're filthy and always have their hand out wanting something. We never see any men between the ages of 14 and 40. It's too much of a coincidence that they're not around. To show you how bad their army is, the 51st ARVN Regiment landed in the northern Arizona two days ago and began what was to be a four-day sweep toward us. Granted, we've had it easy since, because all we've done is acted as the blocking. But so far they have not made any contact with the enemy and they are already a day behind schedule. I don't know if they're being overly cautious or they're inept, but not making contact in the Arizona is like not hitting any traffic on the freeways in LA during rush hours. Each morning a squad and I go out to a designated spot in the treeline, tie in with other squads from our company, and sit and wait for the ARVN to flush the NVA toward us. The only excitement we've had to date has been watching the air strikes supporting the sweep and laughing at the fly that flew into Allen's mouth as he slept.

Lately, I've been having a little problem with some of the guys in my platoon. Some of them try to get sent in out of the bush by faking everything from sickness to bad backs. I can't say that I blame them, but when I don't let them go they get all bent out of shape at me. Some of the black guys call me a racist and charge that if they were white, I'd send them in. Either way I can't win. If I sent them all in the Skipper would be on my ass, and if I don't, the guys are pissed at me. To tell you the truth, Grandpa, if I could send someone in, it'd be me. This combat crap is for the birds. See ya.

Mike

Chapter 11

Mike and Allen, as had been their routine for the past few days left the perimeter at sunrise and headed out to the blocking position, to the tree they had discovered the first day. It was an ideal spot. Not only did it afford relief from the searing heat but from there they could see any movement in the paddies. The ARVN's should have advanced well past their position by now, but the latest report still had them over a klick away so the Marines settled in for another long boring day.

Not long after they made themselves comfortable, a "Killer Team" from Third Platoon exchanged a few minutes of small talk as they passed through the position and headed east across the paddy.

Although no patrols were supposed to be sent out for fear of friendly firefights with ARVN forces, the CO needed to know what was going on around him. Instead he decided to send out four man "KTs" to recon all the treelines up to a klick from the hill.

Mike was lying casually against his pack dreaming of Jody and home when he heard the muffled explosion.

It woke everyone who was sleeping and brought the rest of the men to their feet.

"Ron, what the hell was that?" Mike asked as he felt the intense heat of an adrenaline rush

"I'm not sure, but I think it came from over there." Allen pointed in the direction the KT had gone."

Cupping his hands around his mouth, Mike yelled toward the treeline. "Hey, you guys okay?" The jungle was alive with silence. He looked at Allen. "Try raising them on the radio."

Allen made several attempts yet no answer came.

Something was wrong. Without a second thought Mike grabbed his gear and darted into the paddy.

"Come on, Ron, bring the radio."

Mike had almost reach the treeline when he saw a Marine standing on the trail stark naked. He motioned for Mike to follow him and twenty meters into the brush he found three Marines moaning and lying in their own blood. It was obvious that the naked Marine had used his clothes to try and bandage one of his buddies. Mike went to work immediately and, by the time Allen and the rest of the squad had caught up, he had clamped off and stopped the bleeding on the a Marine who had a lacerated Femoral artery.

While Mike bandage a nasty gash on the forehead of another member of the KT Allen radioed for a medevac.

No sooner had Mike finished tying the battle dressing when he heard the naked Marines say "Hey, Doc, are my guys going to be ok?"

"Yeah I think so that guy over there with the leg wound is the worst. He's pretty bad. Lost a lot of blood but, if we can get him back to First Med soon, he'll be okay, I think.

How'd it happen?"

"I don't know. I think Mac tripped a 'Bouncing Betty'. I saw that sucker shoot up in the air about three feet, and.... There was nothing I could do. It got all of us."

"Doc, Doc, I think you'd better get over here. Something don't look right with this guy." The urgency in Allen's voice sent Mike scurrying on hands and knees back the least wounded of the trio

The Marine's lips had turned blue and Mike was unable to find a pulse.

SHIT!

Immediately, he placed one hand on the Marines forehead, and the fingers of the other hand under the chin and titled the jaw upward. Then with his ear close to the man's mouth he listened for any signs of breathing.

Nothing.

Pinching the nose shut, Mike blew two full breaths into the Marine's mouth, and then slammed his fist down hard on his chest. Deliberately, he positioned the heel of his right hand on the sternum, and with smooth downward thrusts he compressed the chest fifteen times before moving back to the head, and administering two more breaths.

"Come on, man, don't give up. Breathe, you bastard, breathe," Mike pleaded. Looking at the dying man with fear filled eyes Mike resumed the cardiac massage.

The others watched with eager anticipation as dying man's eyes fluttered, but he still showed no sign of life.

Mike was desperate. "Get that fuckin' medevac here quick."

The CPR didn't seem to be working, but continued long past the time he knew it would do any good. Arm-weary, and near exhaustion, he finally gave up.

Defeated, he fell back to a sitting position in the tall grass, removed his soaked skivi shirt and wiped the dripping perspiration from his face. He stared at the lifeless black figure at his feet.

I failed. That Marine shouldn't have died. His wounds weren't that serious. What did I do wrong? Should I have started an IV? What could I have done more? I'm tired of this shit. I don't want to be God. I want to go home.

Mike felt Allen's hand on his shoulder. "Come on Doc, chopper's comin'."

The rest of the squad had already moved the others to the LZ, so he and Allen rolled dead man's body onto a poncho and carried it to join them.

"Delta 2 Alpha, Delta 2 Alpha, this is Sunshine, over."

Wilson picked up the handset and spoke. "Sunshine, this is 2 Alpha, go."

"Ah, roger, 2 Alpha, we are on station. Can you mark your location?"

Wilson turned his head, and yelled at Allen. "Ron, pop the smoke." He watched as Allen pulled the pin and sent the canister flying into the open field. "Sunshine, be advised we have you spotted and have popped smoke."

"Ah, roger 2 Alpha. I see green smoke, over."

"That's affirm, Sunshine, come on in."

The pilot maneuvered his bird, with the logo of the "Purple Foxes" on the tail, in a descending spiral until it was only a few feet above the trees. The rhythmic "whomp, whomp whomp" of the spinning blades filled the air around them. Two big eyes painted on the nose of the chopper hovered a short distance away from Mike and slowly inched forward into the tiny LZ. Allen was directly in line with the pilot's view and guided him in with hand and arm signals.

Sitting side by side, the faces of both the pilot and co-pilot were hidden by the white helmets, and dark visors. They looked like aliens behind the windshield. Working in tandem and as a team, they expertly moved the bird closer. The door gunner leaning out the side door concentrated on the ground and assisted the pilot.

The rotor wash pelted everyone with dirt, grass, and pebbles as the back wheels touched. The wounded were rushed on board first. Mike and Allen followed with KIA's body, and set it on the floor near the back ramp.

"Keep an eye on those two, they're in bad shape," Mike yelled to the crew chief, who nodded and patted him on the shoulder.

Mike took one last look before starting down the ramp, and as soon as he was off, the blades picked up speed. The pilot brought the chopper straight up until it was clear of the trees, then lowered the nose, and accelerated forward, hugging the tree tops for a few hundred yards before quickly banking and gaining altitude.

The squad gathered up the equipment and returned to their position where they spent the remainder of the afternoon. Then at 1800 they headed back to the perimeter to join the rest of the company.

Mike had just started heating his dinner when Sullivan came over the crest of the hill and joined him.

"Doc, Captain wants to see you up at the CP, right away."

"Now? I'm getting ready to eat, sir. Can't it wait a few minutes?"

"I'm afraid not."

Stirring the beef and potatoes one more time, he tasted it for temperature then grabbed the can off the makeshift stove, and headed for the CP. Walking alongside Sullivan, Mike ate on the way.

"What's this all about, sir?"

"You'll see."

Mike smirked and glanced at the Lieutenant out of the corner of his eye. *Gee, thanks. I could have figured that one out myself.*

At the command post, Mike noticed a number of unfamiliar faces sitting around the captain.

"Have a seat, Doc, I'll be with you in a moment." The CO continued his conversation with the officer on his right.

Mike found an empty ammo crate to sit on and placed his depleted C-ration can on the ground next to it. He was really starting to worry about why he'd been called here.

Had they found out that I lied about how the old papasan got the gash on his chin? What else could I have done wrong?

The CO finally leaned forward and rested his arms on his legs. "Doc, I don't think you know Lieutenant Duffy, and Staff Sergeant Niccoli from Third Platoon."

"No, sir, I don't." He acknowledged both men then turned his attention back to the CO.

"The reason I called you here is that I've heard some things, and I personally wanted to talk to you about them."

"Okay, sir." Mike was really concerned now.

"The members of the squad you were with today told us about the events this morning."

"Skipper, I tried my best, but I just couldn't save him."

"I know you did son, but that is not why I called you here." The CO looked directly into Mike's eyes. "I want you to know Corpsmen are not supposed to be pointmen."

"I was just doing my job sir."

"Taking off on your own into that treeline is not just doing your job

"Sir, I wasn't alone. Ron Allen and the rest of the guys were right there with me."

Lieutenant Duffy interrupted. "Yes, and they told us they couldn't keep up with you. Doc, I want you to know how much I appreciate you helping my men like that. The Captain has given me permission to write you up for a citation and I will get started on that right away."

"Sir, all that really happened today was a man died, and I couldn't do a damn think to save him. Going out there was no big thing. We've been in that area before and it was safe. Like I said, I knew the rest of the squad was right behind me."

"That's not the point. There are still plenty of booby traps in the area and, in my book, for you to take off on your own is something worthy of recognition. Do you think the others will be all right?"

"Yes, sir, they should all be fine in a few weeks."

"Thank God. We owe you a lot."

Embarrassed, Mike could only say, "Thanks."

On cue Mike stood when the others did and shook hands as they were extended to him.

The Skipper was the last and continued to hold Mike's hand as he spoke compassionately. "Doc, we all share your sorrow at losing another Marine, but I'm sure you did all you could to save that young man's life." Letting go, he put a hand on Mike's shoulder. "You rate the medal, son, not for the one you lost but for the one's you saved. You and the other Doc's deserve a lot of credit for how you've taken care of our Marines."

"Then the credit should go to my nurses back at Jacksonville Naval Hospital. They insisted that we learn as much as we could before we came over here."

"Well, they taught you well. Now you take care, and if there's anything I can do for you, let me know."

"Yeah, there's one thing I know most of my guys would like."

"What's that?"

"Find us some gooks so we can get even."

The CO slapped him on the back and winked. "I'm with you. I'd like nothing better. I've got a feeling you'll get your wish sooner than you think. See you later, Doc."

Several men from the squad were waiting at the platoon CP when he and Sullivan returned.

"Hey, John Wayne, what do you think this is, Iwo Jima?"

"Naw, we got ourselves a real gungy squid."

"I always heard Corpsmen were supposed to be intelligent, but ours, I don't know."

Mike smiled at the good-natured teasing. "You're right, I used to be smart, but you see, after living with you Marines for so long, I think I've caught that dreaded Marine Corps disease."

"And what's that?" Allen asked impatiently.

"Shit for brains."

Playfully they pounded him about his head and arms for a few seconds. The laughter seemed to relieve the tension of the last few hours.

"Get some, Doc."

"One more thing, Squid." Allen starred seriously at Mike. "To show you what we really think of you, we all got together and took a vote." Pulling an E-tool from behind his back, he handed it to Mike. "We've decided that it's your turn to dig the SHITTER."

Everyone howled with laughter.

"All right, all right." Sullivan's words interrupted their fun. "Listen up. I've got some good news and some bad news."

A low grumble came from amid the group.

"First, the ARVN sweep has been canceled. They're heli-lifting them out at first light tomorrow. Second, it's been confirmed. Our battalion will be leaving An Hoa and relieving the 26th Marines at a place called Dai La Pass. The lucky bastards are going home as part of Nixon's withdrawal plan. In other words gentlemen we're moving closer to Division Headquarters in Da Nang."

Smiles covered the faces standing before him.

"Now, the bad news. Tomorrow morning we'll make a five klick hump to the northwestern part of the Arizona and set up on Hill 29 over near the 'Razorback'. The Recon observation post on the ridge has been reporting large numbers of NVA in the area and, from what I understand, we're goin' over to see if we can draw them into a fight."

Wilson and Weller waited until the re-supply chopper was completely off-loaded before rushing on board. They had only been on Hill 20 for an hour, but the rest of the platoon couldn't wait for them to leave.

Wilson was driving everyone nuts. He was going on R & R to Australia the next day, and had talked about nothing else for the last two weeks. As far as Weller was concerned, there was only sheer happiness. He was going back to the world. For him, in just a few short days, Vietnam and the fighting would be nothing more then a memory.

With mixed emotions Mike watched Dan Weller stride up the ramp and give a final wave. He was happy Dan was going home, where life would once again be normal. But there was also felt sadness, knowing he might never see his buddy again. For, despite their unfriendly first meeting, they had become close friends and he had learned to love him like a brother.

Watching the bird take his friend from the battlefield, Mike couldn't help but think, nine more months and that'll be me. He raised his arm at the disappearing Chopper but let it fall realizing his friend could not see him. Mike stared out at the empty paddy in front of him. *I wonder if our lives will be as exciting or as intense as this year of hell? Will there ever be anything post about our fears or traumas, or will they be with us now and forever. Will we be able to learn to live with them? Will our lives really ever be normal again?* Mike shuffled his feet and looked to the sky. *This war has led to too many unanswered questions but one there was one thing we'd all learned and that is how very special each day is that we are alive. A gift, to enjoy, and to cherish as though each one was our last.*

With both Weller and Wilson gone, Sullivan promoted Cronin to acting squad leader, and Lance Corporal Bobby Kelly from third squad to the new platoon radioman. Kelly, a wiry, freckle-faced kid from Nebraska, loved the Corps and constantly stressed that fact to anyone who'd listen. He was one of those fortunate people who would always have that aura of adolescent excitement, an infectious smile and eyes that made people comfortable. He rarely needed to shave, and looked even younger than his eighteen years. Because of that, he had been saddled with the nickname "Kid". Besides the Corps, all Kid ever talked about was his daddy's farm and the Nebraska football team.

Mike and Allen had just finished erecting their hootch when they spotted the OV-10 Bronco. The double-boomed turboprop spotter plane was circling like a vulture above the treeline where they had lost the ten men a few weeks before.

Mike wondered what was going on over there this time as he watched the Bronco dive toward the earth. A rocket left its rail under the right wing, and a puff of white smoke dispersed into the air above the trees as the Bronco disappeared in the bright sky. Seconds later, two Marine A4 Skyhawks thundered out of the sun and released what appeared to be two-hundred and fifty pound bombs. The black and gray clouds floated upward long before Mike heard the explosion.

With the blast, everyone on the hill suddenly became interested spectators. Swooping in from a different direction the jets once again dropped another load of bombs. On their third and final run, an orange fireball of napalm engulfed the entire treeline.

The propeller-driven Bronco reappeared low over the burning treetops inspecting the work.

Out of the corner of his eye, Mike noticed the Skyhawks heading directly toward him. The planes were racing side-by-side, wing tips only yards apart. As he watched, they roared only a hundred feet above the ground, violently shaking the air and ground around him. Right above him the pilots hit their afterburners and executed a perfect "Victory Roll," sending the grunts below into frenzy of cheers.

Mike nodded, and wished that Chris Graham and the others, who had been hit there could have seen it.

The planes slowed, and circled. As they flew by the hill one last time, they wiggled their wings and the pilots flashed a hearty "thumbs up" from the cockpit.

"You think they know it was our unit that got chopped up over there?" Kid asked, looking up at Sullivan.

"Yeah. I think they know."

"Payback's a motherfucker, ain't it, Lieutenant?"

Sullivan only smiled, and slapped Kid on the back.

Early the next morning Mike sat stoically in his hootch lacing his boots. Shortly he'd join Cronin's squad going over to the treeline to do a bomb damage assessment of yesterday's attack. *We've already lost too many friends over there, he thought. I don't see any point of going back into that area again. It's just plain stupid.*

Mike checked his watch and decided he had enough time for a final cigarette. Leaning back against his rucksack, he turned his head to Allen who had awakened only minutes before.

"Hey, Ron, you ever get the feeling you ain't gonna to make it?"

"Sure, all the time." He reached and accepts cigarette that Mike offered.

"No, I mean a real strong feeling that you're gonna get killed."

Allen frowned. "What's you talking like that for?"

"I don't know. I've got a feeling I'm not coming back from this patrol."

"That's crazy, you're too ugly to die."

Mike smiled, appreciating his friend's attempt at levity. "Yeah, but if it does happen, I want you to have all my stuff. My radio and camera are in here." He pointed to the pack.

"Nothing's gonna to happen to you, man."

"Hopefully you're right." Mike crushed out the cigarette and looked intently at Allen. "But if it does, write Jody and let her know what happened. Tell her I loved her. Okay?"

Allen nodded. "Sure."

"Thanks, Ron, you're a good friend, I want you to know that."

Standing slowly, Mike put his helmet and flak jacket on, and left without another word.

With the temperature soaring to one hundred and twenty degrees the patrol went by way of the supposedly deserted village of Phu An 2. Only minutes after they left the ville and entered the large paddy on the other side they received several rounds of sniper fire. But with no one hit, Cronin simply called in mortars from the hill and continued toward the objective as if nothing had happened.

The pointman's route of march then took them through a patch of elephant grass where the vegetation cut visibility to only a few yards. The stifling air was calm and devoid of even the slightest breeze.

Mike suddenly became concerned about heat casualties as body temperatures elevated to dangerously high levels. He had just started to move up alongside Cronin to talk to him about the problem when he heard the explosion.

"Corpsman."

By he time Mike reached Cannonball, he was on ground holding his leg.

Mike didn't see any blood and Cannonball didn't appear to be in a great deal of pain.

"You hit?"

"Back of my leg."

Mike examined the area, and didn't see anything except a slight tear in Cannonball's pants. "Drop your trou, man, I don't see nothin."

With the pants down, Mike finally saw the wound. A tiny piece of shrapnel about the size of a dime had lodged in the right thigh. It appeared to be no worse than a bad cut and the metal came out easily. He looked back at the hole in the ground and realized how lucky Cannonball had been. Apparently, most of the explosion had been taken by his flak jacket, which was torn to shreds. Sitting on the ground wrapping the battle dressing around the wound Mike slowly released a sinister smile across his face.

"Hey, Cronin, we're going to have to cancel the rest of the patrol and get Cannonball back right away."

"Can't we call in a medevac?"

"No way, he's not that serious. I'm sure you don't want to risk a chopper getting shot down for something like this."

"Then why can't we continue?"

"Well, we're still a good klick from the treeline and I'm afraid that if he keeps walking on it, it could cause serious damage. I can't be sure if I got all the shrapnel out or not, but I don't want to take the chance. I think you'd better call the Skipper and tell him we have to come back."

Cronin eyed Mike suspiciously. "Okay. Kid, bring the radio over here." He glanced at Mike one more time. "Are you sure we can't continue?"

Mike put on his best grave expression. "I'd strongly advise against it. Tell the Captain that if we continue and an artery ruptures, Cannonball could be in serious trouble." Mike turned his head and winked at Cannonball and Kid.

Cronin spent the next several minutes explaining the situation to the Skipper.

"Yes, sir, I understand. No problem. Will do, sir. Over and out." He handed the handset back to Kid and smiled. "Okay, guys, saddle up. Thanks to Doc, we're heading back."

It was late afternoon by the time they entered the perimeter. Mike accompanied Cannonball to the company CP, where he'd have to wait for the evening supply chopper to take him to the BAS in An Hoa.

Returning to his hootch he heard Allen's voice echo from under the poncho. "Shit, I thought I got rid of you. Does this mean I have to put up with you again? I've already sold your camera and radio."

"Yeah, you're stuck with me, Bro." Mike crawled in alongside his buddy, and opened a can of turkey loaf.

"Heard you did a super job of sandbagging the patrol."

"Shhh, will ya? You'll get me in trouble."

Allen grinned. "Why? Everybody knows about it and, from listening to the guys, they thought it was great. What, do you think you're the only one who didn't want to go back into that area?"

"Well, I figured why get anyone else hurt. It wasn't like that patrol was gonna end the war. We were only going to assess the bomb damage and, you know as well as I, we wouldn't have found a damn thing."

"Hey, man, I ain't criticizing ya. I'd a done the same thing."

"Yeah, well, my mama didn't raise no fool."

After finishing a light dinner of turkey loaf and can of applesauce, Mike threw the empties into the cardboard box at his feet and began to remove his boots. A steady drizzle beat a steady pitter-patter on the pastic poncho that protected them as Mike laid back on his air mattress.

"Hey, Ron, I'm gonna catch some Zs. Don't wake me unless it's real important, okay?"

"Sure. I'll put you on the '4 to 6' radio watch."

"Thanks." Pulling the liner over his shoulders Mike curled up into a ball, and closed his eyes. He had no trouble falling asleep.

Somewhere around 2300 hours Mike was startled by the sounds of gunfire. Poking his head outside the poncho, he noticed that the sky above the recon position to the north was lit up like a Christmas tree.

Sitting up Mike rubbed the sleep from his eyes. "How long's that been going on?"

"Just started." Allen extended a half empty cup of coffee toward him. "Want some?"

"No thanks."

The fighting intensified for the next few minutes as scores of tracers ricocheted off the rocks into the night sky.

"That's a bad spot, man," Allen said. "I've heard that place has been overrun four times in the last year."

"Shit. I'm glad we ain't up there. Why do you think they keep sending people up there if it gets overrun all the time?"

"'Cuz it's the one spot where you can see everything going on in the valley. They can spot Mr. Charles and have arty on him before he knows what hit him."

Both sets of eyes jumped southward when they heard the shells leave their guns in An Hoa. They followed the whistle in the darkness as artillery rounds passed overhead. Impacting seconds later on the ridge, the resulting explosions echoed through the canyons, making it seem like hundreds of rounds had hit the ground at the same time. Above in the rain, a steady barely audible drone of a propeller-driven

plane circled the recon position. Mike scanned the blackness.
Suddenly the night disappeared, forcing him to shield his eyes as three,
two hundred thousand candlepower basketball flares were released and
floated toward the earth. A red streak resembling silly string radiated
from the black above the flares and reached to the ground. The
distinctive brrrrrr caused by resonance inside the empty cargo
compartment signaled that "Spooky" had begun to work out on the
attacking enemy soldiers.

　　　　Originally called "Puff the Magic Dragon," the converted C47
twin propeller plane armed with three mini-guns could each put out six
thousand rounds per minute. With all three guns firing at the same
time, which was rarely happened, it could put down eighteen thousand
rounds per minute. Grunts always loved these modern weapons of
mass destruction because they knew that anyone caught in the open
when Spooky did its thing was destined to visit his ancestors, and that
meant one less soldier they'd have to do battle with.

　　　　Mike relaxed against the dirt mound at the back of the hootch,
cupped a cigarette perfectly, and watched the spectacle. "Ya know
them Recon guys are bad dudes."

　　　　"Yeah, man, them's crazy fuckers, but they're good," answered
Allen.

　　　　"Did you ever work with them?"

　　　　"Naw. You?"

　　　　Mike nodded. "When I was at Pendleton . . ." Another burst
from "Spooky" delayed his words. "They gave us Raider training."

　　　　"Raider training, what's that?"

　　　　"They taught us how to paddle in off a ship in tiny rubber boats,
how to sneak up on an objective and attack it without being noticed.
You know, all that commando stuff, like learning how to climb cliffs
and repel down mountains or out of helicopters."

　　　　"That must have been interesting."

　　　　"Yeah, it was real bitchen stuff. I enjoyed it a lot. I was even
going to volunteer to go Recon, but when I found out I would have had
to extend to go to jump school, I said forget it. I don't want to spend
any more time in this man's outfit than I have to. But one thing's for
sure, I've got a lot of respect for those guys up there."

　　　　"I know what you mean." Allen motioned his head toward the
recon post. "I hope them poor bastards up there make it. Not only for

their sake, but ours, too. 'Cause if they get their asses waxed, you know who's going up there tomorrow, don't you?"

"Us?" Mike gave Allen a bemused smile.

"Doc, you's a fuckin' genius. Who said squids was dumb?" Allen turned on his side and pulled the poncho liner over his shoulders. "Ah, fuck it, we only got a week left out here, I'm goin' to sleep. You got the radio?"

"Yeah I'll take it. Hey, Ron." Mike hesitated. "How short are you?"

"Thirty-two and a wake-up. I'm so short I can parachute off a dime. Now will you let me get some sleep?" He poked his head out from under the poncho liner, smiled, and winked. "See ya in the morning, BOOT."

Mike sat upright; legs crossed Indian fashion, and looked down on his friend. *God, thirty-two and a wake up. It ain't never going to end for me. Vietnam is a mind game that only the strongest survive. He wondered if he could maintain that kind of strength?*

As he put on the last of his gear Mike watched a swarm of helicopters circle, land and take off over near the battalion CP on the Hot Dog. For well over an hour the flyboys had been at the business of extracting the rest of the battalion from the Arizona. They were almost done but none of it mattered because Delta Company had been ordered to stay in the field an extra day.

Figuring the NVA was watching the battalion leave, the CO decided to send Second Platoon over to the "Hot Dog" to set up a night ambush. He hoped to surprise any gooks that might come around to scrounge through the battalion's trash looking for cans of food or ammo the grunts may have left behind.

Sullivan had carefully planned the route of march so that they'd be concealed in the foothills the whole way. In order to avoid detection and maintain their stealth capabilities, he ordered the slings removed from all rifles and the rings taped down. Faces, hands, and arms were camouflaged, and they wore only cartridge belts and soft covers.

For the first klick, the patrol went smoothly with no sign of the enemy. Then movement on their starboard side halted the column. Freezing and dropping to a knee along with the others, Mike saw flashes of color moving swiftly parallel to their position. The tall grass and brush waved and rustled as if being blown by the wind – except there was no breeze. Attempting to focus on the object and see what it was Mike's heart quickened when the movement stopped. Intently, he stared into the jungle shrubs where he had last seen the motion. Seconds later, his concentration was shattered by a mighty roar followed by a swift the charge at him. Dozens of rifles spit death toward the enemy, which they instantly realized, was a tiger. Only ten feet from where Sullivan stood in stunned silence, the magnificent feline crashed and died. The creature had faced its only known enemy with the courage of all great warriors and as majestically as it had lived, died without a whimper.

Approaching the animal, Mike felt profound compassion as the sprawled beast gasped its final breath, blood still oozing from every hole.

"Delta 2-6, Delta 2-6, this is Delta 6, over," the radio squawked.

"6, this is 2, go."

"Ah, 2-6, have you run into any unfriendlies? Over."

"Ah, that's a negative, 6."

"Then what was all the firing about? You're under orders to avoid all contact, over." The Skipper's voice was stern, authoritarian, and plainly irritated.

"Be advised 6, we were attacked by a tiger."

"Say again your last?"

"We confirm one orange and black four hundred pound Bengal tiger KIA, over."

There was a brief pause on the other end of the line. "Are you shittin' me, 2-6?" The captain snickered. "Lieutenant, how the hell am I supposed to report that one to Battalion?"

Grinning, Sullivan glanced around at his men, and shrugged. "Well, how about if we confirm four NVA KIAs wearing tiger striped camouflage uniforms?"

"Very funny, Lieutenant, but I don't think that'll work."

Sullivan could almost hear the laughter in the CO's voice. "Sir, do you want us to continue with our mission, over?"

"That's affirm, but I'd advise that you backtrack or change your patrol route."

"Aye, aye, sir."

"But whatever you do, keep me informed."

"Ah, roger that."

"And Lieutenant, one more thing.

"Yes, sir?"

"Make sure you take some good pictures."

"Most definitely. 6, out." Handing the handset to Kid, he rejoined the men still photographing the animal. "Okay, finish up. We have to get moving. Cronin, take the point and head west for about twenty minutes then get us back on course."

Taking one last look at the carcass Sullivan turned to Mike. "You know, Doc, it's a shame something so beautiful has to die."

"Yes Sir, just one more casualty of this fucked up war." Mike shook his head. "What a waste."

Hi Grandpa,

Got some good news for a change. In a few weeks we're saying good-bye to An Hoa and will be moving permanently to a place called Dai La Pass.

Several of my buddies have gone back to the world and Ron Allen is a two-digit midget, which means he is short. I wish I was going with him. I'm sick of this place; you can't believe how bad it is. We keep losing guys yet never seem to accomplish anything. I'm convinced they don't have a plan to win this screwed up war. You know, Grandpa, growing up, John Wayne and Audie Murphy were my heroes - - along with you and Dad of course - - but nothing I've seen over here is like what I saw and heard. I used to watch all the movies, from "Battle Cry" to the "Five Sullivans," and I wanted to be just like those guys. They made it look so easy and glorious. They'd charge farmhouses or beaches and come away a hero everytime. But, you know, I realize now they left out one extremely important detail. The pain. They never showed the pain of seeing friends die, the pain of seeing bodies mutilated, the pain of living like an animal, and the pain of fear.

How did you cope with this shit when you were in the war? You and Dad must be a lot stronger than me, 'cause all I want to do is come home. I wish you would have told me a little more about the horrors of it all and less of the glory, then maybe I might not have been so gung ho. I am sure I still would have gone but may have been better prepared. I know one thing, when my kids ask about the war, I'll make sure I tell them how ugly it really was.

So far I haven't seen much glory. I'm not saying we shouldn't ever fight a war, but if people really knew what war was like they wouldn't be in such a hurry to start them. I'm convinced that if you want to find a true antiwar person, find someone who's been there. Guess I'll close for now. You take care, and write soon.

Mike

Chapter 12

Mikes noticed the smiles spread across tired and unshaven faces, as Delta Company boarded the six helicopters at exactly 0930. After seventy-five brutal days, they were leaving the Arizona. It had taken a heavy toll - - thirty-three members of the company had been killed or wounded.

Arriving back in An Hoa, the filthy Marines were directed to the same tent area they had occupied the last time. Mike and Allen sauntered around a small bunker complex, and were delighted to see the Top and several pogues standing behind barbecues made from fifty-gallon drums cut in half. Pans of macaroni salad, cottage cheese, and chips filled the tables. Ice glistened in the fresh morning sun, as it cooled dozens of cases of beer inside trashcans. The aroma of sizzling steaks, and the juice dripping onto the charcoals, was torture to their long neglected taste buds. Dropping their gear, they joined the others already forming a line.

The Top, beer belly hanging over his belt buckle, and half a cigar sticking out of his mouth, held a brew in one hand and a long fork in the other. As each paper plate passed, he plunked a steak on it, took a swig of beer, and constantly urged the men in his gruff bellowing voice,

"Move along people."

When he was sure everyone had finished gorging themselves, the Skipper jumped up on one of the bunkers.

"Men, listen up! I want everyone to grab a beer. That's an order, on the double." He waited while several dozen men scurried to the trashcans. "Marines, let me say how proud we are of the job you did in the Arizona. You were outstanding. It is an honor to serve with you. As you know, a few of our friends who went with us didn't come out. No matter where we go, or what we do, we shall never forget

them. So let's lift our beers and offer a toast to them, and to you.
OOH-RAH."

The men loudly echoed the toast, and as Mike chugged from his
can, he couldn't help but remember all the faces of the wounded he'd
treated.

"One more thing, the Colonel has authorized me to tell you that
the showers will be turned on early, especially for Delta Company."
Looking down at his watch he hesitated a few more seconds. "Shower
call will go in zero five mikes."

A cheer erupted as the nearly drunk grunts raced for soap,
towels, and shaving gear.

In the showers, they were like kids on Christmas Morning.
They allowed the water to pour over their heads and down their bodies.
They moaned with pleasure as its relaxing warmth flowed to the floor,
turning a dark brown color as it entered the drain.

"Man, this is better than getting laid."

Mike rinsed the soap from his eyes. "Hey, Cougar, let's not go
overboard about this. It's good, but not that good."

"Yeah, you're right, Doc, but unless you can find me a cyclo-
girl right now, it'll have to do. You done with the shampoo?"

"Yeah, here you go."

Mike stepped from the showers, and quickly dried himself
before returning to his tent. He felt like he'd been reborn as he put on
clean clothes and socks that had been left for each of them. Sitting on
the bunk he allowed himself several minutes to really enjoy this slice of
heaven. The aches and pains he'd experienced over the past few
months seemed to have miraculously disappeared, and now - - best of
all - - he'd finally have a chance to get a good night's sleep.

It was back to work as usual the next morning as the battalion
prepared for the move to Da Nang. Excused from the working parties,
Second Platoon was told to get all their gear together and wait near
their tents.

"Hey, Allen, what's this all about?" Kid asked. "Where we
going?'

"How the fuck should I know? I ain't no General." Allen
dropped his gear angrily and sat on the ground alongside Mike who

was busy reading Harold Robbin's, "A Stone For Danny Fisher."
"Doc, why are we always the ones who get screwed?"

Mike glanced quickly at his friend. "It don't mean nothing, man, you know that."

"The scuttlebutt I got was they were sending us out to Liberty Bridge."

From across the road, Cronin injected his two cents. "Naw, I heard we're going up to Hai Van Pass. It's supposed to get hit and they want us in reserve." Wilson, who had returned from R & R only the day before, laid against his pack, and slowly pulled his softcover down over his eyes. "Will you guys shut the fuck up? You sound like a bunch of old ladies. Just wait till they tell us, will ya? You know the green machine don't do anything that makes sense." He stretched his arms out to the side. "Man, after all those beautiful women in Australia, I gotta come back here, and look at you animals. Now I know someone has it in for me. I hope when I die they bury me face down so the whole world can use my ass as a bicycle rack." He started to roll over but noticed Sullivan and Sergeant Greene hurrying toward him. "Okay, guys, gather round." Pushing himself off the ground Wilson brushed the dust from his butt, and waited for the Lieutenant to speak.

"Men, Battalion's sending us out to guard the water purification station over near Second Battalion's compound." A chorus of moans and groans echoed about him. "Six bys 'll be here in a few minutes, so don't wander off."

Allen looked immediately to Mike. "See what I mean?"

"You ever been out there?"

"Nope, but I'll bet ya it's the pits." Stomping over to his pack Allen angrily threw it on his back. "Ain't this a bitch? Rest of the company gets to stay here and skate while they send us back out to the bush."

The Lieutenant overheard Allen's complaining, and moved toward him. "I'm sorry you don't like your assignment, Marine, but I've got some more bad news for you."

Allen's head dropped like a beaten fighter. "Ah, fuck, what now?"

"Your flight date came in. You start processing next week." Sullivan allowed himself a wisp of a smile.

At first the words didn't seem to register, then the famous toothy smile belonging only to Ron Allen radiated across his face. He was speechless as he started shaking hands with everyone before turning back to Sullivan like he forgot something. "When do I leave, sir?"

"Ten days."

"No shit? Well, sir, I'd better not start a long conversation, 'cause I won't get a chance to finish it. I'm so short, I can sit on a dime and my feet won't touch the ground. You know, Doc, I'm so short you'd have to dig a hole to kick my ass."

Mike shook his head and let his eyes roll to the sky. "Oh no, are we gonna have to put up with this crap for the next week?"

"Huh? What'd you say, boot?" Allen cupped his hand around his ear. "You'll have to speak up, I can't hear you, I'm too short."

Two trucks pulled up and covered the small group with black diesel exhaust. The acrid smell of the fuel filled their nostrils as all twenty-eight men climbed over the side rails into the truck beds. Grinding into first gear the driver lurched the multi-wheeled vehicle forward, which sent a cloud of dust up into the air behind. While they bounced down the road Allen was busy writing the number of days he had left on the cloth cover of his helmet. Mike, on the other side of the truck, sat staring vacantly at the countryside until he spotted the compound off to his right about four hundred yards away.

The small camp was completely enclosed by the usual layers of concertina, razor wire, and tanglefoot placed throughout the wire. Reinforced sandbag bunkers were spaced every ten-yard around the dirt perimeter walls while outside the camp to the left two boarded-up rectangular buildings stood only yards from the entrance. What they were Mike didn't know, but they sure would allow someone to sneak up real close to their position undetected. He didn't like that.

The main entrance was actually two gates, one ten yards behind the other, that opened in toward the camp. A large concrete bunker topped by sandbags and a fifty-caliber machine gun presented a menacing welcome inside the second gate. The interior of the compound was completely taken up by two round water tanks.

When the trucks stopped, the platoon jumped down and straggled into the camp where Sergeant Greene immediately assigned each man his defensive position. Mike and Allen wandered around and found residence for the CP in a smaller reinforced bunker across from the fifty-cal.

Inside, the wooden planks covering the floor assured them of dry footing regardless of weather. Whitewashed walls and electric lights brightened what would normally be a normally dark room. That alone would make reading and writing on night radio watch easier. Six field cots filled the square space and, despite the heat outside, the bunker was unusually cool.

Days passed uneventfully, and the platoon settled into a comfortable routine. Three times a day, meals were brought to them by mechanical mule from Second Battalion's mess hall and, at 2200 each night, mid-rats comprised of sandwiches and coffee were delivered to the front gate.

Their time was spent doing nothing more strenuous than cleaning weapons or talking to local kids outside the perimeter wire. By the end of the first week everyone was overjoyed with their good fortune, especially since they'd heard that the rest of the company was working hard, painting, cleaning, and packing gear. It looked, for once, like they had actually gotten the best of it.

Sunning himself, lying on the sandbags near the front gate, Mike looked up and saw Allen bounding up the road toward the compound. He had left earlier that morning to finish his out-processing.

"Well, Doc," said Allen. "Tomorrow I'll be checking out and leaving for Da Nang, and in two days I'll be on that Freedom Bird for home."

Mike sat upright. "I'm happy for you, man. Your replacement came out about an hour ago." Mike pointed to a bespectacled PFC sitting off by himself. A pale, clean face showed the same fears that many of the veterans had known their own first days in country. His carrot red hair had recently been cut high and tight, and his eyes held the shine of youth and innocence. The brand new utilities, boots, and flak jacket hung like a sign "New Meat" around his neck.

"What's his name?"

"I'm not sure. Thompson or something like that. The Lieutenant wrote it in his notebook."

"Damn, I feel sorry for the poor fucker."

"Yeah, can you imagine having a year to go?"

"Nope, but it don't mean nothing. They can kill ya, but they can't eat ya." Allen glanced toward the road. "Speaking of eating, here comes chow."

The mule puttered up to the front gate, dropped off two green containers filled with the evening meal, and a five-gallon carton of cold milk. One metal box held sliced Virginia ham and mashed potatoes, while the second was filled with corn, coleslaw, and dessert.

Allen was given the honor of serving himself first because, as he said, he was so short, he might not have time to wait in a long line.

With a plate in one hand and a cup of milk in the other, Mike joined Allen on the roof of a bunker. The sky to the west had turned a mixture of bright blues, reds, and oranges above the mountains. As they ate, a cool breeze from the ocean swept over the camp, making Allen's last night indeed a beautiful one.

"Damn, Ron, I can't believe you're leaving tomorrow"

"I know, Doc, I can't believe it myself. Just think, forty-eight and a wake up and I'll be on my way home."

"I'm going to miss not having you around, you dumb Jarhead. I can't begin to tell you how much I appreciate all you've done for me. I wouldn't have made it this far if it wasn't for you."

"No sweat, man, just keep your ass down, and get back home. You're a good man, Doc, I won't forget you." Allen extended his fist toward Mike. "Give me some power Bro."

"Say, listen, Ron, when I get home, Jody and I are getting married. How'd you like to be one of the ushers in my wedding?"

"I'd be honored, Doc." The warm smile quickly turned serious. "Maybe you'd better check with Jody first, and see if she really wants a 'blood' in her wedding."

Annoyed, Mike glared at his friend. "That's a low blow, man. I want you there, and that's all that counts. There's only one other guy that's closer to me than you and we grew up together. So don't give me any of that racial bullshit, 'cause it don't wash with me and you know it."

"Sorry, Doc, I guess it's just that I've seen it happen too many times. Over here things are different, we depend on one another in the bush. We are truly brothers - there's no skin color out here - but it seems like as soon as people get back where it's safe, things have a way of changing. You see how different guys are even in An Hoa."

"Yeah, I see your point, but that's not me. I look at a man for how he acts, and his attitude toward me, not the color of his skin." He shoveled a spoonful of ham into his mouth and washed it down with the last of his milk. "I had to fight a war in a foreign country to find Utopia, where we all are truly equal."

"I know that man, I feel the same way." Allen fidgeted, avoiding his friend's eyes. "Doc, there is something I have to tell you."

"Go ahead."

"Remember a few months back when you asked me why I joined the Corps?"

"Yeah. You said something about sharecropping. So what?"

"Well, that was a lie."

Mike shrugged. "So? We all lie once in a while." He grinned. "Even me."

"The real reason I joined was to escape jail. Ya see I killed this 'brotha' back home who was beating up on a lady I knew. I whopped on him so bad he was unconscious for two days before he died."

"Well, good for you, I'll bet the woman really appreciated the help."

"That's just it, I didn't know it at the time, but he was her pimp. She even testified against me. I had gone to school with her, and I never knew she was a whore. Anyway, the police arrested me on charges of manslaughter. At my trial the judge gave me a choice. He tells me I can either go to jail, or into the Corps for four years. I didn't hesitate, but the felony is still on the books, and if I foul up or get kicked out of the Crotch, I go right to jail."

"Do you get to collect two hundred dollars for passing go?" Mike's smile showed he was pleased with his little joke. "It makes no difference to me, man, I still want you at the wedding."

"You sure?"

"Yeah."

"Okay, I'll be there. You let me know where, and when." Allen grabbed Mike in a playful headlock and shook him around a little before letting go. "Thanks, Brother."

"Come on, we've got a surprise for you."

With darkness settling over the camp the two men entered the CP bunker where Allen's going-away party began. Sullivan had bought several cases of beer, and a fifth of bourbon at the PX, while the platoon's care packages were raided for food.

Everyone had already consumed numerous beers by the time Cronin crushed an empty red and white Budwiser can against his own forehead.

"Well, Mr. Allen, what are you going to do when you get out?" asked Sullivan.

"You won't believe this, sir, but I ain't getting out. I'm going to re-up tomorrow before I leave."

Mike nearly choked on the swig of beer in his mouth. "You're what?"

"I'm reenlisting."

"How come you never said anything about this before."

"I didn't make up my mind until a little while ago."

"What made you decide to stay in?" Sullivan asked, lighting a C-ration Kool and opening another beer.

"Well, sir, it's a long story, but basically I figured what could I do on the outside? The Corps gives me a better life than I could ever hope for living in the South. Besides, I really enjoy it."

"Well, I'll be. Allen, a fuckin' lifer." Mike winked toward Sergeant Greene. "No offense, Sarge."

"That's right, squid, and in sixteen years when I'm retired, you'll still be teaching school." Reaching for another beer he turned the conversation toward Sullivan. "Hey, Lieutenant, Doc's going to be a teacher and a coach when he gets out. What's you going to do?"

"I'm not sure yet. I think I'd like to travel for a while before I settle into any one routine. In college I majored in Industrial Design, but it really doesn't appeal to me anymore. One thing I do know, I ain't staying in the 'Crotch,' that's for sure."

CRRR-RUMP. CRRR-RUMP. CRRR-RUMP.

The first three mortar rounds impacted outside the wire, sending chunks of earth onto the bunker.

"Contact 6, inform him we're taking incoming." Pulling on his helmet and flak jacket, Sullivan motioned to his other radioman. "Come on, Kid, let's get down to the command bunker. Doc, you'd better hustle up to the aid station. Ron, you stay here."

"No can do, sir, Sergeant Greene needs a radio with him at the far end of the compound."

"Okay, be careful."

Everyone was in position by the time the second barrage hit, minutes later. The first casualty, Hayes, stumbled into the Aid Station having caught some shrapnel in his shoulder. Mike had little trouble treating the superficial wound, but was constantly forced to flinch as debris rained down on the aid bunker. The mortar rounds were being walked expertly in toward the center of the compound. With each explosion Mike found himself praying helplessly that the roof was thick enough to keep the mortars from penetrating his shelter.

Suddenly there was silence.

Once he was certain the rounds had definitely ceased, Mike poked his head outside to inspect the damage. One by one others reappeared from their bunkers and took up positions in the fighting holes.

Mike noticed Sullivan and Kid running toward the far end of the camp. He was close on their heels when he rounded the water tank and noticed men digging furiously with their hands into a pile of rubble. The bunker appeared to have taken a direct hit and was completely demolished. The smell of burned plastic from the sandbags and wood mingled with the cordite and dust.

Men were screaming directions at each other as Mike moved up alongside Sullivan. "Who's in there, sir?"

Sullivan didn't answer at first, but when he did it was barely audible. "Sgt Greene, that new guy, and Ron."

The name hit Mike like a sledgehammer.

Leaping onto the pile of debris he threw stuff aside as fast as he could. "Hold on, Ron. We're coming, man. Hold on. Hurry up, you guys, get this shit off them."

One by one the entombed men were slowly pulled out. Greene was first, then the new guy. Finally, Mike latched onto Allen's shirt and dragged him from the rubble by the shoulders. His face was caked with red dust, and his clothes were torn and soaked dark with blood from more then a dozen wounds in his body.

"Ron. Ron. No! Come on, wake up, man. Please, wake up." He screamed the words as he shook his friend's lifeless body. " Wake the fuck up, goddamn it."

Tears filled his eyes and ran down his cheeks as he cradled his friend in his arms and rocked him back and forth. "I love you, buddy."

Sullivan put a firm hand on Mike's shoulder. "Doc, he's gone. Let some of the other guys take care of him."

Mike placed his friend's battered head softly on the damp ground, and then with his hands and arms covered with Ron's blood, he walked away. When he finally mustered the courage to turn around, all three were being zipped into the green body bags.

Why? Why is it always the good guys that get it? Why can't it be the assholes that die?

By the time Mike returned to the CP bunker, Sullivan and Kid were sitting on a cot talking quietly. Mike felt numb and empty as he walked over to his bunk, and flung his helmet hard against the wall.

"Fuck it, man, just fuck it all. None of these fucking gooks better cross my path or I'll blow their motherfuckin' asses away." All the rage that had built up suddenly came pouring out. "There ain't a hundred fuckin gooks worth Ron's life. I'm sick of looking at arms and legs gone, guts hanging out, and guys in so much fucking pain they don't even feel it. I'm tired of seeing the light go out in a friend's eyes after learning to love them, and wondering if I did everything I could to save them. I've had it, Lieutenant. I'm telling ya, you'd better keep them fucking gooks away from here."

"Easy, Doc, we all feel bad. He was our friend, too, remember."

"Yeah, and he was going home. It was over for him and they wasted him. For what? To save this fucked up country, and these fuckin people. Bullshit! Let them fight their own goddamn war. Nobody cares about this place anyhow. They certainly don't care about us."

"Doc, I know you're hurtin' bad inside. We all are. But we have to keep going, and do our jobs. You can't hate so much that you condemn all people because of a few. Ron wouldn't want that, and you know it."

"I don't give a damn. It ain't right, Lieutenant. He went through three hundred and sixty-four days of this hell, only to get killed the day before he goes home, and the gooks walk around here doing nothin'. Where's the justice in that?"

"No one ever promised fairness in this life. Look at Thompson. He wasn't here long enough to get his boots dirty. I don't know why things like this happen. But they do. A lot of good men have died and are going to die before this thing is over. Doc, it's your job to get as many of the wounded home as you can. Just think how many wouldn't be alive today if it wasn't for you Corpsmen. You guys do one hell of a job."

"Yeah, I'm so fuckin good I couldn't even help my best friend. I don't buy all this stuff anymore, Lieutenant. It's a bunch of shit."

Mike swung his feet up onto the cot and lay down. He placed his right arm across his forehead and stared at the ceiling in silence. He wanted - no he needed - revenge, not rationalization. For Ivan, for Larry, and now for Ron. He didn't care any more who was right and who was wrong. He had to get even with someone- anyone - for taking away his friends.

Still angry, he bolted upright, and grabbed an unfinished bottle of Jim Beam. He chugged large gulps until the pain was gone and sleep came quickly.

Grandpa,

We move to Dai La Pass in a week and a half. Hope we get to kill a few more gooks there then we did here. I heard Nixon sent the Army into Cambodia to clean out their sanctuaries. It's about time, but I wish he'd turn us loose in there. We'd kick some ass. I really don't feel like writing much, but I wanted to tell you Ron Allen was killed yesterday. One day before he was to go home.

Mike

Chapter 13

Dai La Pass was nestled in a horseshoe-shaped canyon on the western slopes of the ridgeline that also housed Division Headquarters. Compared to An Hoa, it was a small compound. A ravine divided the camp into two separate sections. On one side a three-by-four block of garrison tents, on the other, five hardback hootches sat up on a plateau. The mess hall at the far end of the ravine and the movie theater that doubled as the EM Club, were the dominant structures in the camp. The LZ was actually outside the perimeter wire that ran down one slope of the ridge, across the front of the camp and up the opposite slope. Dozens of reinforced fighting holes were spaced behind the wire. On the western slope of the canyon a switchback road snaked its way to the top of the ridge, where fortified permanent bunkers looked out onto the Hoa Tin Valley.

For three days, from sun up to sundown the company filled sand bags, built bunkers, cleared vegetation and laid hundreds of yards of tanglefoot and concertina.

Mike and the other Corpsmen in the company were exempt from most of the working parties, but there was a job that they had to perform that was one of the most hated in Nam. Every day a couple Corpsmen would take a working party around to the back of each of the four holers, lift the wooden flap and pull out the four cut-off barrels filled with fecal matter and urine. The stench was unbearable. The final step was to pour kerosene into each barrel, drop a match in to light it, and stir the mixture with a long stick. Often times it took days to get the stink out of the clothes and off the body.

Regardless of how much work they did, most everyone was happy with their new situation. Sleeping in a tent and on a cot, eating three cooked meals in the mess hall with ice cream and cold milk, and taking showers each evening was absolute heaven. But that was nothing compared to being able to go to the club after a day of backbreaking work and drink beer while watching a movie.

When the week ended and the camp finally measured up to the Skipper's expectation, and he had a surprise for "the boys." He had convinced an Australian USO show to do a special performance at the camp. It was the first time many of the men had seen a show in Nam, and they waited in anxious anticipation. The band started playing, and were soon joined by two tall gorgeous blonde singers who wore nothing more than a bra, hot pants, and knee high boots. When they appeared on stage the audience broke into a frenzy that lasted the entire performance. No one ever determined if the girls could sing or not; they didn't care. The band played for over two hours, and for the rest of the evening no one talked about anything but the girls.

Early the next morning Mike joined two squads from Second Platoon as they humped over to the Vietnamese District Headquarters on the other side of Nui Thuong Thon to coordinate patrol activities and night acts. Once outside the wire they discovered that the area was quite different from the Arizona. Dozens of people milled around, and they actually seemed friendly. The tension the men felt walking patrols in the An Hoa basin wasn't noticeable here. Many of the men even laughed and joked with the kids who walked along with them. During breaks they'd mingle with the villagers, accepting food and drink freely.

Everyone, that is, except Mike. He purposely kept his distance and made sure his feelings were known to any "gook" that came close.

The patrol had been nothing but routine until they started to cross a knoll and heard the all too familiar sound of an explosion up ahead. Out of instinct they froze, but before they could move forward to check it out, they spotted a middle-aged woman running toward them, screaming hysterically. Bai and Wilson rushed to meet her.

"Doc!" Wilson gestured Mike forward.

Shuffling up to where the three people were standing, Mike stopped in front of the woman, whose white Ao Dai was covered with blood.

"What's up?" Despite her tears, Mike never looked at her.

"Seems this woman's family stepped on a booby trap up ahead, and they need your help. You'd better get up there and see what you can do."

With memories of Ron Allen etched deep into his brain Mike slowly pulled the rifle off his shoulder and let the butt plate rest on his boot. "Yeah, well, do I have authorization to treat civilians in this area?"

"What the hell difference does that make? One of them's hurt pretty bad." There was a hint of anger in Wilson's tone.

"Plenty, and you know why."

Putting his hand on Mike's shoulder, Wilson spoke calmly. "Come on, Doc, go do what they pay you for. Ron wouldn't want you to be that way, and you know it. Now go with her."

"Yeah, okay."

Mike trotted a short distance behind the woman, and by the time he rounded the bend in the trail she was kneeling over the wounded, her panic-stricken brown eyes were begging him for help.

When Mike realized both of the victims were children, his stomach sank, and suddenly he felt a sense of urgency. Kneeling alongside he first bandaged the bleeding wounds of the less serious of the two, before turning his attention to the cute little girl of about four laying motionless in a pool of her own blood. Multiple shrapnel wounds covered her entire body and she was missing her left hand.

The child was barely conscious, and with each moan of pain Mike's heart hurt a little more. Quickly wrapping a tourniquet around her arm. He couldn't help notice how his hand dwarfed her tiny forearm as he picked it up in order to slid the IV needle into a vein.

You stupid jackass. All your self-pity bullshit may cost this baby her life. I know she has to be in a lot of pain, but how much morphine do I give a little kid? No one ever taught us about taking care of babies. How is anyone supposed to handle all this shit?

Rather than risk giving too much, Mike decided not to give her any at all. Instead, he just held her hand and looked up sorrowfully at Wilson.

"Is the Medevac on the way?"

"Bird's in-bound, ETA zero five mikes."

"Tell 'em to hurry." He stroked the little girl's head gently.

The helicopter landed and with the mother holding the IV bottle, Mike ran up the back ramp. Wilson carried the other child on board and set her on the floor next to the mother.

"I'm going to stay with her, Ok?" Mike said to his squad leader with tears in his eyes.

"Ok Doc, catch you later." Wilson raced off.

As they flew, Mike pulled the little girl tightly to his chest, mainly to keep her warm, but in a way he hoped he might pass some of his strength on to her.

Landing at First Med, he rushed the little girl past the waiting Corpsmen into the sandbagged emergency room, and laid her on a stretcher supported by two metal horses. He stepped back and let the doctors and nurses do their jobs.

The duty nurse, seeing Mike's anguish, moved to his side. "She'll be fine. We'll be taking her to surgery right away. You can get back to your unit. We'll take good care of her."

"Thanks." Mike faced the mother, this time looking into her eyes, and smiled weakly. "She's going to be okay. Babysan number one."

Her eyes sparkled as she nodded. Saying something in Vietnamese she left with one of the First Med Corpsmen.

The ride back to the AO left him severely depressed. He had taken his anger and hurt out on everyone, and it almost cost an innocent child her life. He didn't like himself much right now, and for the first time he realized that the war, like it had done to so many others, had completed the process of changing him. His lean body, covered with sores and rot, now felt as if it had aged twenty years. He had become hard -- calloused to death, mutilation, and killing. Life and death meant nothing to him, and the values he'd so strongly believed in all his life were slowly eroding away. He consciously avoided making friends with the new men, and no longer thought about whether his side was winning or not. All that mattered was getting him, and his Marines home alive, regardless of what it took.

Tomorrow they'd be going back into action and he was actually looking forward to it. He didn't like the rear. It gave him too much time to think. He could fight the enemy, but there were no weapons to kill memories.

How could I have ever thought war was noble or glorious? General Sherman was right. "War is hell."

That night, like he had been doing a lot lately, Mike got drunk.

Told to bring only helmets, weapons, flak jackets, and cartridge belts, the Company fell out on the LZ at first light. Three CH-46s, two Cobras, and a Huey command ship landed a short time later, shut down their engines, and then, as was typical of the military, they waited.

Mike and the new Corpsman, Steve Heller, found a comfortable spot among some rock, and settled in. Heller, assigned to Second Platoon only the day before, was an athletic, rugged-looking six-footer from Trinidad, Colorado, who carried himself in such a manner that he was liked even before someone got to know him. His large blue eyes and movie star features could make most women melt, particularly when he flashed his dimpled smile. It was also obvious he worked out with weights because his arms and chest bulged under the green t-shirt even when relaxed.

Unlike Barker, he and Mike got along well right away.

Mike was in the process of showing Steve how to fill out a medieval tag when the CO called the company together.

Captain Andrews, rifle slung on his shoulder and thumb hooked under the sling, stood on the raised LZ.

"Okay, men, listen up." He paced as he talked. "For the next few months the rest of the battalion will assume the responsibility of Division reserve. Our company is assigned to the Division's Pacifier operation. It is a swift striking, highly mobile heliborne task force. We'll be able to react to any situation on short notice."

A low grumble radiated up from his Marines as they looked at each other.

"The idea is to drop us in, buckle with the enemy, then pull us out the minute the area is secured. Some days you may have to sit here all day and do nothing. It all depends on what is happening out in the bush. Our area of operation will encompass the entire Division AO. One day we might be attached to First Marines, and the next to the Seventh. The package will include one Huey command and control ship, two OV-10's as forward air controllers, three CH-46's, four Cobras and four F4 Skyhawks. So, as you can see, we'll be loaded for bear. Questions?" He scanned the men once again. "Okay, then that's all for now. Make yourselves comfortable."

The sun remained hidden behind heavy cloud cover most of the morning, keeping the temperature bearable. Many of the men were napping when the word finally came down to saddle up and move to the LZ.

The chopper's blades beat the air irregularly at first, but soon developed a rhythmic whine as they increased velocity. Second Platoon loaded while the sleek Cobras, already airborne, circled overhead. Mike and Sullivan knelt side by side on the hard steel floor as the CH 46 buffeted and shook on lift off.

By the time they reached flying altitude, Mike could see the tension in Steve's eyes, so he inched over next to him.

"Relax partner, you'll be fine. Hell, they can kill ya but they can't eat ya."

Steve swallowed hard and forced a smile. "Wow, that's comforting to know. Thanks, I'll remember that."

Leveling, the three birds formed a right echelon formation and headed south at full speed. Mike kept a vigil out a window, and soon began to recognize the terrain features. When they crossed the Son Vu Gia River, he poked Sullivan on the arm, and motioned downward.

"The Arizona!"

Sullivan looked and nodded matter-of-factly.

The Skipper's command Huey came into view circling above the An Bangs.

Immediately, their ship began descending. They were still a few hundred feet above the ground when they heard the clink, clink, clink, of metal hitting metal, followed by rays of light appearing in the floor. The 50-Cal positioned in the side door opened up on the jungle below.

The grunts moved to the windows and returned the fire. Rounds that penetrated the 46's thin skin wounded two men almost immediately. The volume of enemy fire became so intense that the pilot aborted the landing and sought altitude. As the Cobras moved in to work over the treelines, the 46s headed east some two miles before dropping to treetop level and accelerating back toward the LZ.

The enemy quickly redirected their fire at the landing and slow moving birds. Even before the wheels hit the deck, the Marines were running out the back, racing for the cover of paddy dikes. Rounds burst from all directions as Mike, running down the ramp, saw a Marine go down shot in the leg. Without stopping to care for him, Mike dragged him back on board with help from the crew chief, and then ran for his life.

Before he could reach the safety of a paddy dike two of the choppers were airborne. The third, hit by an RPG, was forced to shut down its engines, and its crew joined the grunts out in the open paddies. Meanwhile, the volume of fire from both sides was increasing.

"Corpsman, Corpsman up."

Mike took off. Dodging bullets, he sprinted across the open ground and dove for cover behind the closest dike. Scared and breathing hard, he mustered the courage to continue toward the wounded man. Jumping up, Mike had taken four strides and was almost at full speed when something hit him. The force spun him to the ground, rifle and helmet flying in opposite directions. His heart pounded, as he lay on the ground afraid to look down, expecting to see his own blood. The nylon of the flak jacket was shredded, and there was a crease in the protective material that covered the right side of his intestines, but no wound. His body quivered as he fought to regain composure.

Relieved, he took a deep breath, pushed off the hard ground, and ran to Barnes, who had taken two rounds. One had passed clean through the right leg, while the other was apparently still lodged in his stomach. He was bleeding profusely and going into shock. Mike didn't have time to drag him to the protection of a dike, so he lay on his belly and used Barnes' body as a shield as he treated him.

Rolling over onto his back, Mike removed several battle dressings from his bandoleer, tore the plastic off, then rolled back onto his stomach again, and wrapped one tightly around the leg wound.

"Take it easy, man, you're gonna to be okay." Mike paid no attention to the sounds of the battle going on around him. Every fiber in his body worked to save Barnes' life.

"Ah shit, it hurts."

"Relax, DB, we'll have you back home in no time."

Mike started the IV but couldn't raise the bottle high enough for gravity to start the fluid to flow. "Fuck!"

He realized the only way he was going to get it to work was to kneel. But as soon as he got to his knees bullets exploded all around, forcing him to dive back to the relative safety of the ground.

Damn, I have to find some way to keep the bottle up, yet keep myself from getting killed.

Looking around, he finally realized what he could do and yelled over his shoulder at Rivas, only a few yards away.

"Hey, toss me your bayonet."

Pulling the blade from the scabbard hanging from his cartridge belt, Rivas tossed it near Mike's foot. Mike slid it onto Barnes' rifle, taped the bottle to the stock before jamming the bayonet into the dirt. An RPG exploding nearby caused him to instinctively cover Barnes with his body. The light sprinkle of debris was absorbed by his helmet and flak jacket.

Satisfied he had done all he could, Mike left Barnes, and set out to treat several others who had been wounded to a lesser degree earlier in the firefight.

"Mike!"

By now the firing had stopped completely. Mike turned toward the voice and saw Steve motioning for him from the other side of the paddy. Jogging across the dried up field, Mike plopped down next to his partner.

"What's up?"

Steve's voice trembled as he spoke. "This guy caught a bullet in the neck and it crushed his trachea. You wanna take a look and see if it's okay?"

Positioning himself on one knee, Mike pulled the blood-soaked bandage away from the wound.

"He couldn't breathe, so I did a Cricroid. I didn't have an airway tube so I just inserted the hollow part of my pen." Steve watched from over his shoulder as Mike inspected the tiny incision in the throat.

Standing, Mike patted Steve twice on the cheek, the way his grandfather did whenever he was pleased with him. "You did good, partner. Welcome to the Nam." He saw the relief in Steve's eyes.

With a second wave of helicopters carrying Third Platoon landing behind him, Mike left to prepare the wounded for evacuation.

The eight man recon unit that had been pinned down strolled casually out of the brush and past Third Platoon as they replaced them in the tree line. Each of the ragged and tired looking Recon Marines had a battle dressing tied somewhere on his body. One of their group, his faced covered with camouflage paint and wearing a bush cover, broke away and limped slowly toward Mike. As he moved closer Mike saw he had a battle dressing on his arm and one on his leg, but more noticeably, he carried a Unit-1 medical bag.

"Hey, Doc," said the Recon Corpsman. "Name's Meyers, you ain't got any extra morphine by any chance, do you? I'm out and one of my guys is hurtin' bad."

Mike reached into his leg pocket and pulled out the cigarette case and handed him a syrette. "Can we give you any other help?"

"Naw, but thanks. You guys pulled our bacon out of the fire and that's good enough. I'm sure if you hadn't showed up they'd be zipping us into body bags right now." He adjusted the bandage on his arm and looked into space. "Well, I'd better get back to my guys. Catch you later. Thanks again."

An hour later with all the wounded medevaced, the company was flown back to Dai La Pass.

Getting off the choppers, Mike and Steve headed directly to the BAS to see if they had received any word on their casualties. Mike entered the front door, removed his helmet and torn flak jacket, and dropped them to the floor.

The battalion surgeon at the forward BAS, Doctor Moyer, wearing the silver bars of a Navy Lieutenant, was busy writing notes in a health record folder as he sat on the treatment table.

"Evening, sir."

"Hello." Moyer closed the folder and looked up.

"Sir, this is HN Steve Heller. He's a new Corpsman with our company."

"Nice to meet you, Steve." Sliding off the table, Moyer put the folder down and extended his hand

"Sir, you should have seen what Steve did out in the bush today. He..."

"I already know. They called from First Med." He turned toward Steve. "They were very impressed with your field surgery, young man. Saved the man's life, so I understand. Outstanding job."

"Thank you, sir."

"By the way, we've been informed all the casualties you took today will be fine."

"That's great news." Mike smiled, and winked at Steve. "Way to go, partner."

"Now, how 'bout a cold beer?" Moyer opened the refrigerator, pulled out a "Bud" and popped the top. "I think you guys deserve a few of these."

One beer led to another and another as they sat and talked. By the time they quit it was midnight and they were all very drunk.

With the arrival of June, Da Nang Airbase, and Division Headquarters came under rocket attack for ten straight nights. Delta Company was given the assignment of searching the sandy flats along the coast south of Marble Mountain for the launch sites.

As the choppers left at dusk, the veterans in the company were angry. They knew that trying to find rocket firing sites was like trying to find fleas on a beach, and they reasoned they were being sent out just so the rear area commandos wouldn't have their sleep disturbed.

In Second Platoon alone booby traps claimed three wounded in the first hour on the ground. The soft sand sapped the leg strength of every man in the unit, as they were constantly moving all night. For the next three nights the routine remained the same. Each morning they'd chopper back to camp without having accomplished anything. Mike could see that everyone was extremely tired and irritable.

In the hootch area tempers flared more than usual, and several fights broke out. A dozen men were put on report for various offenses, from fighting to disrespect, to disobeying a direct order. All over the camp, tension hung heavy in the air as blacks and whites began to separate. It was most noticeable in the EM club where the two groups sat apart and eyed each other suspiciously. Hispanics were split, but mostly paired with the blacks. It wouldn't take much to ignite either group.

Hoping to keep a lid on things, the CO ordered the bar closed during the movie. This irritated some of the men even more.

Corpsmen were the only ones who could really communicate with both sides, so Steve and Mike decided to wander among the groups and talk to the men in an attempt to douse the flames. The lights went out and the movie started. It was a good comedy, and many of the men who hadn't laughed or smiled in days did just that. As a result the tension eased.

Halfway through the movie, the projector stopped, lights came on, and the Gunny jumped up onto the stage.

"Attention, men. All personnel from Delta Company return to your hootches." There was some urgency in his voice. "Get your gear, and report to the LZ on the double."

The scraping and rattling of benches sliding across the cement floor was mixed with the voices of rushing men. Except for a few pogues the theater emptied in minutes.

Mike, like the others, wondered what was going on as he sprinted across the ravine to his hootch. *We've never been called out after dark. I hope we're not going out again looking for rockets. This company will really explode.*

Within ten minutes, the company was assembled at the LZ, fully armed. The CO had gathered the platoon and squad leaders together while they waited for the helicopters to arrive.

"All right, listen up. Here's the dope. A company from 7th Marines is currently under attack down in Antenna Valley. It is estimated they are surrounded by two companies of NVA." He paused and eyed the small group. "Men, we're going in to reinforce, and help them hold the position until a reactionary force from LZ Baldy can counterattack. When we land, First Platoon will reinforce the western section of the perimeter! Second and Third Platoons, you'll take the north and east sections respectively. I'll take Weapons Platoon and link up with their CP." Mike could see the fear in his eyes as he gathered his thoughts. "This isn't going to be a tea party gentlemen, so make sure your Marines are ready and understand that, before we go in. Any questions?" He scanned the group. "Alright then, dimissed and God bless."

The sounds of three CH-53s landing sent everyone rushing back to their platoons. Only the chopper's lights twinkled in the darkness as platoons raced into the rear of the birds. Mike dropped down onto the red canvas seat, chambered a round and checked the safety switch. As they lifted off, he placed the flash suppressor against the floor between his feet, and held the rifle with his hands and thighs. Illuminated only by the eerie red hue of the night vision lights, he looked into the face of each Marine and realized they seemed different. They appeared grim and serious. The hate he had seen earlier in the club was gone, as determination and worry took over.

How can I not love these guys? They can hate each other's guts, but as soon as anyone else tries to mess with a brother Marine, they'll have to take on the whole damn Corps. This truly is a special brotherhood. I guess that's what makes the Corps great. They don't even think twice about risking their lives to save another Marine. As the Gunny says, 'there is only one color in the Corps and that's green. Marine Green.'

Mike fidgeted as their flight approached the fifteen-minute mark. His fears were now consuming his every thought. He tried to pray, but the adrenaline rushing through his body wouldn't allow him to concentrate. His right leg bounced up and down nervously, and he felt the dinner he'd had earlier fighting to escape his body.

Suddenly, the birds began to circle, and the sky was bright with illumination. Red and green tracers slashed through the air. The pilot maneuvered the collective, sending his ship descending rapidly toward the LZ. Dozens of rounds ricocheted off and through the 53s as they landed.

Several severely wounded Marines were rushed on board as Delta Company sought cover in the fighting holes. Safely under cover Mike looked back and was alarmed to see one of the choppers completely filled with casualties. The noise from mortars, RPGs, and rifle fire, coupled with the spinning of the helicopter blades, sent stabbing pain into his ears.

He hadn't been on the ground for more than thirty seconds when the first call came.

"Corpsman Up."

Half crawling, half running, he hustled over to the wounded man and dragged him into the safety of a fighting hole so he could treat the wounds. When he finished, he brought his rifle up over the side of the hole to fire at the enemy, and froze in sheer terror. Hundreds of enemy soldiers were moving up the hill on line.

Cobras zipped down, making pass after pass, pounding the slope with rocket and mini-gun fire. Despite the slaughter, the NVA seemed to be multiplying. The bark of AK-47s and the crack of M-16s volleyed back and forth as the men on both sides fought viciously for this little piece of God's earth. Claymores spit death with booming roars. Mortar tubes and the artillery from LZ Baldy rained tons of shells down on the NVA. It was a battle more reminiscent of World War II, or Korea, than Vietnam.

Mike quickly dismissed the assaulting troops; that job was up to the Marines. Calls for help filled the air sending him racing from one hole to the next.

"Corpsman."

"Corpsman up."

"Get a Doc over here."

Blood covered Corpsmen from both companies scurried about in the open to care for the mounting number of wounded. Although several were wounded themselves, they disregarded their own pain to provide medical aid to the grunts.

After bandaging a shrapnel wound, Mike climbed out of the hole and was on his way to the next wounded man when an RPG exploded only a few meters in front of him. The blast lifted him off his feet and drove him into the ground.

Stunned, he felt himself slipping into a deep fog. The ringing in his ears blocked out the sounds of battle. As he lay on his back staring up through the smoke and haze, he struggled to regain his senses, but his body refused to respond. Groggy, he rolled onto his stomach, but still felt like he was floating in a dreamland. Unsure of how much time had passed, Mike's mind finally began to clear, and his eyes eventually focused on objects around him. The pounding in his head was brutal but he forced himself to crawl into the nearest hole, only to discover several wounded men from 7th Marines. Still fighting the effect of the rocket blast Mike could see that shrapnel had ripped huge chunks of skin from one man's arm. Lethargically, he applied the battle dressings and administered his last syrette of morphine.

Except for a thundering headache and a bloody nose Mike had recovered enough to know exactly what he was doing. He moved over to the other Marine, who was lying face down in a puddle of his own blood. When Mike turned him over, the face had no recognizable features. Only one ear was in place and his chest was peppered with chunks of metal and rocks. He was alive, but barely. Mike had already used up three of his four bottles of plasma, and he now agonized over his options. *Do I use my last one now? If I don't he'll definitely die. If I do, he still might die, and there won't be any for someone I'm sure I could save. God damn, what do I do?*

Wrapping a tourniquet around the faceless Marine's arm, Mike inserted the needle. When the IV was in place and flowing, he sat back at the bottom of the hole and popped four aspirin, hoping they would keep his head from exploding.

High above he heard a familiar, monotonous sound circling. Moments later, the distinctive red line of Spooky streaked across the sky. The sound of bullets striking the ground so close reminded him of the times as a kid when he'd take handfuls of rocks and throw them as hard as he could into a pond, only this was ten times louder.

As it had done so many other times, Spooky broke the back of the assault. The NVA withdrew and the night soon became quiet.

Tired, but thankful to be alive, Mike slid over to check on his patient. He was dead. Slumping back against the wall of the hole again, Mike stared at the body. *What were you like? Did you have a wife, a girlfriend? Did you have a kid who will never see you again?*

Except for the occasional pop of an illumination parachute opening and the familiar whistle that followed as the canister fell to earth, the night remained quiet for the next hour. The Corpsmen stayed busy keeping a close eye on the severely wounded and preparing the others for medevac.

The western night sky miles away suddenly lit up in a blaze of tracers and illume. Mike checked his watch -0400. He reasoned that the reactionary force from Baldy must have finally caught up with the fleeing NVA.

With the battle raging out in the valley, the medevac birds landed one at a time on the hill. Forty-five young Americans, who if back in the world would be out on dates, or drinking with their buddies, were on their way to operating rooms or the morgue. They had left their blood and body parts on a hill somewhere in Vietnam for a cause most of them didn't entirely understand.

At first light several squads left the perimeter to search the slopes. Scores of dead enemy soldiers lay scattered everywhere, some as close as ten feet from the Marine's fighting holes. Mike and a few other Corpsmen now administered first aid to ten wounded NVA soldiers that were found among the dead.

Small groups of exhausted, dazed warriors sat scattered were across the hill, the realization of what they had just been through starting to sink in . For the first time in hours they relaxed. A few engaged in idle conversation but most ate breakfast in silence. They were lucky to be alive and they knew it.

Mike walked over and sat down beside L/Cpl Davey Manifold, who only hours before had seen his best friend since childhood killed right beside him.

"Hey Davey, how ya doing buddy?"

"Ok Doc, I guess."

Mike removed his helmet and briskly scratched his head and hair with both hands. "Did I ever tell you about my venture into acting like the "B girls" in the bars on Okinawa?"

"B girls, what's that?"

"You know the ones who sit with you in the bars as long as you buy them drinks and you pay for liquor, but all they're drinking is tea. Then they get a cut of it at the end of the night."

"Naw, Doc, you never told me about that"

Mike lit a cigarette. "Well I was in Charleston, South Carolina and me and some of my buddies went into this bar and we no sooner sat down, when these ladies come up put an arm around each of us and ask if they could join us."

"I bet you guys thought your were in like Flint"

"Naw, I had seen this before and knew what was coming and I said no but my buddies bought them a drink and the women immediately sat on their laps and puts their arms around their necks."

"Damn Doc. Really?"

"Yep, no lie." Mike took a long drag on the smoke then continued. As I sat there I looked around and saw two older women sitting at the bar. A light went on in my head and I got to thinking. Here I am a young good looking stud, maybe those two older ladies would like the company of a cool guy and at the same time buy me drinks."

"You didn't, did you?" A slight grin appeared on his face.

"Yep. I marched right over and sat on the stool beside the blonde. I smile my best smile, and then ask her if she would like to buy me a drink."

"You got balls, Doc."

"But wait, the best is yet to come. She looks at me like I'm from Mars, then turns to her friend and starts making all kind of gestures with her fingers. The friend looks at me and says, my friend is deaf, did you say you wanted to buy her a drink? So guess what? I wound up buying them both drinks."

Through his laughter, Manifold said, "You are a crazy son of a bitch
Doc."

"I never tried that again." Mike playfully tapped Davey on the knee. "Hey, man I got to go check on some of the guys. You take care."

"Doc."

"Yeah."

Manifold stood and extended his hand. "Thanks a lot. You made me feel better."

"Don't mention it. If you need to talk, I'll be around. Catch you later."

It wasn't until midday that Delta Company was flown back to Dai La Pass. That evening at Sunday services, they held a special tribute to their friends, but the chaplain's sermon was geared toward the

"... Regardless of what you think of this war, men, most of us are sharing something not many of God's children ever experience. It is called Brotherhood. You men share a love for each other that will be with you always, regardless of your background, color, or religion. The closeness you feel to each other over here is a gift from God. If only we could get the rest of the world to feel as much love for each other as you feel for your buddies over here, we'd never have to fight again. Remember and cherish this feeling; it will probably leave you when you are safe back in the world. Be proud of each other and never forget what war is like. Tell every one of the horrors of war, so maybe someday boys like you will never have to see friends die. God bless you. Now, let us pray for our fellow comrades who died last night."

Hi Grandpa,

Seven months down and only five to go. I can't wait. Guys say that the last half of your tour goes pretty fast. I hope so. Normally, being a Corpsman I'd have been pulled out of the bush by now, but we aren't getting any replacements because of Nixon's pullout, so I'll probably be with the company another month or two.

We had one hell of a firefight the other night. It was real hairy so right now we're standing down for a few days. Bravo Company is taking over our Pacifier duties, and tomorrow the CO is making transportation available for anyone who wants to go to Freedom Hill for the day. Freedom Hill is the big PX area over near Division Headquarters. He wants the men to have the opportunity to spend a pleasant day cruising the PX, eating at the cafeteria, or seeing a movie. I'm sure most of the guys will just hang around the USO and talk to the "Donut Dollies." But I'm also sure a few will make their way into "Dogpatch," and enjoy the favors of the women there. I'll probably be seeing them a few days later with a needle and penicillin. But that's okay, they owe it to themselves. I'm not going to go to Freedom Hill, though. Heller, a Corpsman from Third Platoon, and I have decided to visit our wounded out on the hospital ship Sanctuary anchored in the harbor. We've wrangled a ride from the CO's driver into Da Nang City for a case of beer.

We'll, I'm going to the club for a few beers and to see the movie, so I'll close for now. Take care and God bless.

Mike

Chapter 14

The dock in Da Nang City bristled with activity as Becker pulled the jeep into a parking space but kept the engine running.

"I'll be back at 1700. Is that okay?" Becker asked.

"Yeah, that'll be perfect." Mike planted his right foot firmly on the ground and pulled himself out by holding onto the side of the front windshield. Before he and Gibson headed toward the launch, Mike removed his flak jacket and left it on the front seat of the vehicle.

Shannon Rodgers, a slender, firey-eyed six-footer corpsman from Geneseo, Illinois, was still limping from the shrapnel he had taken in the leg during the battle in Antenna Valley. He and Mike had come in country only weeks apart, but had rarely seen each other during that time.

The old World War II "Mike" boat bobbed and weaved in the choppy water as the two men climbed on board. The sailors in blue dungarees on the front and back undid the ropes from the cleats on the pier, and jumped in only seconds before the boat pulled away from the dock. The gray rectangular landing craft plowed smoothly through the water, leaving a wake that sent the smaller sampans rocking back and forth, and the occupants struggling to keep them upright.

Ten minutes later the coxswain was expertly maneuvering the craft alongside the large white ship and held it there while it was secured to the ramp by rope. Mike and Rodgers thanked them and climbed the fifty metal steps suspended from the side of the ship.

Reaching the top, they stepped onto the quarterdeck and followed correct Navy procedure by saluting the flag at the stern, then the Officer of the Deck.

"Request permission to come aboard?"

"Permission granted."

Dropping the salute, they moved to the Master-at-Arms room, pulled their 45s from their shoulder holsters and checked them in.

It took only an hour to locate and visit with each of their men. The launch wasn't due back for a while so the two ground pounding sailors, who had never been on a ship before, decided to wander around and see what the Navy was really like.

Like fish out of water they blundered down one passageway after another. Somewhere on the upper deck they entered a ward filled to capacity. All the patients wore sky blue pajamas.

"Hey, man, what is this ward?" Mike asked one of the men lying in bed near the entrance.

"General Medicine. Everyone in here either has a fever, malaria, or some other illness not associated with combat,"

Looking around, they noticed several of the ship's Corpsmen in undress whites and two nurses sitting behind the desk at the nurse's station charting in medical files.

Rodgers, never known for being shy, immediately went over and struck up a conversation with a delicious looking brunette nurse. The idle chatter soon got around to which hospital they'd been stationed at, and when Mike mentioned he'd been at Jacksonville, the other nurse, a petite blonde J.G. named Sara Anderson, looked up from her chart.

"Were you really? My roommate and one of the Corpsmen in orthopedics were there."

"Is that right! What's his name?"

"Kenny Howe."

"I know Kenny. Do you know if he is down there right now?" Mike was excited at the thought of seeing an old friend.

"No, he's not. I'm sorry." Sara said genuinely sad. "He just left on R & R two days ago, but my roommate Sandy is down in the room. She's working nights."

Mike tilted his head and thought about the name he had just heard. *Naw, it couldn't be.* "Ma'am, your roommate, was she at Jacksonville the same time as Kenny?"

"Yes, I think she was. Do you know her?"

"If her last name is Case, I do."

She smiled. "That's her."

"Damn, it's a small world. Could you do me a favor, ma'am?"

"Sure. What?"

"When you see Miss Case, tell her Mike Lombardo said to say "Hi." I think she'll remember me."

"Why don't I call and have her come up?"

"Naw, don't do that. She's probably sleeping."

"So what? She can sleep any time. I know she'd be upset if I didn't." Before he could object, Nurse Anderson turned and was dialing the phone. Mike couldn't hear what she was saying, but within a minute she looked back at him. "Kelly said for me to tell her little brother not to go away. She'll be up in about ten minutes and she told me to let you know she's mad at you for not writing."

"What's this brother stuff all about? I didn't know you had a sister over here," Rodgers asked.

Mike's cheeks rose in a smile. "I don't. Miss Case used to tease me about how much I looked like her kid brother. He was her favorite because he was the nicest and she could always beat up on him without his getting mad. We joked about it so much I just started calling her 'Sis'." Mike grinned. "It got us into trouble one time though. I was giving A.M. care on CCU behind the curtains when Miss Case said something I didn't hear. I yelled back like I normally did, 'What'd you say, Sis?' The curtain flew open and before I knew it the old hag of a head nurse was in my face. She lectured me about military courtesy and all that jazz right in front of my patient. When she finished with me she ushered Miss Case into a treatment room and chews her out but good. We could hear it all through the door. I really felt bad about that."

"Good move, slick."

Putting away the chart, Sara stood and placed her hand on Heller's shoulder. "I'm sorry, fellas, I'd love to sit here and chat with you some more but I do have to get back to work or I'll have a head nurse on my ass."

Looking at Mike, she smiled. "I hope you and Sandy have a nice visit. You two come back and see us again, anytime. Take care of yourselves and God bless."

"Thank you, Ma'am. It was kind of you to take the time to talk to us."

Anderson winked, turned and walked away without another word.

Both pairs of eyes were glued on the back of the uniform dress as it wiggled its way to the other end of the ward.

"Mmm, damn. She's fine." Rodgers said.

Mike could see that he continued to lust at her as she'd paused to talk to a patient.

"Hey, man, I'm gonna wait outside for Miss Case, okay?"

"Yeah, sure, go ahead. I think I'll ahem ... just stay right here and... do a little recon of my own."

Before Mike could get to the door Rodgers, had caught up with Nurse Anderson, and was once again actively engage in conversation.

Opening the hatch, Mike stepped out into the bright sunlight on the deck. A strong whiff of salt air filled his senses as he walked to the rail. He gazed at the beautiful green coastline, allowing himself a few minutes to think about Ivan and Larry and the good times they had in Jacksonville.

He heard the heavy metal of the hatch opening, and when he turned he saw a familiar face stepping through it onto the outer deck. Her honey-blonde hair was cut shorter and she appeared tanner, but even under the starched white uniform her figure was still impressive.

"Hi, Miss Case, do you remember me?" Mike asked while nervously spinning his cover round and round in his hands.

"I sure do. How could I ever forget my favorite Corpsman?" With that special smile of hers, she moved forward, wrapped her arms around his neck and gave him a hug. Her body pressing tightly against his awoke an excitement that had been dormant for many months. He had forgotten how good a woman's hug could feel. Stepping back he looked around to see if anyone was watching then moved closer to the rail.

Sandy spoke in her familiar soft Pennsylvania accent. "It's so great seeing you again. I can't believe this." She placed her warm hand on his forearm. The ocean breeze pushed the scent of her perfume toward him. "How long has it been?"

"I guess about two and a half years." His palms were sweating and he felt like he was on a first date.

"You know, Mike, this is really ironic. It's almost like some mysterious force brought you out here."

He frowned. "What do you mean?"

"Last week Kenny Howe - you remember him, don't you?"

"Yeah, his bunk was across from mine. Your roommate told me he's here."

"Well, Kenny and I were looking through my photo album when we came across pictures of the party the nurses threw for you and the others when you left Jaxs."

"That was one hell of a party. I think I was sick for two days." Mike scrunched his face as he recalled kneeling at the toilet that night.

"You weren't the only one. Anyway, I asked Kenny if he had ever heard from you."

"No, we didn't keep in touch. I'm not much at letter writing."

"Yeah, that's what he said. Anyway, later I got to wondering where you were and what had become of you. I was even going to try to get your home address. That's why I think it's strange that you showed up all of a sudden."

"That's weird -- almost like mental telepathy."

"Have you kept in touch with any of the other guys?"

"Yes, Ma'am, a few, but I guess you hadn't heard Ivan and Larry were both killed last year."

Her smile disappeared. "Oh God no. I didn't know. I'm so sorry." She compassionately touched his arm. "You guys were very close, weren't you?"

"Yes ma'am."

"Now tell me, what in the world are you doing out here?"

"Well, ma'am..."

"Wait a minute. What's all this 'ma'am' stuff? I think you can call me Sandy. There's no one around."

"I remember the last time I got familiar, we both got our fuc..." Mike blushed as he caught himself. "You'll have to forgive me. I guess I've been around the grunts too long."

"Oh, that's okay," She laughed. "I've heard it once or twice before."

"Yes, ma'am I am sure you have."

"Sandy."

"Okay, Sandy." The name didn't feel comfortable coming from his lips but he said it anyway. "A buddy and I came out to check on some of the guys from our unit who got hit the other night and."

"Were you at that battle in Antenna Valley two nights ago?"

"Yes, I was."

"My God, it must have been awful. I work on the Orthopedics Ward and many of your boys are my patients. All they talked about was how great their Docs were during the battle." She paused and looked toward the shore. "One guy in particular, who had shrapnel wounds all over his chest, kept worrying about his Corpsman. He kept asking me if I had heard about any corpsman casualties. He was worried cause he saw an RPG explode and his Doc go down. He blacked out right after and never knew if Doc was ok or not"

Mike allowed a hint of a smile. "Well, I just saw Rivas and he now knows the Doc is ok."

"So that was you?"

"Yes."

"Thank God you weren't hurt."

"Got a mild concussion but no holes in my body thank you."

"From the way the Marines describe the battle, it must have been a very frightening."

"Well, you can't believe too much what grunts tell you. They're habitual liars, especially when talking to a pretty woman."

She chuckled.

"Sandy, before I forget, I want to tell you how fortunate I am to have had you as a nurse and a friend." In the back of his mind he kept thinking about how we wished they were back in the world so he could take her out for dinner to say thanks, but what about Jody would that be fair to her? "All the things you taught me at the hospital have really come in handy over here. I know it's helped me save some lives. For that I'll always be grateful."

Her eyes softened. "Thank you. That was sweet of you to say, but you guys, you're the ones who deserve all the credit. I've seen the boys come in, and if it wasn't for you Corpsmen, a lot more would be dying."

"Yeah, well." Embarrassed by the compliment, Mike shuffled his feet and decided to change the subject. "So how long did you stay at Jacksonville?"

"Until eight months ago, when I got orders here. What about you? What have you been up to? How's it going for you out there?" She pointed toward the coastline.

"Okay. I'm with a super bunch of guys and my platoon leader is the best in the Corps. You'd like him, he's a great guy."

"If you think that much of him, I know I would." She moved closer and her voice turned serious. "You know Mike, I often wondered. With so many of the other Corpsmen dating nurses at the hospital, how come you never asked me out?"

Caught completely off guard, Mike stammered. "Ahhh, I don't know. I guess I was scared but, more so, I think I was just too young and naive. Don't get me wrong. You'll never know how many times I wanted to, but I could never get the guts." Realizing she wanted to hear more he continued. "I think an even bigger reason, was that our schedules never seemed to jive. Remember, when I got off graveyard, you went on, and by the time we were working the same shift, I was getting ready to leave."

The hatch sprang open, and Rodgers stuck his head out. "Hey, partner, sorry, but we gots to go, boat's comin'."

"Okay, go ahead, I'll meet you at the gangway." Mike didn't want to leave and was disappointed the visit was ending so soon.

"Gotcha."

The door closed and Mike turned his attention back to Sandy. "Well, I guess it's time for me to shove off. Please tell Kenny I said 'Hi', will ya?"

"I will." Reaching out, she grabbed his hand and held it gently between hers. "Listen, Mike, two weeks from Wednesday several of the nurses and corpsmen are getting together to have a picnic at China Beach. I wasn't going to go because it will be mostly couples, but if you can come we'd be able to spend the whole day together. Kenny has been dating my roommate and will be back by then too"

"Um... I'm not sure I can make it. Supposedly, we're heading out to the bush in a few days."

"Please, try. Here's my address. Write and let me know. But I won't take 'no' for an answer." Sliding her arms around his neck, she kissed him lightly on the cheek. "Please take care of yourself, Little Brother."

Mike leaned back and stared directly into her beautiful brown eyes.

"I will. You too, ok?" Reluctantly, he pulled away and walked to the door. Before opening it he turned for one final look. He had to tell her about Jody. "Sandy, I have to tell you I am..."

"Hush. See you in a few weeks," Sandy said with a smile.

Mike waved and left her alone on the deck. Seeing Sandy, smelling her perfume, reminded him how much he had cared for her. *I should have told her I was engaged. Ah, it don't mean nothin', but boy, did she look good.*

Rodgers was waiting on the Quarterdeck with a big grin on his face. "You, Casanova, you."

"Well, guy, some of us got it and some of us ain't."

"Yeah, but look who got that Nurse Anderson's phone number?" Rodgers waved the piece of paper he held in his hand.

"Well enjoy your paper, cause I got a date to go on a picnic with Miss Case." Smiling, Mike threw an arm around his friend's shoulder and headed down the ladder to the boat.

The jeep was waiting when they arrived, and the entire way back, to Becker's delight, all Mike and Rodgers talked about was Sandy and the other nurses they had met. They got back to the camp just in time for chow.

After dinner, Mike took off his boots and stretched out on his bunk. He couldn't shake Sandy from his mind. He had argued with himself most of the afternoon over what to do. He was beginning to feel guilty, like he was cheating on Jody. Opening a book, he hoped that reading would take his mind off her. No sooner had he started when the door swung open and Ramirez, one of the new squad leaders, entered.

"First Sergeant wants to see you in the company office ASAP."

"Thanks, Scott." Mike dropped his feet over the side of the cot and sat up. While he laced his boots, he began to wonder what the Top wanted. A thousand thoughts raced through his mind as he tried to recall everything he'd done over the last few days. As hard as he tried, he couldn't remember doing anything wrong. Maybe something was wrong at home? Blousing his boots he headed out the door and across the compound. He was really worried. No one ever got called in to see the Top for a friendly chat.

Cautiously, he entered the office and ambled to the doorway that led to the Top's office. He struck the doorframe hard three times.

"Get you ass in here, Doc," the Top yelled in his gravel voice.

Mike quickly removed the cover he remembered was still on his head, and stood at attention in front of the desk. "You wanted to see me, First Sergeant."

Leaning back in his swivel chair the Top looked up, stared and sipped menacingly on his coffee.

"I've got some bad news for you..."

Oh, shit, someone must've died.

"...I really don't know how to tell you this but..."

Well, come on spit it out.

"...I've just been notified that you have been promoted to E5 effective today. Congratulations, squid."

Relieved, Mike reached out and shook the hand that had been extended to him. "Thanks, Top." He turned and started to walk away.

"Whoa, Doc, not so fast. Where do you think you're going?" He had already started to come around the desk.

Mike stopped in at the door. "Uh, nowhere." He had hoped he could have gotten out of the office because he knew what was coming.

"Come with me." The First Sergeant walked him out the door and straight over to one of the hootches that had been converted into a staff NCO Club.

Entering the hardback hootch Mike saw every E5 and above in the company squeezed into the tiny hut. He closed his eyes and shook his head as the group began to form two lines. "Wait a minute. Remember Navy personnel wear rank on one side only, so..."

"Sorry, Doc, you're one of us. You get those stripes pinned on both sides."

Mike could only close his eyes and shake his head. "Well, lets get this over with so we can drink some beer."

Grandpa,

I was promoted today. I'm now the equivalent of a Sergeant, only we're called Hospitalman Second Class. It means more money but the bad part was that I had to have my stripes pinned on. It works this way: Two guys line up on each side of me and at the same time they both let fly with a thundering punch to my arms. They turn me around and do it again. This continues until everyone my new rank or higher has taken their turn. I'll tell ya; the pain shot through to my brain sometimes like a lightning bolt. I'd just start to recover from the two punches when the next pair was already loading up. A few of the guys were nice and didn't hit me too hard but some, oh my, it hurt like hell But the seventh or eighth group, my arms were so numb and I didn't feel it anyway. Last year, when I made E-4, I also got kneed in the thigh. They do that to represent pinning on the "Blood Stripe" which I don't even rate.

The one good thing was we got to drink free. I'm a little drunk right now, that's why my handwriting is so bad, but I wanted to let you know about my promotion tonight. I won't have time to write tomorrow 'cause we're going to the bush. A couple of my friends just came in to my hootch and want me to go to the club with them and celebrate some more, so bye for now.

Hey don't I outrank you now.

Mike

Chapter 15

Mike woke early the next morning and the bright sunlight penetrating the hootch hurt his eyes. Waves of nausea exploded in his stomach as he felt around under the rack for his Unit-1 and the bottle of lifesaving aspirin. Using what seemed to him like superhuman effort he swung his legs over the side of the cot and shook six white tablets from the clear plastic bottle. His head throbbed and his arms ached, as Mike washed the painkillers down with a warm R.C. Cola. Holding his head in his hands he heard the screen door open and a voice speak, but it hurt too much to look to see who it was.

"Doc, trucks leave in twenty minutes, you'd better get a move on."

"Ugh. Okay... I hear ya. I'll be there, but I can't promise what shape I'll be in."

"You look terrible." Wilson chuckled.

"Thanks, but I'll bet I feel worse than I look."

Slowly gathering his gear, Mike stood, wobbled back and forth, and fought the urge to puke. Every step was an effort, as he made his way outside. The cool morning air felt good as he climbed up onto the truck for the ride out to the northern AO to relieve Delta Company.

Most of the men were looking forward to the new assignment. It meant less fighting and more skate time. In the month that Delta had occupied the position, they had not engaged the enemy or lost a man.

By the time they arrived at the position Mike had recovered considerably and was actually able to hold his head up without help from his hands.

The platoon spent most of the first day getting the hill organized. Plotting fields of fire, building hootches, improving defenses, and generally getting acquainted with the area around them.

Early the next morning, Mike joined first squad on a familiarization patrol. Following a well-used trail they quickly covered a klick before coming upon a small farm. The main hootch was set deep in a well-shaded area and as they entered, the temperature dropped nearly fifteen degrees.

"Okay, guys, take a break, " Wilson said as he removed his helmet and flak jacket. Sitting down, he motioned for Kid to bring the radio. "Call in checkpoint one." He waited for Kid to finish the transmission then continued. "In twenty minutes call in checkpoint two and keep calling in checkpoints every twenty or thirty minutes after that. When you get to checkpoint six, let me know."

Kid smiled. "Okay."

Mike realized they were going to sandbag the patrol, so he put his gear down and walked over to the farmer who was spreading recently harvested rice on a mat in order to dry it.

"Papasan, nook?" Mike gestured as though he were drinking from a glass.

The old man nodded. "Ah." He pointed to the right with the stick he held in his hand.

Pulling a bucket of cool water from the well, Mike filled the cup and by the time he rejoined the others a mamasan emerged from the hootch carrying a large pot of rice.

Setting it down she giggled and flashed a warm black-toothed smile. "You eat rice. It make you big and strong."

"Thanks, mamasan, you numba 1." Kid grabbed one of the small bowls she had brought, and scooped the rice in with his C-ration spoon.

The rest of the squad followed his lead. Except Mike, he lay down, rested his head on his flak jacket, pulled his soft cover down to the bridge of his nose, and closed his eyes. The last thing he heard before drifting off to sleep was Kid calling in checkpoint four.

Returning to the perimeter near mid-afternoon, Mike had just removed his gear when the Lieutenant joined him.

"Doc, I'm glad you're back. I was afraid I was gonna miss you."

"What's up, sir?"

"They're sending a jeep out for me. I've been transferred to Division S2."

"Shit, sir, they can't do that, we're too good a team. Besides, I just got you squared away. Mike crawled out from under the poncho. I really don't feel like breaking in a boot lieuie."

"I know. It'll be hard leaving the platoon. We've been through a lot, and I'm gonna to miss all you guys." He handed Mike a slip of paper. "Here's my address back in the world. When this thing's all over, I want you to drop by and I'll show you the best damn time you've ever had in your life."

"That's a deal. Don't worry about us, Sir, you owe it to yourself to get out of here. We're all happy for you. Here's Jody's address Sir, you can always get in touch with me there until I find a place of my own"

"Thanks, Doc."

The vehicle pulled up as they were shaking hands. Sullivan climbed into the passenger seat then turned back to Mike.

"Keep your ass down, Squid, and get back home to that girl of yours."

"Yeah, that girl of mine. I'm not too sure any more if getting married is the right for me to do at this time.

"What do you mean?" Sullivan frowned.

"Well, after all this shit I don't know if I can deal with or care for a wife right now up here." Mike pointed to his head. But most of all I worry that with as much as I have changed if there is any room left for anyone in here." He slowly touched his chest and looked away, a tear in is eye.

"I know what you mean Doc. You'll be ok. It don't mean nothing, so you take care."

As the jeep pulled away he flipped Mike a friendly salute, and once again Mike watched a friend leave. Now, only he and Wilson remained from the original platoon that had gone into the Arizona months before.

Soon he would be the only one left because Wilson was down to sixty days and counting.

A week passed as Second Platoon got to know their new platoon leader. Lieutenant Jim Pierce wasn't at all like Sullivan. He was strictly go-by-the-book military, having only recently graduated from Annapolis. Right from the start there seemed to be an underlying tension between him and the rest of the men. Whether it was that the men trusted Sullivan more, with his easy going authority, or disliked Pierce because he was too "Hard Core," Mike wasn't sure. He noticed right away that where Sullivan would listen to suggestions, Pierce never bothered to ask. Sullivan would often cut the men a huss whenever he could and tried to avoid coming down on them about haircuts and shaves. Pierce, on the other hand, ordered the men to shave every day and keep their hair and moustaches regulation. He rarely mixed with the men, keeping pretty much to himself. The evening bull sessions Mike had enjoyed with Sullivan and the rest of the CP stopped.

Pierce also had a routine of walking around the perimeter each morning and inspecting the positions. The men grew to hate his daily walks because they knew someone always wound up getting their ass chewed out for some chicken shit reason.

"Lance Corporal, what's your name?"

"Sir, Brooks."

"Brooks, why haven't you shaved yet?"

"Sir, Doc Lombardo issued me a no shaving chit." Brooks pulled the slip of paper from his pocket and handed it to Pierce.

Without looking at it, he folded it, and stuffed it in his pocket. "I'll have a talk with Doc Lombardo about this, but you will shave ASAP, Marine. Do you read me?"

"Yes, sir."

Halting his inspection, Pierce headed straight to where Mike and Steve were holding sick call.

"Doc, may I speak to you?" He handed Mike the paper. "Lance Corporal Brooks informed me that you issued him this. Is that right?"

"Yes, sir, I did. He has a condition common to black men called pseudofolliculitis barbae. When the beard starts coming back in after shaving, the emerging hairs grow back into the face, taking with it the dirt and bacteria. The result is an ingrown hair or razor bump."

Pierce released a breath of air and looked off disinterestedly into the distance.

Mike could see that Pierce didn't really care, but he had to explain about Brooks. "The more he shaves, the more irritated the condition becomes, until finally the hair will have to be picked out with a needle. So to prevent the condition on those susceptible to it, we've been told to issue no shaving chits."

"Well, in my platoon every man will shave."

"Sir, I'm sorry, but this is a directive that comes down from the Division Surgeon."

"The Division Surgeon is not running my platoon. You take care of Brooks some other way, but everyone will shave."

"But sir . . ."

"No buts about it. That's an order." Pierce turned and walked away without further discussion.

Steve moved alongside Mike. "What are you gonna do?"

"Fuckin' dick head. I'm gonna let Doctor Dunn handle it. We'll see how far GI Joe gets with him. Can you handle the rest of sick call?"

"Sure, go ahead."

Mike found Brooks and the two of them took the jeep to the BAS.

Doctor Dunn was irate when he heard that Pierce would not abide by his Corpsmen's decision. Without hesitation he stormed over to the company office to spoke to the company commander.

Ten minutes later he returned and handed Mike a memo signed by the CO to give to Pierce. "I told the captain I was backing any treatment my Corpsmen prescribed and wanted all his people to understand this. He agreed with me and said he'd make sure Pierce understood it in the future. If you have any more trouble with him, let me know."

"Thank you, sir, I will." Mike couldn't help but feel a little smug. "Now we'd better get back, I've got a patrol this afternoon."

As soon as he got back Mike handed Pierce the note, then readied himself for the patrol. Pierce never said anything more about the incident and Mike didn't really care 'cause in two days he'd be on his way to meet Sandy at China Beach, and nothing was going to ruin that.

Getting to see her again, and getting away from Pierce for a few days was something to look forward to. Today's patrol and tomorrow's Med Cap were the only things he had to get through before three days of sheer bliss.

The Med Cap was scheduled for the village of Truc Dong, two klicks down highway 540. As soon as the road was swept for mines, Mike, Steve and Wilson's squad boarded the truck loaded with two large boxes of medical supplies. Pierce, sitting royally in his jeep, led the way as the drivers raced at a wild thirty-five miles an hour, kicking up a wake of dust that never seemed to settle. As soon as they reached Truc Dong, the kids surrounded the vehicles ran alongside begging for food, cigarettes, or anything they thought the Marines might be carrying. Slowly, to avoid running into them, the truck rolled toward the hootch at the far end, which would be used as an Aid Station.

The squad set up security and helped unload the gear. Pierce disappeared in search of the village chief. Mike and Steve unclasped the medical kits, and took out the supplies they were sure they'd need, before setting up their equipment.

"Hey, Wilson, can you get one of the guys to fetch some water from the well?" When he nodded, Mike tossed him a plastic five-gallon jug.

For the next hour they cared for patient after patient and the line of people waiting didn't seem to be shrinking.

"Oooee, Mike, will you look at this." Steve walked the middle-aged woman over to the table where Mike had just finished treating a kid with impetigo.

"Ouch." He inspected the six-inch gash in the woman's leg.

"From what I can make out she was using a sickle to cut rice and accidentally sliced herself."

"Well, this'll take a few sutures" Mike looked at the crowd of people then back at Steve. "You want to do it?"

"Naw, you'd better handle it, I haven't done too much suturing in my career."

"Okay, I'll take care of it." Mike pulled on a pair of surgical gloves and uncapped a hypodermic needle. "Hand me the Lidocaine, will ya?"

Steve picked up the small bottle, and sponged the rubber top with an alcohol swab. "Here you go."

"Thanks, do me one more favor?"

"Sure, what?"

Mike inserted the needle into the vial and withdrew about 2cc of the numbing agent. "Give her a tetanus shot, then finish screening the rest of these people."

Without waiting for a reply Mike wiped the skin around the wound with a clean swab, then stuck the needle into the skin at a number of separate locations around the wound, each time injecting a little fluid.

The woman gritted her teeth and winched, but it was obvious that she had I high threshold to pain.

After making sure the wound was cleaned he ripped open a package of five-0 silk suturing thread with his teeth and slipped it into the curved needle.

The Lieutenant, who had finished talking to the village elders, walked in as Mike waited for the Lidocaine to take effect.

"What do you have there?" He put his face close to the wound. "Nasty looking cut. Can you handle it?"

"I think I'm capable." Mike was a mildly irritated at Pierce's lack of confidence. He would have said more but he remembered his R & R and decided to keep his mouth shut.

"How many stitches are you going to have to put in?"

"I think about twenty-five should do it."

"Wow, that many, huh? Well, I guess it'll take awhile so I'll just wander around. Let me know when you're done."

"Will do, sir."

Putting the suturing needle in the silver clamp Mike locked it in place before inserting the tip about an eighth of an inch from the edge of the jagged skin. Applying firm pressure and a twist of the wrist he passed the needle through the wound until it came up through the skin on the opposite side. Using the tweezers and clamp he tied a surgical knot and drew the skin flaps closed. He repeated the procedure until the wound was completely closed. *Pretty good job even if I do say so myself. Shouldn't leave much of a scar.*

Steve had taken care of the last patient and was already loading the gear back onto the truck.

"Hey Wilson, go find Super Marine and tell him we're all done." Suddenly thirsty, Mike walked over to one of the more enterprising kids, and paid two dollars MPC for two cans of cola. After taking a long swig from the can he climbed into the truck, sat on the sandbags spread around on the floor and waited for the others.

Minutes later, Steve pulled himself up onto the steal bed

"Here you go, boss." Mike tossed his fellow corpsman one of the cans.

Pierce and Wilson returned minutes later and got into the jeep. The truck driver swiveled in his seat and looked directly at Mike. "We ready to go?"

"Home, James." Standing, he pointed like Washington crossing the Delaware and laughed. He felt good. It had been a good day. At least no one had gotten killed and tomorrow he'd be partying.

As he ate breakfast in the hazy sunlight, Mike couldn't believe that in a few hours he'd actually be with Sandy. His mind had been working overtime the last few days thinking of nothing but that and now the day had arrived. The excitement and anticipation had kept him awake most of the night, but he wasn't tired. On the contrary, he felt better then anytime since he had been In Country.

Whistling happily, he packed his gear and slipped into the new pair of pants he'd gotten from supply especially for the occasion.

"Man, don't you look good," Steve said, when he saw Mike in his clean duds.

"Yeah, I even took a bath in the river early this morning."

"Well, that's a first. Here, use some of this. It'll hide the smell of the Nam." He tossed a green plastic bottle of "Brut" which Mike caught in both hands.

"Thanks."

Mike sat down to enjoy a smoke and a last cup of coffee with Steve as he waited for the supply truck. Mike sat down to enjoy a smoke and a last cup of coffee with Steve. Suddenly, their conversation was interrupted by the Skipper's voice on the radio.

"Delta two-six, be advised that we have a chopper down approximately one klick west of An Bang 3. Have your people ready to move out as soon as the birds arrive. Your mission will be to rescue the survivors, then set up security around the crash site. If the chopper is beyond repair, destroy it and get the hell out. If it's serviceable, you'll be staying until we can bring a team in there to get it out."

"Ah, roger that," Pierce murmured, as he marked the location on his map. "Six, can you tell me first, was the chopper was brought down by hostile fire, and secondly, are there any bad guys presently in the area?"

"That's affirm on both counts. Estimates are there could be at least a company of NVA regulars." The radio hissed. "Musk Ox has already plotted artillery and it's on call from An Hoa if you need it. I'll give you the coordinates in a minute, but I think your people need to know that one of the men down with the chopper is Lieutenant Randy Sullivan."

"Lieutenant Sullivan's chopper is down in the Arizona," Kid turned and yelled to the entire perimeter as soon as he heard the words. Saddle up and get down to the LZ."

Mike removed his new shirt, put on his helmet and flak jacket, jammed a magazine into his rifle and marched toward the LZ.

"Where you going, Doc?" Pierce asked, as he walked up alongside. "You're supposed to be going on R & R."

"Later."

Pierce nodded approvingly.

The helicopters arrived and within a half hour of the transmission the platoon was over the crash site. Circling continually, the pilots were unable to find an area large enough to land the large CH-53 so they settled for a spot half a klick to the east.

Once everyone was finally on the ground, Pierce moved the men quickly toward their objective. Disregarding booby traps, the platoon raced through the brush. They had only covered two hundred meters when what appeared to be a large force of NVA opened up on them from ambush.

Several Marines at the front of the column went down wounded in the initial volley. Wilson, reacted swiftly to the situation, moved his squad forward, and immediately attempted to gain fire supremacy. As they laid down a base of covering fire Pierce organized the rest of the platoon and Mike hustled up to join Wilson at the front. Cronin and several others were lying helplessly in a clearing surrounded by waist high grass.

"Cover me," Mike yelled.

Before Wilson could object, Mike bolted toward the men. A hail of AK-47 rounds was aimed in his direction as he dove alongside the nearest casualty. Breathless from the run he quickly applied a pressure dressing over a bullet wound in the thigh.

"Greg can you make it back to the treeline on your own?" Mike panted, as he tied the knot on the bandage.

"Yeah, I think so."

"Find Doc Heller, and get him to give you some morphine, I need to get to those other guys."

Crawling as low as he could, Mike inched along until he spotted Cronin and Ramirez both men were completely unprotected and in the open. He could see that only half of Ramirez's face remained, and a row of bullets had perforated his chest. Cronin on the other hand was moaned and was barely moving.

Mike was on one knee, about to dash into the open to retrieve him, when he saw a gook across the clearing level his rifle toward Cronin. Instinctively, Mike jumped up and began running, firing his weapon on fully automatic at the NVA soldier. Unable to react quickly enough the gook's head exploded sending huge chunks of flesh and bone in all directions.

Mike pulled Cronin back into the safety of the grass, and had just started to treat the wounds when the round slammed into his arm, knocking him down. As he stared up at the royal blue sky, he had felt as though he'd been blindsided by Dick Butkus. Blood quickly soaked his shirt as it leaked from the hole in his left arm. He began to feel a little lightheaded and realized he had to get Cronin back to the treeline before he passed out.

Mustering all his strength, he crouched and grabbed Cronin by the suspender straps. He started to drag the unconscious body to safety when he heard the AK open up. Flying backwards amid a swarm of bullets, he saw several slam into Cronin causing his body to jerk in spasms. The firing suddenly sounded hollow and far away. Time seemed to stand still as Mike struggled to understand what had happened.

Looking up he saw Steve kneeling over him. *Good. At least he can take care of Cronin. What are you doing? Damn it, Steve, don't worry about me, Cronin's hit bad. Take care of him first.*

The words were registering in his brain but nothing came out of his mouth. Through the haze he watched Steve turn his head toward someone and, despite the buzzing in his ears, he heard him say, "Cronin's dead and Mike's hit in the gut and arm."

Unable to move, Mike felt Steve place the wet pressure dressing on the left side of his stomach, and the stick of the IV needle in his arm. Moving in and out of consciousness he wasn't sure how long it had been but the next thing he knew was he was being carried to a chopper. The swirling blades sent thousands of pebbles and blades of grass to assault his body.

The last thing he remembered before passing out again was being placed on the floor of the chopper.

When the gunships entered the fray, the NVA abandoned the firefight and everything was again quiet. Once all the wounded were safely airborne, Pierce got the platoon moving toward the objective and finally found the wreck of the chopper a half hour later. As they set up a hasty defensive perimeter Sullivan and four others appeared from their hiding place and quickly moved inside the circle.

"Wilson, Kid, Hughes! Sullivan shouted, the moment he saw them all. "God, am I glad to see you guys. I thought we'd bought it for sure."

"We're glad we could get here in time." Kid shook Sullivan's hand. " We'd have been here sooner but we had to land almost a klick away, and then we got ambushed ourselves."

"I knew old Second Platoon wouldn't let me down. Damn, it's good to see you guys again. I'm glad to see ANYONE again." Sullivan laughed nervously.

"Lieutenant. I'm Jim Pierce." Pierce had come up from behind and extended his hand.

"Please to meet you, Jim. I'm Randy . . ."

"Yeah, I know. Come, join me, I have to inspect the chopper." The two officers walked off alone toward the Huey. "You know, Randy, your men have a lot of respect for you. You should have seen the way they fought to get here." Pierce removed his helmet, and wiped the sweat from his forehead with his forearm. "It's a pleasure to command a unit so well trained. The squad and fire team leaders knew exactly what to do without me having to tell them. It made my job easy."

Sullivan stared at his fellow officer and knew he meant it. "Thanks, but these kids are good. They learn so quick and I found if you respect their judgment they'll bust their butt for you." He looked around to make sure none of the men were close enough to hear. "If you don't mind me saying, I think you've got your shit together and they'll follow you without a doubt, but from what I've heard you've got to ease up on them a little."

Pierce looked into Sullivan's eyes. "But we were taught... "

"I know what they taught you basic but it's hard enough over here for them without a bunch of boot brown bars coming down on them all the time." Sullivan put a caring hand on Pierce's shoulder. "As far as them being mine, well, you're wrong. They're all yours now. They followed you here, not me."

"Thanks that means a lot to me." Pierce was happy for the vote of confidence.

"Now, is there anything I can do to help? You're in charge."

"Yeah, I'd appreciate it. We've got a long way to go and I've got a feeling the gooks might be waiting for us."

"Okay, let's do it." Sullivan spun around and saw Steve taking care of the pilot who'd been injured slightly in the crash. "Hi, Doc, how's it going? Where's that crazy squid buddy of yours?""

"He got hit, sir."

Sullivan felt like he's been punched in the gut, and the smile left his face as he pounded a fist into his thigh. "Shit! How bad?"

"Pretty bad. He lost a lot of blood before I got to him and by the time we put him on the chopper he didn't look very good."

"Yeah, well, Doc's tough. It'll take more than that to do him...."

"Yeah, he is."

"You know, Randy," Pierce said. "Doc postponed an in-country R & R with some nurse from the Sanctuary to come on this mission when he heard you were down."

"Really? He shook his head. "Well, that's just like him."

Pierce shook his head. "I'll tell ya, he and I don't always see eye to eye, but I wouldn't trade him for anyone. He's got a lot of guts, and his Marines definitely come first."

"Yeah, he can be kind of a smart ass and renegade at times, but he grows on you, doesn't he?"

Pierce nodded as he pulled out two thermite grenades and handed one to Sullivan. Both men yanked the pins at the same time and tossed them into the damaged Huey. As soon as it ignited Pierce yelled out to his men. "All right, people, we got choppers inbound so lets get movin'. Jones, put a couple of your men out on the flanks. Wilson, your squad's got the point. Alright, let's go. Lieutenant, could you hang in the back and handle rear security?"

"Gotcha."

"Let's get this cluster fuck spread out. We don't want to be caught out here after dark." Pierce took up his spot in front of Kid then turned and said, "Call the choppers and inform them we'll be at the LZ in thirty mikes."

They were able to reach the LZ only minutes before the choppers arrived. Relieved to be getting out safe they boarded quickly.

Steve was sitting on the floor staring up at the control cables still shaking from the events of the past few hours, when he recognized the crew chief as the one who'd flown the medevac for Mike.

"Hey," he said, as he touched the crew chief on the arm. "Do you happen to have any information on our wounded?"

"Sure do. We were able to get them all back but unfortunately one guy didn't make it."

"Oh please no. Which one?"

" Must have been your Corpsman cause he had several bandoleers of battle dressing across his chest. "

Steve's heart sank and he couldn't move for several seconds. His eyes flooded with moisture as he struggled to gain his composure and inch over next to Sullivan. "Sir, the crew chief just told me-- Mike's dead."

That evening Steve and Sullivan went to Mike's hootch to gather his personal effects. While packing, Sullivan came across a photo album then sat on the cot to look at it. Leafing through the pages he looked at the scores of 35 mm snapshots. A lump stuck in his throat as he scanned the pictorial history of his friend all the way back from Field Medical School at Camp Lejeune. Flipping to the last page he couldn't keep his emotions in check as his lip quivered uncontrollably. There, smiling up at him in vivid color were Cronin, Weller, Wilson, Allen, Mike, and himself, arms draped around each other's shoulders, on the beach at "Stack Arms" enjoying a beer.

Sullivan spoke reverently to the picture. "You really loved the Corps, didn't you, Squid? It figures you'd get it helping someone else, but that's the way you'd have wanted it. I'll always remember you, and hope that wherever I go you'll be there to watch my rear. Semper Fi sailor.

Securing the pack Sullivan put the album under his arm. "Steve, I'm gonna to take the album. When I get back to the world I'll personally give it to Mike's girl. I think she deserves to know exactly how much he meant to us."

"Great idea, sir. I'm sure Mike would have wanted one of us to go see her."

"Yeah I think so too. Can you take the rest of the stuff over and turn it in at supply?"

Steve nodded grimly, pausing before he answered. "Sure, no problem."

"Thanks. I've got to get going. They want me back at Division for a debriefing. You take care of yourself, and if you're ever near Division Headquarters, stop by."

After a quick handshake, Sullivan hopped in the waiting jeep, and headed out the front gate.

He never looked back.

Chapter 16

The door of American Airlines flight number N730 closed with a dull thud, sealing in the surprisingly eerie silence of its passengers. The sounds and odors of a land, which had brought them so much pain and suffering, were now locked out by the pressurized cabin.

Hard-eyed combat veterans leered out the windows as the engines roared and the jet rolled steadily along the taxiway. Turning slowly onto the runway, the plane stopped. Palms sweat, as their hands tightened on the armrests. The turbines revved to maximum speed before the brakes released. The"Freedom Bird" lurched forward and increased speed with every yard. Like in George Orwell's "Time Machine," the landscape of Vietnam sped faster and faster into their past. Finally, the nose smoothly rotated upward.

The instant the wheels left the ground a thunderous ovation bounced off the cabin walls. Some men clapped, others whistled, but almost all shouted obscenities back at the Nam. It could no longer hurt them. They had survived.

As the plane climbed, Sullivan looked at the beautiful green hills and paddies before reclining the seat and closing his eyes. Five months ago, he thought, when my Huey went down, I never believed I'd see this day. Now it has finally happened and the past year is only a memory. He shifted in his seat so he could get one last glimpse out the window at Vietnam disappearing quickly behind the plane. One things for sure, the relationships I forged over here will never be duplicated and I know that from now on, everyone I meet will be consciously or unconsciously judged by the men I met over here.

But it don't mean nothing, I'm going home!

The twenty-two hour flight made refueling stops on Guam, Wake Island, and Hawaii, and it was nearly 4:30 a.m. when Sullivan was awakened by the excited voices in the darkened cabin.

"Look! Street lights, and cars on the road."

" That has to be the San Bernardino Freeway. It leads right to Norton Air Force Base.

"Damn, we made it."

"Yeah, man, the good ole' USA."

The excitement and emotion filled every fiber on his body as Sullivan realized that he was finally back in the civilized world.

Upon the wheels touching the airstrip, the pilot's voice echoed over the intercom. "Let me be the first to welcome you home, gentlemen. We are extremely proud of you. You have served your country honorably. Thanks for a job well done. Good luck to you all."

The words sent a chill up Sullivan's spine.

The cabin then came alive with the sound of Bobby Vinton's "Welcome Home Soldier."

"... No more marching and fighting for me.
I'm just a soldier,
a coming home soldier.
I know that I've done my best..."

After claiming baggage and clearing Customs, Sullivan and three other officers hired a taxi for the trip to L. A. airport.

The sun was just coming up over the horizon by the time the cab pulled up in front of American Airlines terminal. Now, instead of cautiously moving into a ville, as they had on so many previous sunrises, they strutted to the ticket counter.

Sullivan felt nervous and edgy waiting in line. *Too many damn people. I can't keep my eye on them all. Why are they staring? Do we really look different?* He was disappointed moments later when he learned that the earliest flight he could get to Denver didn't leave until 11:00 pm.

Once everyone had finally purchased their tickets, the group made their way to the coffee shop for a much needed, much anticipated first breakfast. They ordered complete meals of pancakes, eggs, bacon, hash browns, juice, toast, and coffee. As they chowed down they laughed loud and often, thoroughly enjoying their first day back in the World.

"Guys, check out them two broads over there." Sullivan motioned toward two hippie-types sitting at a table near the window.

"They've been scoping us out for about ten minutes. You think they'd like to come over and join us?"

"I don't know, but will you look at the lungs on that one in the flowered shirt." All eyes immediately focused in on the women's braless chest.

"Man, it sure is good to see round eyed woman again."

"What do you think? Should we ask 'em?"

"Yeah, go ahead."

As Sullivan thought about what his opening line would be, he saw the two leggy blondes, their love beads dangling, leave their table and start walking toward him.

Instinctively, all four men started to get up when the girls stopped at the table and the big-breasted one said, "They shouldn't allow you filthy imperialistic baby killers to be around civilized people. Your Fascist war is immoral and illegal." She raised two fingers. "Peace." Then both girls just turned and walked away as nonchalantly as if they had just paid the Marines a compliment.

Sullivan felt the veins in his neck bulging. "Fuck you, bitch." He jumped out of his chair and started after her, but his friends grabbed his arm and pulled him back.

"Sulli, it ain't worth it, man."

"What do you mean 'it ain't worth it'?" The two women had stopped to pay the check, but Sullivan continued to yell in their direction. "I lost too many friends to have some asshole broad talk to me like that. I'll kick that fuckin' piece of shit's ass all the way back to Hanoi."

The other patrons looked on in stunned silence. The women turned laughing, and with one last taunt of a peace sign, they walked away.

The Marines finally sat and slumped in their chairs. Angry and hurt none of them spoke as they stared at the plates, and suddenly feeling like unwelcome criminals.

A silver-haired woman, who was sitting at the next table with her husband, tapped Sullivan on the shoulder. "Don't you boys pay any attention to those hippies. We are very proud of all you."

He managed a weak smile. "Thank you, ma'am, but it don't mean nothin."

Excusing themselves the Marines quietly got up and left the restaurant to catch their flights

Wanting to be alone Sullivan said good-bye to each friend and went outside. He leaning against the rail, listened to the roar of jet engines and looked sadly out at the planes. *Damn, I miss my platoon, my guys. I wish I could be with them right now.*

As he turned back toward the street he heard a young boy standing nearby speak excitedly to an elderly man holding his hand.

"Look at all the ribbons on the man's jacket Grandpa. I want to grow up and be a soldier just like him."

"You bet, Tommy, but he's not a soldier. He's a MARINE."

Sullivan's neck suddenly stiffened, and his chest stuck out a little farther.

The man extended his hand. "Welcome home, gyrene. Semper Fi."

"Ooh-Rah, Sir."

With tears in his eyes and his lip quivering the old man put his arm tightly around his grandson, smiled and walked away.

Had to have been a former Marine from a previous war Sullivan thought. Suddenly, he felt good and proud. He reached into his AWOL bag and pulled out a tiny green address book. Flipping to a page near the center he stared at the lone name, then closed the book with determination and turned toward the street. He immediately flagged a cab.

"Take me to Whittier."

"Sure thing, son." The gray-haired driver watched Sullivan climb in beside him and close the door before he started the meter. As he accelerated down the road he looked over at the uniform. "You just back from Viet Nam?"

"Yes, sir, last night." He pulled his cigarettes out of his sock and held up the pack. "Mind if I smoke?"

"No, go ahead." He waited while Sullivan rolled the window down and lit the cigarette. "Well, how does it feel, being home?"

How does it feel? Well, after this morning not as good as I'd imagined it would after all those months away. "Different," he finally said. "I feel a little naked without a weapon. All the cars and people make me feel pretty uncomfortable. Everything's moving too fast back here."

The driver headed the car onto the freeway ramp. "That's what most of the boys say. I felt that way too when I came home from the Big War." He rambled on about the battles he had fought in during World War II. Sullivan listened politely but wasn't really concentrating on what the old man was saying. He was nervous and apprehensive at the task ahead of him

The yellow Chevy exited the highway and the driver stopped in front of the green stucco Hollis home. Paying the fare, Sullivan grabbed his bag, got out and stood looking at the house. It was exactly how Mike had described.

The wall. The big palm trees. The well manicured front lawn. His stomach churned and he had to take a deep breath to calm down. With his courage mustered he tugged on his uniform coat, and marched toward the front door. The chimes of the doorbell echoed as he waited. Finally, the brown wooden door swung open and a voice came from behind the darkened screen door.

"Hello, may I help you?"

Clearing his throat, Sullivan answered. "Are you Jody?" He suddenly felt very awkward and wanted to be some other place. Even now he still wasn't sure what he wanted to say.

"Yes, I am." She pushed open the door, eyed the rows of ribbons on his chest, and smiled. "What can I do for you?"

"My name is Randy Sullivan. I was Mike's platoon leader in Vietnam, and I just came by..."

"Get your Goddamn ass in here, Marine!" The voice came from somewhere inside the house. Sullivan strained to see who had called out to him and before he could say another word, what he thought was the ghost of Mike Lombardo stepped forward into the doorway.

The two men embraced as tears filled both their eyes. They looked at each other, both wanting to say something but neither able to speak. For several minutes, with Jody smiling and looking on in tears, they hugged and rocked back.

Finally, Mike forced the words out, "Welcome home, buddy. It is so good to see you"

"Doc, it is so good to see you too. We all thought you were dead for Christ's sake."

"Where'd you hear that? I was shot up pretty good but I'm fine now. Come on in." Mike put his arm around his friend and led him to the living room.

"God, I can't believe it. They told us you died on the medevac to 1st Med."

"I wonder why they said that"

"Well, Steve asked the crew chief, and was told that the guy who died had bandoleers of battle dressing across his chest."

Mike thought for a few seconds and nodded. "Ah, I'll betcha I know what happened. Some time during the flight I regained consciousness and my bandoleers were choking me so I yanked them off." Mike simulated removing them. "I just tossed them and they must have fell across Simms and that crew chief must have thought he was me. I heard later he died on the flight. He..." Mike dismissed the thought from his mind. "Anyway, I'm not really sure what happened 'cause right after that I blacked out again. The next thing I remember was looking up at a gorgeous nurse." He glanced out the corner of his eye at Jody. "Not as pretty as you, babe."

"I don't care as long as she took good care of you. How about I get some beer?"

"Thanks, that'll be great." Mike watched her get up and head to the kitchen before turning back to his friend. "Now tell me what happen after I got hit? Were you hit?"

"No, I lucked out only minor scratches. Pierce did a great job of getting through to us. They swept through the gooks and saved our ass."

"Pierce? That asshole? Well, at least he did something right for a change."

Jody returned with the beer, then as was a ritual they had developed in Nam the two men toasted, and chugged the entire can before they took a breath.

After a short quiet burp Sullivan continued. "What, you didn't like him?"

"Naw, we didn't exactly get along."

"That's not the impression I got. He had nothing but praise for you. He told me how you gave up an In-Country R & R to go on my rescue mission."

"Yeah, ain't I stupid?"

"Did you know he and Kid got killed a month later?"

"No, man. How?"

"Booby trap."

"God, those damn things caused more K I As then bullets. How 'bout Wilson and Steve?"

"Wilson went home safe. I saw him just before he left."

"And Steve, did he make it out?"

"Yeah, he got transferred back to 1st Med a few weeks after you got hit, but I never saw him again." Unbuttoning his coat Sullivan finally relaxed.

"Well, I'm glad he was safe at least." Mike turned to Jody, who had brought the two beers and sat beside him. "Sweetie, why don't you go get changed, so we can take this jarhead out to 'Steak and Stein' and give him the best damn meal he's ever had."

"Okay. Give me about twenty minutes."

"Good. We've got plenty to talk about."

Jody picked up the empty cans off the table, and then gave Mike a peck on the cheek.

With Jody gone Sullivan leaned forward. "So how bad were you hit?"

"Pretty bad. I was in the hospital for over four months. I just got discharged a few weeks ago. Now I'm a PFC." Mike laughed. "You know - - private fucking civilian. Do you know those Navy lifers wanted me to get discharged in my Navy blues. I told them to kiss off. I fought and bled in my greens and I was going to be discharged in them. What were they gonna do, shave my head and send me to Nam? Seriously though, I was real lucky. No major damage. Except for a few scars no one will ever know I'd been wounded." Grinning, Mike sat back on the couch. "Enough about me, tell me what you been doing. You look great."

"Not much. Got back to the world this morning." Sullivan stared solemnly at the coffee table. "Doc, would you do it again?"

Mike pondered the question for a moment. "Yeah, I thought about that a lot in the hospital. Yeah, damn right, I'd do it again. We were right for being there and helping those people. We did a good job, and nobody will ever be able to tell me anything different. You know, while I recovering I read *Henry V*. I remember you telling me and Allen about it." It was still hard to say his buddies name without choking up. "You were right on, it almost could have been written about us."

"Doc, I'll tell ya, I feel so bad sitting here safe with all those guys still over there."

"I hear ya bro, but we will always have a little part of us over there."

Their attention was suddenly drawn to the television screen as they focused on a news report showing pictures of fighting in Vietnam.

Walter Cronkite finished the report as he always did. "Seventy-four Americans were killed in combat throughout Vietnam as heavy fighting is reported south of Da Nang. And that's the way it is, November first, 1970."

"God, nothing changes." Sullivan said sadly.

Mike looked with respect and pride at his friend. "We did."

Sullivan offered a sardonic smile. "Yeah, but remember, it don't mean nothing."

"Semper Fi sir.

Glossary

ACTUAL - a word use to designate a unit commander.

AN HOA(pronounced An Wha) - Name of the base camp for 1st Battalion 5th Marine.

ARVN (Pronounced ar - van) - Army of the Republic of South Vietnam.

BAS - Battalion Aid Station, the 1st line of Doctor staffed medical treatment.

BATTALION - Unit composed of 4 rifle companies and 1 Headquarters and Service Company.

BLOODS -Term used to refer to black soldiers.

BODY BAGS - Plastic zippered bags used for dead bodies.

BOOT - Marine term for a new guy.

BOUNCING BETTY - A booby trap buried on a trail that hurls an explosive charge into the air when tripped. The charge "bounced" about waist high before exploding.

BUCU(pronounced boo-coo) - Vietnamese for many or much.

BUSH - Anywhere outside a base camp. The enemy territory where most of the fighting took place.

C4 - A plastic explosive that could be molded to shape and could easily be attached to a target.

CO - Commanding Officer.

CP - Command Post - units of platoon size and larger where activities of the unit are planned.

C-RATS - C-rations or prepackaged military meals eaten in the bush.

CHIEU HOI (pronounced chew-hoy) - Open arms - a program that allowed the NVA/VC to surrender.

DIDI MAU LIN (pronounced dee-dee maw lin) - Get out of here right now.

DINKY DAU (pronounced dinky dow) - To go or act crazy.

DUNG LAI (pronounced dung lie) - Come here.

FRAG - Short for fragmentation grenade.

FREEDOM BIRDS - Name given to the planes that took the soldiers home from the war.

GOOK - Derogatory slang for any Vietnamese person.

GRUNT - Any infantryman.

H.E. - High Explosive mortar or artillery round.
HOOTCH - Any shelter constructed in the bush. Also a Vietnamese peasants home.

KIA - Killed in Action.

KLICK - 1 Kilometer

LAY DAI - Come here.
LP – A Listening Post, a position usually manned by 2 marines located a distance away from the parent unit at night to monitor enemy movement. During the day it is called an OP.

LZ - Landing zone – a place for helicopters to land.

NAPALM - A jelly-like mixture that was combined with gasoline to form a very explosive compound.

NVA - North Vietnamese Army troops.

NUMBER 1 - The best.

NUMBER 10 - The worst.

POGUE - An administrative type Marine.

POP UP - Hand held illumination signals that when expanded shoot a star cluster of different colors into the air. Each color has a different meaning.

RPG - Rocket propelled grenade.

SPOOKY - Sometimes called "Puff the Magic Dragon". It was an AK-47 fixed-wing airplane whose guns can cover every square inch of a football field in 60 seconds.

SRB's - Service Record Book.

Made in the USA
San Bernardino, CA
04 May 2016